LISTEN, HONEY
SHORT STORIES

BY THE SAME AUTHOR

Wretched Beast
The House of the Easily Amused
Orchestra of the Lost Steps
Talking Down the Northern Lights
Riding Planet Earth
The Bone Talker
Tell Me Everything
Sky Kickers
A Few Words For January

SHELLEY A. LEEDAHL

LISTEN, HONEY
SHORT STORIES

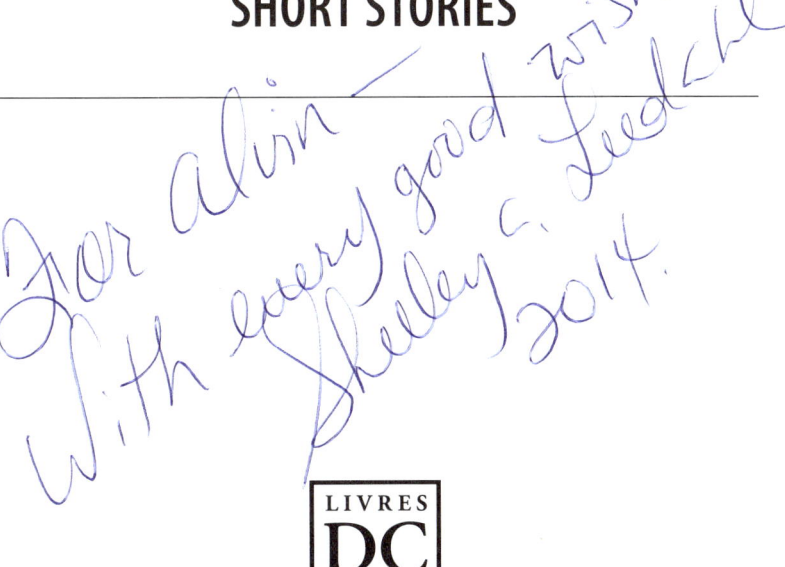

Cover illustration by Christiane Beauregard.
Author photograph by Greg Richardson.
Book designed and typeset by Primeau Barey, Montreal.
Edited by Angela Leuck.

Copyright © Shelley A. Leedahl, 2012.

Legal Deposit, Bibliothèque et Archives nationales du Québec
and the National Library of Canada, 2nd trimester, 2012.

Library and Archives Canada Cataloguing in Publication
Leedahl, Shelley A. (Shelley Ann), 1963-
Listen, honey / Shelley A. Leedahl.
ISBN 978-1-897190-80-7 (bound).
ISBN 978-1-897190-79-1 (pbk.)
1. Title.
PS8573.E3536L57 2012   C813'.54   C2012-902387-6

This is a work of fiction. Names, characters, places, and events are either products
of the author's imagination or are employed fictitiously. Any resemblance to actual
events or locales or persons, living or dead, is entirely coincidental.

No part of this publication may be reproduced or stored in a retrieval system
or transmitted in any form or by any means, electronic, mechanical, recording,
or otherwise, without written permission of the publisher, DC Books.

In the case of photocopying or other reprographic copying, a license must be
obtained from Access Copyright, Canadian Copyright Licensing Agency,
1 Yonge Street, Suite 800, Toronto, Ontario M5E 1E5 <info@accesscopyright.ca>

For our publishing activities, DC Books gratefully acknowledges the financial
support of the Canada Council for the Arts, of SODEC, and of the Government
of Canada through the Book Publishing Industry Development Program (BPIDP).

   Canada Council   Conseil des Arts
                       for the Arts   du Canada

Printed and bound in Canada by Groupe Transcontinental.
Interior pages printed on FSC® certified environmentally responsible paper.
Distributed by LitDistCo.

DC Books
PO Box 666, Station Saint-Laurent
Montreal, Quebec H4L 4V9
www.dcbooks.ca

For Greg Richardson

ACKNOWLEDGEMENTS

What writers need most is time. The following organizations and retreat centres helped provide that great gift: the Saskatchewan Arts Board, the Canada Council for the Arts, Hawthornden Castle International Retreat for Writers (Lasswade, Scotland); Hambidge Centre for Creative Arts and Sciences (Rabun Gap, Georgia); and Fundación Valparaíso (Mojácar, Almería, Spain). I was fortunate to receive the Wallace Stegner Grant for the Arts and accompanying month-long retreat at the Stegner House, in Eastend, SK.

Flowers to Jim, Helen, Kirby and Laurel Herr (aka parents, brother and sister-in-law) for offering their SK and AB homes when I required fresh landscapes, and to Greg Richardson for lending an ear in this book's final stages. I am grateful to Angela Leuck for wise editorial suggestions, and also for minding my home and dog while I spent two months writing in Sooke, BC, at The Land Conservancy Cottage.

The excerpt from Heather Cadsby's poem "Quick question" appears in her poetry collection Could be *(Brick Books, 2009). Mary Oliver's "Wild Geese" first appeared in* Dream Work *(Atlantic Monthly Press, 1986). The poem is often anthologized.*

Thank you to the editors of Descant *and* Rough Cuts *(US), in which "The Song of the Dog," and "Apples by an Open Window" appeared; and to CBC Radio Saskatchewan for the broadcast of "Natural Disasters."*

Of the dozen stories in this book, "Johnny Dead Bed" has had the longest life: it first appeared in NeWest Review, *then as a chapter in my novel* Tell Me Everything *(Coteau Books, 2000). It returns as a stand-alone story in this collection. W. D. Valgardson gave his kind permission for the use of a quote from his story "The Cave," which appeared in* What Can't Be Changed Shouldn't Be Mourned *(Douglas & McIntyre, 1995).*

CONTENTS

- 1   Heads Down, Keep Low
- 25   The Song of the Dog
- 47   Light Housekeeping
- 65   Johnny Dead Bed
- 83   Natural Disasters
- 97   Listen, Honey
- 111   Paraplegic Sex
- 137   Rabun County
- 155   Scenes From a Family On Fire
- 179   The Lay of the Land
- 193   We Don't Say *Negro* Anymore
- 205   Apples By An Open Window

"You do not have to be good. You do not have to walk on your knees for a hundred miles through the desert repenting. You only have to let the soft animal of your body love what it loves. Tell me about despair, yours, and I will tell you mine. Meanwhile the world goes on."

–Mary Oliver, "Wild Geese"

"They said the mother went back into the house-on-fire. They said the father went too. They said the parents didn't know the baby was already out and safe. It grew up as best it could."

–Heather Cadsby, "Quick Question"

HEADS DOWN, KEEP LOW

I love to fly. I love the flight attendants' bilingual safety demonstration that even the children ignore. The page-sized windows framing clouds, mountaintops, and rivers like worm-trails in sand. Above cities I count blue and green postage stamps: the swimming pools one envies, the private residential tennis courts. I dig the headsets and eclectic music, the inoffensive movies, the fold-down trays with their circular indentations for beverages. I treasure the guessing game of Who Will Be My Seat-Mate? as passengers self-consciously file down the aisle searching for their letter and number, and the apologetic faces of strangers as they scramble over my tucked-in knees. But what I most love is the absolute liberty flying affords: the vague, comfortable knowledge that while the world zooms along beneath me I can't be responsible for a single thing. It makes me believe that time has stopped, or I've reincarnated. Here I am, the slate is clean. Free as a child again.

We're lucky to be leaving: snow's been gusting in thick as gesso for the last two weeks. It's transformed washing machines, mattresses, upturned shopping carts and Toyotas into hulking, soft-shouldered animals. Yes, snow–more than anything else–defines Labrador for me. When I arrived in Goose Bay last year I was delighted to see folks gassing up snowmobiles, not cars, at the pumps. Once, while passing through Sheshashit en route to a meeting in Northwest River, I witnessed a hillside burst into colour and theatrics: kids in bright snowsuits, blurring down the slope on scraps of cardboard. What a postcard.

Someone's left an unabused *Globe and Mail*–that most treasured of airport finds–apart from a wallet full of cash, or a Nikon–in the modest waiting area. I snatch it and see that Labrador's splashed across the news again, thanks to Nain's wildly high suicide rate. I know Nain. I travelled up there on a milk-route flight with Ximena on one of her nursing jaunts. Three of the passengers were in handcuffs. Noxious trip, and really not worth it except for the gargantuan inukshuks and the cursive landscape. I turn the page, see what else is making headlines, and am peripherally aware of another body. A man in a grey and white paisley scarf and a handsome black dress coat–that brings undertaking to mind–claims a seat at the table next to me. He spreads his hands on the surface like it's a piano and he's Glenn Gould. Diamond-crusted wedding ring. White gold, thick band. I watch a thin ghost rise from his coffee and feel suddenly and irrationally aware of my toque-meringued hair, the oversized plaid coat–purchased at a used-clothing sale organized by the English wives who try to make the PMQs as cosy as a military base can be. The coat floats around me like a weird life-jacket. After a minute or so of checking his phone, my conspicuous neighbour faces me and asks: "Coming or going?" I'm surprised he's the type to chit-chat. Sometimes all it takes are those small wheels of boredom to open one up to conversation: we have an hour to kill in the Goose Bay airport, and I've beaten everyone else to the only thing worth reading.

"Flying to Saskatoon," I say, and know I'll ask his destination, too. This propensity to interact. An almost physical hunger to *connect*. Perhaps it's my small-town Saskatchewan upbringing... an echo of the Tommy Douglas spirit of democracy and co-operation, the import of community, my own father's socialist values embedded like grain dust and chaff in my ripened skin. "Going home to see family." My parents moved to the city when Mom first got sick. They coexist in a seniors' high-rise beside a shopping mall with a Disney-themed mini-golf. Dad likes it. He takes to spectacle. Mom says he's strapped Canadian flags and whirlygigs to his electric scooter. I can just see him whizzing around Wal-Mart, pinwheels spinning. Beep beep! "How 'bout you?" I ask, moderating my tone, measuring for excessive earnestness. Some men read me the wrong way. "Where you headed?"

"Home to Toronto." He lifts the corners of his white paper napkin and shakes it as if straightening the crisp sheets of a very small bed; he doesn't directly address me. Could be shy. Or arrogant. Jury's out. "What brought you to Goose Bay?" he asks.

Goose Bay. A funny name, really, but many places are strangely-named. I think of communities in my home province: Moose Jaw, Cutknife, Elbow, Turtleford, Rapid View–blink and you'd miss it–and the numerous locales christened with optimistic names, as if the reference alone might invoke good fortune: Plenty, Success, Conquest, Goodsoil, Stalwart, Biggar, Strongfield, Lucky Lake–towns now imploding like abandoned barns. One almost feels embarrassed for those great whales of the prairies: backs broken, paint baked and buffeted off, sometimes leaning at impossible angles. Even *Saskatchewan* is good for a chuckle on fresh ears. Ximena, my latest ex–a public health nurse cum textile artist from Valparaíso, Chile–said *"¡Salud!"* each time she heard it. I miss that woman. Of all the former lovers who hate me, she hates me best.

"Work... I'm a sculptor." This is usually enough to dead-end a conversation with anyone, and particularly a Teutonically-jawed stiff with a briefcase that might be worth more than my first car. I expect he's the type who doesn't let you step ahead of him in the grocery queue when you have a single jug of milk and he's sporting a full cartload containing much produce and bulk food items that require weighing. "And you?"

He slides out of his coat and releases the scarf. "Pharmaceutical sales. We've never had anyone up here before, and I wanted to see the area, so...."

Ah, a salesman. Everyone lives by selling something, my brother used to say, and he would know. If I remember correctly, Chris sells farm equipment now, but he could sell anything, and often did. As a teen he whipped up fabric beer holders on Mom's Singer sewing machine. He metamorphosed our father's ties into striped, solid, and paisley slings his rowdy friends wore to keep beer at-the-ready on their chests; Chris's friends wore them to keep their beer at-the-ready on their chests. After high school he worked as a travelling salesman with a trunk full of pantyhose. He had this *shtick* he jazzed up for parties, affecting a French accent as he manipulated the nylon legs: *Allô, my name is Claudette Roberge and these are my Claudette Roberge pantyhose.*

Look... you can stretch zem, pull on zem, tie zem in a knot! Zey will never bag nor tear, even in the center seam and beneath. Watch, ordinary nail file, yes... look no run! He parodied himself like no one else I ever knew, and made up outrageous stories as if to compensate for the ones our card-playing parents never shared.

Everyone loved him.

§

We board. I shove my bag beneath the seat ahead, hoping the straps won't fling into the aisle of their own volition and trip someone. A flight attendant, say, balancing hot drinks. Happened once. Just a little scalding. I choose the window side but there's a chill coming through the glass, so I scooch into the aisle seat and attempt to look confident so no one displaces me. It's damn cold here, too. Glad I double-socked: at least my feet should stay toasty.

"So we meet again." The salesman buckles into the seat directly across from me. I smile in my best non-encouraging way. Too early for extended small-talk. I just want to sit, and rest, and count the nicks in my palms and knuckles: the wire I use in my work often springs back, as if exacting revenge. I reach to close the window-slide:

nothing but ink out there. Six in the morning. Hours of darkness left. And its -24 Celsius, a ludicrous temperature in most parts of the world, but a cold Labradoreans embrace. Not me. In the last few years I've been donning toque and mittens earlier than necessary, my tolerance—like my skin and hair—becoming thinner with age. Fellow travellers lurch down the aisle like somnambulists. A father with a preschool-aged daughter. She's dragging a spongy doll—with a menacing visage—by its three-toed foot. An Inuit elder, face etched like a soapstone engraving. A threesome of adolescents in bomber-style team jackets, names stitched on one sleeve, hockey position on the other. Give them a few minutes; they'll be the loud ones. Someone's gone heavy on dime-store cologne.

"When were you last home?" Persistent fellow, this salesman, but a voice like butterscotch. And I'm too bloody polite to ignore him.

"Two years since I last graced my parents' home." I count backwards. "Nine since I laid eyes on my brother."

"Long time." The salesman's hands are spread on his thighs now. Arthritis? Perhaps it hurts less to keep his thick fingers splayed.

"Yes, a long time. We sort of drifted apart." I think about the children we were, riding air-mattresses on northern lakes, and how those, too, drifted away from each other, though we began from the same point on shore. We'd only close our eyes against the sun for a moment, but open them to find we'd strayed outside the safety of the buoyed area into the treacherous zone of speedboats and water-skiers, where you could get your head swiped clear off. Three buoys between us, then six. Strange, this coming loose, especially as there are only the two of us, but it happens so easily: one person skips a Thanksgiving, the other cancels at Christmas—too busy, too far away, too broke to make the trip home. Or just too disinclined.

Perhaps I shouldn't have been surprised. The four years between us were enough to keep us in separate schools and give us different frames of reference as we were growing into the strangers we'd become. By the time I'd gained an appreciation for The Stampeders, BTO, Grand Funk, The Who–*his* music–he'd already progressed to some other band, new expressions, more original ways to make our parents fume. The game was perpetual catch-up, and I never really did.

Stragglers are still boarding. A middle-aged man with a five o-clock shadow, his fly unzipped. I hold my breath as he approaches, then passes. He smells like gasoline. Snowmobiles. The north. A pair of teenaged girls wearing matching ear muffs giggle about something or someone in the malicious way only adolescent girls know how to. I check my watch–we should be in the air already, bulleting toward Saskatoon via St. John's, Toronto, Regina. Before this, countless other arrivals and departures: Montreal, Paris, Mexico City, Edinburgh, Berlin, as well as a dozen short-term destinations. I am returning home via a life that has transported me to cities and experiences I expect my family could never fathom nor respect.

I've never once heard my brother introduce me as an artist. The last time I saw him he was living in a cowboy town not far from that bigger cowboy town, Calgary. His house was a prairie gothic movie set: indoor-outdoor carpeting, a TV the size of a picture window, his old albums stored in blue milk crates scavenged from a confectionary, a few minor hockey trophies on a brick and board shelf, his girlfriend's daughter's 8 × 10 school photographs hanging too close to the ceiling, and one plant–an aloe vera with its ends snapped off–beside his kitchen sink. In his basement: a rusting "beer fridge." The whole place reeked of disappointment.

It seemed we shared the same abysmal luck regarding relationships. Chris boasted a litany of girlfriends; he went through them like some men graduated cars, test-driving each new flame for a year or two, then trading them in on a different model. Not newer, not better, just variations on a theme. His women smoked and cursed and knew how to "put up" fruit and vegetables for the winter. Several of them were single mothers. They made pies from scratch–I admired that–and sometimes wore slippers to Safeway.

I only met three of his partners, and even then I hardly spent enough time with them to construct a fair impression, but Evelyn, the anti-feminist, stands out. In our scant hours together she took numerous digs at Chris while simultaneously defaming females *en* total. When he spent more than five minutes in the bathroom: *What are you, a woman?* I was hoping it wouldn't work out for them, and *voilà!...* soon enough it did not.

I slide off my scarf and try to bunch it into a pillow-shape. I'm a poor sleeper at the best of times–even a fifteen minute nap would be a gift. No one has so much as squinted at the seat beside me; I'm thankful for small islands of luck. "Sorry about this delay, folks," the pilot apologizes over the speakers. "We've been waiting for another passenger but he's not arrived." The engines rumble beneath my bottom. Oh, to be returning to Saskatchewan by choice and jetting toward a happy occasion, but alas, our mother is dying. We boomerang home.

§

Two flights attendants. Joyce sports the ubiquitous short and permed hairstyle that women of a certain age often go for. My hand flies to smooth my own hair–straight as string, with a proclivity for static electricity. I wrap the front lengths behind my ears, briefly wonder if, being of a certain age myself, I should cut it, or get the omnipresent perm. The style was common in my hometown back in the day, even among men. I bugged Chris when he got a perm, told him he looked like a forty-year-old lesbian. (Ha, ha.)

Joyce heaves a suitcase into the overhead compartment as if she's throwing a bale into a truck. A younger and alarmingly slender flight attendant seems to regard her senior through a gauze of wide-eyed awe. First I think that she must be freezing: no meat on the bones. It's a challenge not to see people sculpturally. The girl looks about sixteen; the more birthdays I count, the younger everyone else becomes. I'd swear my accountant's too young to have a driver's license. I had a doctor in France who had a butterfly tattooed on her wrist. *This* young woman–her name tag says Helene–sports purple-black hair in short braids, and I notice that her eyebrows are almost completely plucked away. Her hand frequently flashes up to her name tag, as if she's confirming her identity. First flight? That's my guess.

    I hear the distinctive slap of cards being fan-shuffled in the seat before me. I try to guess what they're playing. Cribbage? Some variation of rummy? Card games, like music, are a universal language and I'm well-versed in it. Mine is a family of several thousand card games–*Ooh la la!* my Norwegian grandmother cooed when dealt a good rummy hand (deuces and jokers wild). Playing cards trumped all else in our family. It seems now that we hardly even talked; conversation concerned only the game at hand. I didn't realize how few stories we shared until I'd moved to Labrador, where everyone dished out at least a few decent tales. I suppose we had the ever reliable drama of extreme prairie weather at our family's daily beck and call, and, with luck, a debilitating illness, farm tragedy, or some other untimely death to pass along with the canned spaghetti and boiled hotdogs, but no lively characters, no legends, no mythologies to speak of. I wonder if story-telling–it seems romantically "Old World"–could be something one tired of: the same narratives dredged up from the archival well to fall upon already enlightened ears, nary a syllable changing with each telling. Kith and kin would know all the details, intonations, and punch-lines, almost as if he or she personally experienced it, but just like a person who persevered in the popcorn line and thus walked into a movie fifteen minutes late, one would never know the whole and true story.

§

I went far away. High school diploma in one metaphorical hand, suitcase and sketch book in the other. The great escape. By the time I had a few years of college (Rhode Island School of Design) beneath my belt buckle, I'd developed a rich resentment of my family's domestic rituals and effects. Fellow students' parents–from Boston, Montreal, New York–sported art in their homes, not the black velvet masterpieces in burnt wood frames that garishly loitered on the walls in our simple house, time-zones away, and were hung–insult to injury–always far above eye level. My art school friends drank wine with evening meals–proper *dinners* which did not pour out of a can or take three minutes to boil or fry. They did not eat at 5:00 p.m., and I'm guessing their mothers never bellowed "Supper!" out a front door, or "went to town" with hair caged up in scalp-torturing curlers, or wore their father's mouse-coloured cardigans and socks–even when their daughters had friends over. Those other lives were scored with classical music or hip jazz, not the right-wing rants of *Hockey Night in Canada's* Don Cherry, or the local radio station's buffet of country music, "Swap and Shop," and funeral announcements. *They* sat around dining room tables discussing things that *mattered:* current events, art, politics, the environment, travel, books. Hell, they talked, *period.*

We played cards. Always. I remember Dad once asking about my "artsy fartsy" new friends. "What do you *do* when you visit if you don't play cards?" I didn't humiliate him with an answer.

I tried to tease stories out of my parents, thinking their tales would possess–if nothing else–a kind of folksy charm, but when I returned home for Christmas and summer vacations, playing cards were cut and dealt within the hour. *Fifteen two, fifteen four and a pair is six.* Audio installation, my early life: the slap of cards on arborite; the calling out of scores; the crunch of pretzels and mixed nuts; chairs scraping across linoleum when someone rose to refill our glasses. And my Norwegian grandmother–with an especially good hand–boasting: *Ooh la la.*

§

"Belted in?" Joyce is hovering. I part my coat to prove that I am an obedient air passenger. "That's fine," she says, "thank you," and her silverish-pink lips spread across her teeth in an unnecessarily broad smile. All is well. She looks like someone who prides herself in her gift-wrapping prowess.

The plane's engine takes on a new, higher-pitched whine. We're finally leaving, thank Christ. The card players ahead are having a merry time of it; their good cheer rankles. I close my eyes and imagine what awaits in Saskatchewan. I feel badly for Mom, that she's going to be the first to go. Is she ready? People's philosophies around death intrigue me. Ximena, lapsed Catholic, strapped by nuns who found her playing medical school with another female Catechism student, still wore a cross and believed. Most of the artists and academics I know insist there's nothing on the other side of a beating heart. I don't think dying means the end, it's just something we go through, and then we're on to the next thing. It's a kind of gate. And my parents will deal with cancer the way they've literally dealt their way through every other tragedy. I'm sure they're still at it, the cards shuffled out and scooped up and fanned right there in the hospital, Dad and any visitors careful not to stumble over Mom's IV pole.

Some things never ever change. The protocol to our familial nights: a drink in the living room to start, then everyone reconvened at the dining room table for Cover-up Rummy, Pay-Every-Hand

Rummy, Rummy-to-a-Hundred, Michigan Rummy, and Cribbage or Thirty-One. My parents don't play the games we engaged in as teens, holed up inside each other's houses during eight-month long winters: Hearts, Kaiser, Chase the Ace, Twenty-One, Elimination, and Asshole, or the ones that got rowdy, like Spoons, which required vast amounts of alcohol and pawing each other. It's how we copped our earliest feels.

I check my watch. Clear black numbers on a large white face: one day I could read a map and menus, the next day I was in Shoppers determining which reading glasses I'd need by reading the instructions on shampoo bottles. We're fifteen minutes behind schedule. It's a short flight to St. John's. Up and down. Hardly worth rummaging in my bag for the novel I keep trying to love. It won a Giller, and all the reviewers claim the author well-deserved it, but I've read the same chapter five times over and still keep mixing the characters, each one as witty as a gameshow host. I wonder if my brother ever cracks a book. Doubt it. I wonder if he's wondering about me, too, in these hours before we reconnect. If he takes a good gander he'll note grey hairs woven among the dark ones, my hand's topography of veins, the fifteen extra pounds of flesh; all the ways the body keeps score of birthdays. And what will we say to each other? What *won't* we say?

I hunch to stare out the window again–only the raw dark, though I'm certain that now we're up we'll soon begin our descent. I'd been wrong about the team jacket trio: quiet after all. The salesman sneezes, and I say, "Bless you."

He wipes his nose with an old-fashioned handkerchief, like my dad uses. "Thank you." Only his bottom teeth show: straight and ivory. A miniature keyboard. "Damn cold."

"Dry air," I say. "You know… airplane air." He's likely a nice enough guy, I decide. More comfortable in jeans and a sweatshirt than that slightly Victorian coat. I'm sure his wife will greet him at Arrivals. Slim, tall, gracious. Perhaps a little too aware of their height parity. They'll share a chaste kiss on the lips, a quick hug. Maybe she'll bring the children–a boy, seven or nine-years-old, a girl in kindergarten, wearing a toque with animal ears. "I just got over something... that time of year."

The man leans toward me. "I've got to spend the afternoon in a cold rink. Son has a hockey game. He's a Bantam."

"Ah," I say. "I grew up in a hockey town. You never really forget that cold."

"True enough." He laces his hands above his safety belt, and I feel welcome to continue.

"I knew the local rink's washroom graffiti like some memorize poetry," I say. *Here I sit, broken-hearted, paid a dime and only farted. Next time I will take a chance, save a dime and shit my pants.* Beside that: *Roman and Doreen, true love 4-ever. For a good time call Sylvia Runningaround. Olivia Rottencrotch was here.* "My brother played defence." I don't tell him that my boyfriends–oh, there was a mixed-up time–played goal and the wings. "My father announced the senior mens' games from the penalty box. He sounded a little like Howie Meeker."

"Well then," my fellow flyer says, "you understand about cold rinks." He peers out his window, and says, "Hey... the lights of St. John's. We're moments from touching down–"

But the plane shoots up. The passengers–us, every one–make a collective vowel sound, and I am instantaneously thrust into a warp where I feel outside my experience, but unalarmed. The plane climbs. Passengers respond with hushed interrogatives– *What in the world? What's going on?*–like one might hear in a movie set on a plane and involving terrorists before anyone realizes there's clear and present danger. Surprise, surprise.

The salesman exchanges my glance. "This is a new one," I say, "and I'm a bit of a flight veteran."

He kicks his briefcase under the seat in front of him, and straightens, tightening his lap belt and adjusting his lapels like there'll be a royal inspection. "Yeah, this is rather weird."

The airplane announcement bell chimes: "Uh, folks, this is your captain. We've just had a warning light indicate that our landing gear hasn't descended, so we're going to do a fly-by over the tower and get them to take a look."

Minutes of silence follow. Finally one of the hockey players calls toward the flight attendants: "Is this normal?" Helene's arms are folded beneath her breasts as if she's holding herself upright. Joyce lifts the microphone and speaks into it. "Not to worry, folks. This happens sometimes. Please stay buckled in."

I want to make a joke now. A little nervous laughter would lighten things. The plane continues ascending and I feel increasingly giddy. "I don't know why," I say to my neighbour, "but I suddenly feel like laughing." He lets out a little goat's bleat himself, and I think we both feel better. Somewhere behind us a woman's suffering boisterous hiccups, which seems even more incongruous than the giggles. I wonder if it's the woman on crutches, or the man with the bulbous nose. There are only twenty or so passengers in total.

My cohort opens a magazine. Distraction. If I'd grabbed my novel at the outset, I could have completed at least a chapter, maybe more. I check the view. The sky seems big; our vessel terminally small. "Guess we have to get up high again to make the loop," my new friend says. He stuffs the magazine into the seat pocket. "It can't be the easiest thing."

"No, I don't suppose it is." But what the hell? I check my watch again. It seems time's standing still as a horse. The minute hand confirms ten minutes have in actuality passed, and we're still circling. "Apparently this fly-by thing takes a little lifetime."

"I don't like landings," the salesman says, and I recall the time Ximena and I fought above Italy because I wouldn't hold her hand during a landing. Sometimes I examine my life and see only one pettiness after another. Where was the largesse?

Suddenly the toddler with the evil doll gives a vivacious scream far too close to my ears. Her father attempts to calm her: "We'll have candy when we land, suckers or anything you want." Public volume's increasing in every direction. Joyce and Helene rendezvous at the front and I try to translate gesticulations. Young Helene is a skittish bird; I take my cue from Joyce, who seems less rattled than she would be if this were a major deal. Joyce is a rock. I like Joyce. I bet she's delivered babies and tamed many a drunk. But how much will this delay affect our schedule? I'm still hours from home and really hope to land on time; I don't want to give Chris anything to hold against me. I've got an hour layover in Toronto; I'll call home with my ETA.

I notice I'm dripping with sweat. Hot flash. They're precipitated by so many things lately: wine, chocolate, dreams, stress, desire. I cinch my safety belt until it's pushing against my hip bones, which aren't especially easy to find. "Okay, something's up." Am I thinking out loud? If so, surely this is the kind of moment where one can't be considered daft for talking to herself.

"That's fifteen minutes now," the pharmaceutical rep says, "since the announcement. Someone should let us know what's going on."

Suddenly the plane plunges, and it's not unlike being on that ride, the Drop of Doom. Again we make a communal noise, as if we're watching fireworks and there's just been an especially impressive flare. I eyeball the barf bag. "We're coming in so low–"

"We're just missing the tower!" someone shouts.

Again the plane swoops up. A woman wails. A coyote in a trap. The bell chimes. "I don't want to alarm anyone," the pilot evenly states, "but you're going to see several emergency vehicles on the airstrip. This is just a precaution." His voice is grave. *Official.* "Our wheels still haven't dropped, and we have a fuel issue. We'll circle then touch down. Keep your safety belts fastened. Flight attendants… the emergency procedures."

"A whisky would go down well about now," the salesman says. His tongue flashes out and wets his lower lip. Ah, a drinker. At my last medical exam I learned about a small spot on my liver; I've been trying to cut back.

"Oh," I say, "agreed." I'm hot and cold, hot and cold. There is no way to feel comfortable any more.

"What the fuck's happening?" People crane to locate the source of this abject outburst. It's the guy with the dramatic profile. "I have shares in this airline! I'm going to be writing a letter!"

The salesman extends his hand, and I'm not sure whether I'm meant to shake it, squeeze it, or simply hold it–same quandary I faced when presented with a penis. "My name's Allan," he says, "and now I'm scared."

§

When your plane's landing gear is on the fritz and you fully expect to end up in a casket with your hair parted on the wrong side, it's amazing how you think of many of the same things you would on an ordinary flight: *Gee, the lights of the city are pretty. I wonder what the temperature's like? My breath must be horrible right now.*

It's become pin-drop quiet. My chest clenches. This is really happening. My mother, riddled with cancer, might outlive me. All these years, and never have I made the time to make peace with my brother, or even tell my own story. I unzip my large purse, and scribble on the back of an envelope. *Dear Mom, Dad & Chris.*

We're having trouble landing. I just want you to know that... I tumble into a canyon of sadness: I have no lover to say goodbye to. Ximena, Jane. The tumultuous years with Sue. All past tense. There's no one–if I survive but am terminally injured–to hold my hand at my deathbed.

    I reach over and close the slide over my window: an eyelid over an eye. I don't want to see. Who knew it took forever to crash? My penned words are a bluish blur. Allan unbuckles, breaking the rules, and crowds in beside me. "Don't worry. We're right over the wings... best place to be."

    "I haven't been home for a long time," I say, my lips wet with snot and tears. I wipe my face against my sleeve.

    He squeezes my knee. "You'll be in the arms of your loved ones soon."

    "Jesus," I say, "that is not reassuring."

§

    I expect the movie of my life to begin at the beginning. It doesn't. What comes is a scene around the family table. Winter, because the furnace kicks in, and I am warming my feet against the metal register beneath the table. Hot air blows up my bell-bottoms. The cards have been returned to their decks. Mom's gone to bed, company's headed home. Dad and I are robotically stuffing barbecue chips into our mouths, and he says, "I saw a UFO once."

    "You're kidding me."

    Bits of chip cling to his lip. "I was a teenager, about your age, coming home from a dance at Clearwater Lake. It was late–after midnight for sure–and just as we crested the hill, this huge, glowing spaceship flew right over the car."

    "No way. You saw a *real* UFO?" Mr. Absolutely Normal? Mr. Married to my Mother? "You're *sure*? I didn't think you even *believed* in UFOs!"

He crosses his heart and fakes a spit into the chip bowl. "It flew right over us. The light was blinding, but Jack didn't stop driving. A second later it was just a white blip in the sky, then gone. But we saw it. Real as a hammer."

My father's best and only story. I'd forgotten.

§

Mom and I in webbed lawn-chairs. Campfire sparks. Woodsmoke in my sweater and hair. It's chilly; we huddle close to the fire. The soles of my sneakers are smouldering. I've got a beer, the label half-peeled. Mom pokes the glowing embers with a stick. "There's something I've never told you." She rolls an orange coal, making it hiss. "I was engaged to someone else before Dad." She stabs the coal, swings it above the fire. I am holding my breath. "He was in med-school... almost finished. I bussed into the city as often as I could. I was working in your grandpa's insurance office then. I came up one weekend when Gerry wasn't expecting me. He... he had another girl. It nearly killed me."

My mother's sole confession, released beneath a smear of northern lights.

§

The flight attendants chant:
Heads down, keep low.
Heads down, keep low.

§

Calgary. I teach at the Alberta College of Art. Thanksgiving weekend. No time to travel back to Saskatchewan, so I plan to spend the holiday with Chris. He lives with Tonia and her daughter Angela. Tonia assistant manages the new Sands Hotel and sounds like a decent person on the phone, except she tags every sentence with "you know." I'm anxious to meet them. I throw together a Greek salad and buy buns from a Kensington bakery. Racing, as always. City traffic is hellish, as if the entire city's emptying like a pail. There are freeway stalls and fender-benders, and above it all, a female reporter in a traffic helicopter uses compound words like "bottle-necked" and "log-jammed" with what sounds like sadistic pleasure.

Dark when I arrive. Tonia's more intelligent-looking than I expected, like someone who maybe got a year or two of college in before flunking out or getting knocked up. Maybe it's the masculine glasses. Grey turtleneck, black dress pants. I wonder if she's made an effort for my sake. I wonder if she's trying to look queer. "Front desk clerk called in sick," she explains, breathlessly, and whisks the salad bowl from me to Chris. "I'm sorry, but there's no one else to take the shift. We'll visit tomorrow, though, you know." She calls into the house's interior: "See you, Ange! Don't be on the phone all night, eh?"

She leaves me facing my brother. He's wearing a Calgary Flames jersey, and he's gained an abdominal tire. "Hey," he says. He gives me a little punch in the arm, and only then do I realize how I've missed him, and pull him into an awkward hug in which only our shoulders meet.

"Hey back, you." I look down at his old man slippers—faux leather slide-ons. I could so easily mock him.

"Let's put this in the fridge," he says, and slip-slides away. "What can I get you to drink? Beer or beer?"

I follow him from the front entrance to the kitchen, the layout similar to the bungalow we lived in as family. "A beer would be super."

"We'll roast the turkey on Saturday," he says.

"That's perfect, I have to leave early Sunday. I've actually got a commission—a small bronze casting for an oil company—and can't spare an entire weekend away. And the teaching keeps me—oh—hello."

The daughter's entered from the shadows. Chris gestures toward the table. "Go ahead, sit." Angela takes one end, and I pull a chair out opposite. I see the table's set with plastic condiment containers–red and yellow–and a vinyl tablecloth, as if prepared for a rain-or-shine picnic. The girl sits cross-legged and immediately begins painting her fingernails the colour of prunes. "Ange, this is my sister, Denise."

"Hi," I say, and stop myself before I reach to shake what would be reluctant fingers. She doesn't look me in the eye. I have taught kids a little older but much like this. It behooves them to pay me the slightest attention, so I make a special effort to remember their names and address them as often as possible. This one has gathered long frizzy hair into a side ponytail: a style which might look attractive on another young woman, but on this one serves only to accentuate a weak chin. She's wearing feather earrings. Shimmery turquoise. A peacock colour. Baby peacock. "How are you?"

She shrugs, and starts in with the brush on her short left nails.

"Well, guess we might as well play cards," Chris says, setting a beer in front of me. "Ange... the cards."

The girl leisurely completes her nail work, blows on the polish, then crosses the floor without lifting her feet. She opens a cupboard and retrieves two decks, bound with elastic hair bands. I recognize the cards: my gift from Spain, imprinted with a photo of the relief by 18th century sculptor Ignacio Vergara–from the façade of the Museo Nacional de Cerámica González Martí in Valencia.

"I'll take this stuff off." I remove used coffee cups and a plasic ashtray further cheapened with the logo of an auto repair shop. "Ange, I'll just set your nail polish on the counter, okay?"

"Whatever." She affords me a solemn nod and we assume our positions: Chris at the head of the table, where I was, and Angela across from me. Now we look at each other. The girl has a wandering eye and I attempt not to be mesmerized. The eye will make me try harder with her. I once told Ximena that I considered my ability to ignore people's "challenges" to be one of my gifts. She said they should put that on my headstone.

§

Heads down, keep low.
Heads down, keep low....

§

We play old-fashioned rummy. Chris doesn't ask about my work and I don't enquire about the satellite dish industry. He's had an ear pierced. A surprising metallic stud. There are new things and there are old things. When he gets a winning card he pronounces as he always has: "Read 'em and weep!" It's clear Angela knows her way around a deck of cards, too: she handles them like she's been working tables at a casino for at least half her young life.

We break after the first two games and Chris trots downstairs to get fresh bottles from the beer fridge. "Can I have one?" Angela asks when he returns with four new bottles spoking out from his fingers. Her mouth hangs open like a door. I can see her grape-coloured bubble gum. *You'll catch flies,* my mother used to say. The girl picks the gum out, stretches it into a string and swings it around her pointer finger. Grape on prune. When the gum's adequately hived around the digit she sucks it back into her mouth.

"Your mom would hang me up," Chris says, "but a sip wouldn't hurt." He passes the bottle and the girl takes a guzzling drink. *No backwash!*

I split the deck into four piles, then eight, and restack them. "Talk to Mom and Dad lately?"

"Last week. Dad's retiring soon, eh?" Chris takes the cards and makes them snap like belts.

"Next year." I stare as my brother works the cards. "Hey, do you realize we've pretty much watched our parents grow old shuffling cards and paying each other in nickels, dimes, and quarters?"

"Nothing wrong with that," he says. "After the games, remember how Mom made coffee and served salmon sandwiches?"

"Or ham."

"Or egg salad."

"On white bread," I add, "diagonally halved, with a bread and butter pickle stabbed through their centres." I cut the deck again when he offers it. "Chips in the bowl... ice melting in trays on the counter. Always the same games, the same Bridge Mixture or peanuts in the same glass bowls, same salt on everyone's fingertips, same clink of coins across the table."

Chris nods and begins the clockwise dealing. "Mom would slap down her sets and run down with increasing speed when she was about to go out."

"And you prefaced your victories with clichés... 'read 'em and weep!' You still do it." I pick up a pen and doodle on the score sheet.

He finishes dealing. "Remember Grandma?"

"Ooh la la," I say, and we both laugh, and damn it feels good. But I need to pull the reticent kid into this. "Ange, we're a superstitious lot, too. Some of us wait until every card's dealt before picking them up. Others fan them as they arrive. I don't even arrange them into suits."

"Wow," the girl says, with unabashed sarcasm.

I don't give up. "We had change-purses specifically for card money. Our Aunt Jean set out a ceramic leprechaun for luck. We always drank–Chris, my artist friends are surprised at how well I hold my own–and we always gambled."

"Okay, you gonna make a play before Christmas or what?" he says, and lightly pinches the skin at my wrist. I swat at him with my cards. The distances between us seem shortened. It's fine. "Sister, it's your draw."

§

Heads down, keep low.
Heads down, keep low.

§

The clock's edging toward 2:00 a.m. and Chris is still going strong. "Dealer's choice," he says, and begins gathering the cards again. He's eight bottles in and I'm not far behind him. Angela's swallowed her share, too.

"Chris, I just can't... I'm beat." I get up, begin placing empties into a carton on the floor beside the fridge. "You said 'one more game' three games ago. I'm done. Finished. *Finito.*"

"Okay, quitter. You're in Ange's room, downstairs." He pushes his chair back, lifts the red jersey and rubs his belly. I doubt he's in good enough shape to play even Oldtimers' now. "Only bathroom's up here, just so you know. Ange doesn't mind the couch, right Ange?" She's cracking shelled peanuts with her teeth; he doesn't wait for an answer. "She usually nods off watchin' late night movies, anyway. Satellite TV, eh Kiddo?"

She says, "All the good shows are on late."

A plain girl, heavily made-up. I feel somewhat sorry for her. One could overlook the wandering eye and recessive chin if she had other likeable traits—a quick laugh, say, or a complimentary nature. I purposely let her win two games. She hasn't directly addressed me all night.

I follow my brother downstairs. Clothes are jammed into drawers that don't quite close, and lipsticks, nail polish, large hoop earrings and cheap bangle bracelets litter the girl's dresser.

I note movie and pop stars on the walls—no originality there—and a half-burned candle in a chipped scallop on an overturned milk crate. Fluorescent stars on the black-painted ceiling. The single bed's been hastily made, a box of Playtex tampons kicked partly beneath it. *If I have to tell you one more time to make that bed!* A landscape of ordinary adolescent sloth. A future as dizzyingly predictable as a rope of chewed gum spun around a finger then returned to the mouth: the flavour gone, the colour faded, the snap extinguished.

Chris drops my overnight bag at the foot of the bed. "Sleep well," he says, and I think he might hug me for real now, but he doesn't. "Night night, Kiddo." I'd forgotten that he used to call me that, too.

§

Heads down, keep low.
Heads down, keep low....

§

Hours later I'm staring at fluorescent stars. Need to pee. *Like a racehorse.* And if I don't have a glass of water I'll wake with one mother of a headache. I pat my way out of the dark bedroom. Halfway upstairs I hear something and stop. I don't want to go further, but I'll never be able to hold it.

§

I roll forward, grasp the back of my neck, head between knees. Allan's doing the same. Static crackling. Cockpit announcement. *Brace! Brace! Brace!*

§

On the couch in TV light. Nightgown bunched around her waist. I do not visit my brother in jail.

§

We land. And people slowly unfold. Shock has settled on our shoulders like snowfall on grass. No one dares speak.

I can't feel my legs as I disembark. A reporter's shoving a microphone into blank faces. An airline representative says she'll be getting in touch tomorrow. "I know it's been a trying experience." She sounds like she's under water.

I stumble into the washroom, steady myself at the mirror; only my reflection makes me real. A few provinces from now my brother will find me as I left him nine years earlier: my face stained, eyes red and burning, body a rag of disbelief. As if no time has passed. As if nothing's happened. We'll shuffle the deck, deal fresh hands, begin our story again from here.

THE SONG OF THE DOG

They'd agreed on him, she was sure of it. Oh, she'd had to be sneaky about it, that was true. Put every contender into some sort of Hollywood context. She'd bring up SPCA photos on the laptop and point out how this one looked just like that little firecracker on *Frazier*, and that one bore an uncanny resemblance to Lassie. "Many dogs have higher IQs than people," she'd said, though even Dion, at nine, could see how this was impossible, because their skulls—and thus, their brains—were so much smaller. "You're funny, Auntie," is what Dion had said. "You're *crazy*."

The thing was, they'd had a dog, and it had just happened to be the *perfect* dog. The *crème de la crème,* in Dion's words. The boy drew great pleasure from the fact that he and the dog possessed the same birthdate. Even that hard-ass Gil had loved their Lab / Shepherd found-in-a-ditch-when-he-was-a-puppy dog. Elton John performed all the usual dog tricks and had at least a dozen above-and-beyonds in his repertoire. How many dogs could sneeze on command? How many could nose their empty water dish over to the sink, or open the back door? They'd even taught EJ to talk: he could say "Mama" and "verandah," and they frequently hauled out their DVD library to prove their claims to naysayers. "See? *Told* you."

As a rule, Nadia was distrustful of anyone who used superlatives, but there was simply no other way to describe the dog than "best boy ever." Then one soggy April morning, Sam-the-Man from the corner house came calling with his new rollerblades. Was Dion around? No, Dion only came on Saturdays, when his mother had her, um, *zumba* class—well, she couldn't exactly reveal that her sis was at "Strip to Fit." Could Elton John pull Sammy on his rollerblades? "Of course," Gil chirped from the kitchen. "He loves that kind of thing." Twenty minutes later EJ and Sam-the-Man were whizzing down the avenue. When the leash snapped, Sammy braked, the dog didn't, and that's how Elton John came to be sitting in an English toffee tin on top of the Heintzman between the metronome and a photo of Gil's parents–with leis on–in Honolulu.

EJ was their *best boy,* their *baby.* Nucleus. Ten years of marriage and one hyper-intelligent dog was all they really had to show for their union. Nadia could not erase the fact that the last time she'd seen him alive, she'd been reading on the toilet, the door characteristically open. Elton John slunk up, and they stared at each other. "His eyes were particularly sad, as if he *knew.*" Then the dog jogged off with the neighbour and it was *au revoir, chien*; goodbye, yellow-brick road. She felt herself sinking into the quicksand of grief, and Gil, it seemed, did not possess the emotional acumen to grieve along with her. "He can't even fake it," she complained to her sister, Marcella. "He doesn't even freaking try."

For her part, Nadia was going off the rails. *Dysphoria,* her therapist diagnosed. Sounds like some sort of tree mould, she thought, or a fungus that grows between digits and makes them cakey. A Greek goddess, wife of Dysphos. She thumbed through the well-worn OED. Etymologically, it was the opposite of euphoria. Well, that pretty much clinched it. She confessed to her therapist that she'd only stayed in the marriage for the dog's sake, and this revelation surprised even her. It was like one of those moments when a drunk says something profound and the party stops momentarily. A moment within parentheses. This counsellor, whom she was encouraged to call by his first name–"Claude" (and she ever struggled to remember whether to pronounce it so that it rhymed with "shod" or with "ode")–supported an imminent and radical change. "A new landscape," he advised, "sea and sand.

Or, maybe you should take in a foreign exchange student. One of those studious South Korean girls, always bowing."

She usually didn't take this man's advice; although he taught at the university and had all the requisite certificates framed at eye level, three things disturbed her. A: He had no receptionist (what kind of a psychologist didn't hire a receptionist?), so you had to walk right in, hike a flight of stairs, wait on a hard chair and be submitted to smooth jazz until you were beckoned into the inner sanctum. B: He never asked about her relationship with her parents. (Shouldn't that be *de rigueur,* she wondered? Didn't this man watch TV?) and C: He was grossly overweight. *Emphatically* overweight is how she put it to Marcella, who disliked *her* therapist for entirely different reasons. If Nadia's doc was in his own right mind, surely he'd do something about the extra two hundred pounds he was packing around like a conjoined twin–Claude 2–that had melted into shapelessness and settled into various parts of Claude 1's body; those surplus pounds would send him to his grave *tout de suite.* Could her therapist be suicidal?

He'd suggested a trip. Could she travel alone? She consulted the map of the world pinned into the basement drywall between stacks of games they no longer played and a rack of clothes she no longer wore but still liked and hoped would eventually come back into style again (although maybe not the stirrup pants) because some Hollywood celebrity with sixteen kids adopted from sixteen countries was seen wearing the same thing, almost.

She chose Spain.

§

The new dog was a looker. Indeed, he'd literally stop traffic, as they would learn. He did not hail from the SPCA.

"I've found the dog," she'd told Gil, waiting until he was in a superior mood. His Colorado Avalanche had just thrashed the team he most abhorred. "Rat bastards," he called the Edmonton Oilers. "Those rat bastards got two breakaways and we *still* creamed them." Nadia never understood this rooting for one hockey team over another. If you didn't know any of the players personally, what was the point? As for watching a game herself: "I'd rather clean the oven," she'd say, "bring on the toxic fumes."

Gil squared his shoulders. "We're not getting another dog. Had dog. Dog died. End of story."

"I don't get you," she said, for the one hundred and forty-sixth time since April. "You loved having Elton John around. Your parents adored him. Dion worshipped him. He was excellent security, and you know the neighbourhood's gone downhill–you've seen the graffiti. Why can't we get another dog?" Then she had an epiphany. Perhaps he felt, as she did, that the height of their matrimonial love was behind them now; only the dregs were left. A few soggy grounds in the bottom of the cup, a brown so dark you couldn't tell it from black. She often sensed that he tried to punish her in what he thought were imperceptible ways. He'd purposely hang up after his parents called without passing her the phone, even after she'd mouthed, "Let me say hi, too." He sped the car and took corners too quickly after she'd had a rollover. Little things and asshole things. And he was getting worse. She wanted another dog? He'd be damned if she got one.

Gil left the TV to check his hockey pool status. Every time she found him in his office he was mesmerized by those bloody stats. She followed him in and said: "Remember that movie, *Where the Red Fern Grows*? From the early '70s, I think."

"Mm. Rings a distant bell." His voice was of one was not really listening, but not *not* listening, either.

She set her palms on the knobs of his shoulders. "Come on, you remember those gorgeous dogs in the show." The great thing about marrying someone your own age, she thought, was that you had the same frames of reference. Of course he remembered. He would have seen the movie *and* read the book by Wilson Rawls. Probably blubbered at the end, just as she had.

"Long ears. Hunting dogs. Shit! Forsberg's down with another strained groin."

She pulled his chair back, wedged herself in. "May I?" Her fingers did a little cha cha cha on the keyboard; a handsome beast appeared. Regal head, sleek red coat, drooping ears, muscled frame: it caught the breath in her throat. "This is the dog. A hound dog. A redbone coonhound."

She could tell the image was making a favourable impression because Gil's brows had knit together and two lines contracted into Vs, like a Chevron logo. This was his happy face. She felt like a mother, stepping back to let the curious get a good gander at the new little monkey in its cradle. She bet Gil was already imagining this spectacular specimen prancing along with him on the Meewasin Trail.

Nadia pounced. "There's a litter advertised in the paper. Two hours away, some small town. I'd really like to see them… tomorrow?"

"Jesus, woman," he said, which was as close as he ever came to an endearment, but he didn't take his eyes off the dog.

It was a *dog's* dog.

Still she gleaned Gil was still far from convinced, and when they pulled up to the farm yard she knew she'd lost a tad more ground. "A trailer," he said. A sorrel-coated dog leapt off the deck. A web of saliva swung from its black lips right to the ground. "Holy hillbilly."

Nadia said, "Bet this is Papa," and scratched the drooling male. The top of its head was the size of a dinner plate. "And there's Mama." A slightly smaller coonhound, teats hanging dramatically low, was guarding the doorstep. "Aren't they beautiful, Gil?"

A hip-less adolescent in low-rise jeans opened the door; woodchips clung to her socks like decorations. "Pups?"

"Um, yes," Nadia said, and felt she was being evaluated. The girl had strikingly pink skin. Sore-looking. The kind of girl who appropriated her life philosophy from three-chord country and western songs that venerated traditional marriages and racism, Nadia guessed. They shadowed her past three generations in Lazy-boys. Bet there's a good case for Dr. Phil in here, Nadia thought. Or maybe for that other show, Jerry what's-his-name, who encouraged illegitimacy and fisticuffs. "How do," she said, low and in passing, her words buried beneath the volume of a game show host on the big screen TV.

The litter was penned into a plywood lean-to connected to the trailer. Light sailed in from poly-covered rectangles that had been hacked through the walls. The floor was covered in pallets. The pallets were mostly covered in scraps of green indoor-outdoor carpeting. "Well, here they are." The girl swept an arm over the mewling pups. Nadia saw colour creep up the girl's neck: a flush of pride? The pup's jowly mother swung into the room between human legs and plopped onto her side. Pups tripped over their own disproportionately-large paws to get to her leaking teats. Nadia noted half a dozen fecal squirts and little ponds of urine. Several puppies had wandered off the rug and were falling through the wooden slats. Hard work, Nadia thought.

"We've got eleven altogether, but two are spoken for. One female and a male. I know which ones." The cable-knit sweater was large enough for two of her, or one third of a Claude.

The pups were scrambling over each other. Some bore a milky smudge on their foreheads. One pair curled together like the yin and yang symbol. "Oh my God... don't they have the sweetest little faces, Gil?" Nadia lifted one long-eared pup and snuggled it against her breasts. "And these paws are absolutely precious."

The girl freed a pallet-trapped male and plunked it back into the squirming pile. Gil kept his eyes on it. "Yeah... they sure are cute." He dropped to his haunches. A pup wobbled toward his hand, and licked it. "This one's got crust or something in its eye." He reached for a larger, clear-eyed pup, and closely assessed it.

The teenager was still loitering, which irritated Nadia, as did the canned laughter in the next room, and the ridiculous pallets. The room smelled like urine-soaked newspaper. "This is going to take some time," she stated. *Please flock off so we can bond here.*

"I'll leave you alone then, but this one–" the teen indicated a small female, "and I think this little guy–" she checked genitalia, "are already sold."

"And how much did you say they were?" This was Gil.

"Three hundred for males, three hundred and fifty for the bitches."

"Fine," Nadia said. She'd already told Gil she'd pay the whole shot.

The girl left then. Sunlight gunned through the windows, and several pups dropped into sleep. Nadia would fall in love with one, then another would catch her eye, and she'd offer it to Gil. She kept mixing them up–they really did look much alike.

"Check out that guy," Gil was saying. "He's the only one not walking like he's three sheets to the wind."

Nadia observed. "You're right... husky devil is all over his brothers and sisters. Definitely an Alpha. You know he'd be more work... harder to train, maybe downright obstinate. You sure you'd be up for that?"

"He's just so much stronger than the rest. I mean, look at *that* little gaffer." Gil pointed to the obvious runt. "This one's almost double his size. We don't want to spend hundreds on a dog that's not even going to survive the drive home!"

In the end, they chose Gil's dog. He thought it was a concession; she saw it as brilliant engineering.

It began to lightly snow, the flakes a mere spritz on the windshield.
"This highway is now officially called Louis Riel Trail," Gil offered.
"Of course everyone will still call it Highway 11."
"And what will we call our new baby?" she asked, nuzzling the sleeping pup. She'd been internally processing names since they'd left the city four hours earlier, but again: she knew how to pick her battles.

Gil was silent for one minute. "Sakic. I think it suits him." He patted the pup, curled now on Nadia's lap.

They passed a curling rink—a long tube of a building—on the edge of a village. Nadia thought how one didn't see many curling rinks anymore. Gone the way of the drive-in theatre, and pop in glass bottles. "Come on. You want to be yelling 'Sakic' anytime you call the dog? People will think you're saying 'sidekick,' or 'sack it.' No, he's a southern dog," she argued, "and he needs a southern name."

"What, like 'Bubba'?"

"No, maybe 'Jefferson,' or 'Lincoln'."

"We're *not* naming our dog after an American president," Gil avowed.

By the time they pulled up to their elm tree in the city, they'd settled, finally, on "Kentucky."

§

Her therapist, she decided, would be proud of her. In Spain she hooked up with a pair of middle-aged Australians who talked her into joining them on a bus trip to Tossa de Mar, a resort town north of Barcelona. Before they boarded she e-mailed Gil; God but it was dull having to maintain this arms'-length connection. The Internet cafés charged a small fortune, but she supposed it was the least she could do. She thought of the kindness he'd shown her before she'd left: counting out her vitamins and scooping them into Ziploc baggies, each one labelled: glucosamine, multivitamin, calcium, B supplement. "Well, you're not going to stop taking your vitamins, are you?" It truly was among the nicest things he'd done for her in years.

At the computer, she tapped out: *Hi, G–, going N to a beach. No Internet. Will write when back.* She examined her message, then added: *I miss Elton John terribly. L, N.* She paid for her time and stepped outside, her eyes hidden behind sunglass lenses the circumference of coffee cups.

§

The new dog was a holy terror. His were not just the typical exasperations, like chewing gloves: Kentucky went after the headboard, couch cushions, the piano's left leg. Gil was incensed; particularly about the Heintzman. "That piano has been in my family for more than a century!" he railed. Kentucky woofed at him. Gil woofed back.

Nadia pleaded. "Give it time... he's still got his puppy teeth."

"More than a century!"

Sometimes she thought how the skin below his ribs would be the best place to pinch and twist. "Jesus, Gil. You don't even play."

Kentucky had been all feet the first few months. When they strolled him, strangers regularly exclaimed: "That's the most gorgeous dog I've ever seen! What breed is it?" Gil and Nadia would beam. But anytime Kentucky wasn't directly within their line of vision, or snuggling under the blankets between them—as he loved to do and soon insisted upon—the dog was wreaking uncommon havoc. He tore into the garbage like a junkyard bear, and was soon tall enough to stand and surf off the kitchen counter. He demonstrated a fondness for their most coveted items: photo albums, autographed books, shoes purchased in Denpasar on their honeymoon.

Nadia: "Well why'd you leave them on the floor?"

Gil: "And where do you advise I keep my shoes... in the fridge? It's about the only place they'd be safe!"

They bought a kennel. Guessing on the size they'd need when the dog was full grown, they erred correctly in favour of mass. "There's your condo, Kentucky," Nadia gushed. "Aren't you a lucky boy?" When they attempted to lock him in he snapped and tried to sever their fingers through the grill.

Nadia made another appointment with her therapist. "I feel like I need to be in therapy *over* my therapy," she told Marcella during coffee. "Before I even get in a *hello*, he has his receipt book out and is waiting for my cheque. And I'm not getting the full hour, either. Fifty-two minutes last time."

Marcella turned her coffee cup in circles on the table. "This business with Kentucky...." Her sentence trailed off like a morning dream.

"What about it?" Nadia had a feeling she wasn't going to like whatever her younger sister had the audacity to say next.

"Um, maybe... I'm just suggesting that *maybe* you should put the human relationships in your life ahead of the dog. Gil's trying, but that dog...."

Nadia stood. "Well holy shit... I *must* be in crazy town now. My own sister's siding against me? Do you know that Gil doesn't even like you that much? Sometimes he groans when he sees you drive up. Sometimes he ducks behind the curtains. And he hates your potato salad, too!" To hell with them both, she thought.

§

In the spring Kentucky destroyed lawn and garden alike, making shrapnel of the solar lights and desiccating coveted tulips, and unlike Elton John, he never did learn to crap in the specified area at the back of the yard.

"This dog's got to go," Gil ordered. The statement became a refrain.

"Over my dead body," she countered.

He'd pantomime that that he was holding a pistol, point it at her head and make clicking sounds with his tongue each time his hand kicked back. "Damn Canadian gun laws."

She downplayed the passive aggressiveness. She thought his silly clicks sounded like an African tonal language, or one urging on a horse, and told him so.

By the end of summer they'd stopped accidentally calling the new dog by the old dog's name. He grew to ninety pounds. One day he chewed up all their paint rollers; the next morning he snapped at a letter carrier and they received a warning from Canada Post.

They had him neutered. The procedure, and Kentucky's subsequent day-long lethargy, afforded Gil particular delight. They bought the dog stuffed animals at the second-hand store; he annihilated the teddies in seconds. They tried obedience school, but his "Recall" was non-existent, and one evening, after he'd wrested away and tore around the enclosure as if possessed–terrifying dogs and owners alike–the trainer suggested that a different school might be more suitable.

Then one afternoon: "Jesus, Gil, he's got your project folder." Kentucky bolted to his *condo,* file firmly in teeth; he was not giving it up.

"You stupid… bastard… dog!" Gil yelled, repeatedly booting the kennel. Kentucky growled deep in his throat, teeth gnashing, satanic. Gil ventured a tentative hand into the kennel. "Fuck!" It wasn't the first time he'd lost blood. He pounded the kennel so hard he cracked the top. Kentucky went into a frenzy. Nadia thought about the Tasmanian Devil from the Bugs Bunny TV show.

Her sweet youth. Who knew adulthood would amount to this? Sometimes a song she'd listened to on her record player as a girl–alone in her bedroom, or with that carnival of long-legged, halter-top wearing girlfriends she once had–still aired on the oldies radio station, and it made her eyes well, her stomach clench. "Dreamer" by Supertramp had the power to do that. Or Peter Frampton singing "Show Me the Way." Still good songs, and to think she'd known all the words since she was fourteen, and innocent, and utterly ignorant of the mess she would make of her life. That's what she cried for. That time. The brief ledge when her life could have gone in any direction, and yet she chose this. Sometimes during these nostalgic episodes she'd lock herself in the bathroom and watch herself cry in the mirror, the way she did after Elton John was killed. Sometimes she crawled into bed; it smelled of dog and revealed claw-torn sheets.

§

"It's abuse," she told her therapist. "Gil's completely flipped."

They discussed cycles. "Gil's a classic," Claude said, unwrapping a butterscotch candy. A Werthers. She wished he'd offer her one. "He has it all out with Kentucky, then an almost loving grace period follows."

"Yes," Nadia said, thinking how cool it would be to have a therapist with a couch. Or maybe a chaise lounge. She'd kill to stretch out right now. "Those in-between times give me hope. And I can't help myself... I'm wild about the hound." Yes, he was an incomparable brat–she'd gotten into the habit of disguising his destructive handiwork when possible, or downright lying about it–but he also snuggled right up against her like a lover or a child, and after she returned from an absence of any length he'd leap onto the couch and throw his arms around her, their faces at the same height. He'd pin her to the ground with his love, any hour of the day.

Claude checked his watch and a shattering silence followed. "See you next week?"

Despite herself, Nadia said yes.

§

She was dreaming of Spain, or remembering. Which was it? Didn't matter. She was in bed, beside Gil, with Kentucky snoring at the foot of the bed. She was in that foggy state between the lived and the imagined.

The Australians had stayed one night and caught the bus back to Barcelona, but Tossa de Mar was cathartic for Nadia in a way the city could not be, and she remained. Currently she was on the beach at Mar Menuda, a few coves north of Tossa de Mar via a glass-bottomed boat. She'd been mustering courage. She was stretched beneath a rented sun umbrella and had just unhooked her bikini top. She slid it off, still on her belly. Well, what the hell? When in Rome and all that. She was conscious of a man reclining against a tombstone-like rock. The breaking waves almost reached him. Gil would snort at his Speedo.

A familiar sound was competing with the surf for her attention. Dog. She propped onto her elbows. Elton John? His death often seemed the effluvium of a bad dream. *Every*thing seemed of another world: Gil's moods; Gaudi's sea serpent in Park Güell and his unfinished masterpiece, La Sagrada Familia–which she photographed from every angle with all the other camera-wearing tourists; La Rambla, where flower venders and silver-painted mimes competed for her euros; the waves smashing against a reef twenty metres from shore. She remembered that she was half naked and squirmed back into her top. The Lab slapped along the shore toward her. Except for a rusty swatch beneath his chin and a white muzzle, he could have been Elton John.

Suddenly everything hurt: skin, eyes, chest. Such effort required in holding back. She watched the dog paddle through the sand toward the next friendly face. Nadia's sunglasses went back on. Gil swung his left thigh over both her legs. Heavy. Kentucky rolled onto his back. Jesus, here I am, she thought, between man and dog, well and truly trapped.

§

January blasted in and Kentucky tore into the New Year's roast Gil had set on the counter. When the fight commenced Nadia was folding clothes upstairs. Always it began with Gil's shouts, then the dog barking back in grave defence. *Now* what? Something crashed. Yelping ensued. She flew down the stairs, swinging around in time to see Gil boot her dog in the ribs. "Gil!" She reeled forward and tried wrenching him away. This time neither dog nor husband were prepared to surrender. Kentucky's fur formed a spinal ridge: he growled and snapped and fancy-danced while Gil taunted and shot out with fist and feet. His right sleeve was torn. A mangled photo of Elton John was abandoned on the hardwood. Gil kicked Kentucky hard, again.

Nadia screamed. "You're killing him!"

"This fucking dog–I hate him! We're getting rid of him. I didn't want the fucking wanker in the first place!"

She yanked Gil back with all her strength and they both slammed against the couch. Kentucky gave up one more coyote howl and retreated to his kennel.

"We're *not* getting rid of him and you did *so* want the dog! You picked him out, remember?" She would leave him soon. He was truly a stranger to her now. Sometimes he still impersonated a human being–that kindness with the vitamins–but he was mostly a stone, a replica. An effigy.

The doorbell rang. "It'll be Marcella," Nadia said, straightening her blouse, "and Dion."

Gil disappeared through the garden doors with his car keys. She answered the front door, not caring that her face had become a grotesque: snot, mascara, fury.

Dion blazed past her, shedding toque and scarf en route. "We heard Kentucky and Uncle Gil." He peered into the kennel. The dog thumped his tail but was otherwise too frightened to move.

"Marcella, the camel's back has been irrevocably broken." Nadia's pulse clocked through her veins. She wiped her nose on her hand. "I've been looking at properties on the Internet with six foot fences."

Her sister's eyes widened. "You and Gil... moving?"

"Nopers."

Marcella clutched her. "Nadia, I know you've had a rough couple of years, but–"

Nadia was not listening. She was considering how people speak of "A boy and his dog," or "A man and his dog," but really, no animal-human bond could be tighter than what existed between woman and dog. And now, and now....

A neighbour had come out to start her car. She waved, her red mittens a blur.

Talk, talk, talk. Her sister's lips kept moving. Nadia was not greedy–a home, a partner, reasonable health, a few good friends, family nearby, and–because by choice there would never be children–a large, faithful dog to follow her through her rooms for a dozen or so years. Was that not basic enough? Suddenly all was confused. Now she wanted to sit with her family around a table and eat roast beef, now she wanted to stand on a sea cliff alone, not caring where her next bite of bread came from, or whether she'd sleep alone or in the bed of another... yes, freedom, that's what she required... not attachments, not the dull idiosyncrasies and complaints of others... first too hot, then too cold... *ugly shoes... that waitress brought the wrong order... there goes gas, up again.... Harper's a nutbar... pick a lane, Buddy.... You wanna drive?* Away, where she knew no one but would learn the names of all the flowers. She had to get away, her life was a too-tight scarf, a noose... she wanted the wind, a simple skirt flapping about her knees....

"Are you okay?" Her sister'd grasped both arms now.

"Yeah. I'm... I'm just really, really tired."

They went inside. Marcella said she would make green tea.

Hours later, the moon bone-white and well-risen over rooftops, the roast beef semi-salvaged, Nadia was awake in bed, cried out, face to the wall. Because the house was old and the curtains fluttered at windows—which groaned counterpoint complaints against age and the elements—Gil had taped thick poly over the glass. Their views were distorted: perpetually two-toned, the sky always white, as if plugged with snow; the bare bones of the elms black and blurred. Rooftops, pigeons, clouds. Everything rendered in soft focus; Vaseline over a lens. And for all of Gil's efforts, little was improved. The plastic stretched across north-facing windows was a bellows. Cold in the house, she thought, cold inside her skin. Gil argued that they should sell, buy a condo. No condos that she was aware of allowed large dogs.

Gil was beside her, but a hands-width of space gaped between them. She wondered why, when things got really bad, people were inclined to lie down. Vertical, horizontal... the hurt didn't go away. The morning Elton John died, she stumbled up the stairs, tapped out eight lorazepams and closed the blankets over her head, like a shroud. She was comatose for seven hours.

"I know why this is happening," Gil said, softly.

Silence or vehemence? She counted to five before speaking. "What could possibly make me not hate you right now?"

"Please, let me talk."

"Gil, we're done. We'll sell the house. After we pay the bank off, we should come out with about eighty thousand each. I'll stay with Marcella until I find a place. You've got your parents here."

The furnace kicked in. "At least let me try to explain. I–" He sighed, and she realized that he was tired, too. They needed a rest home. For the rest of their lives. "It's about EJ, about... about the day he died."

There was no point, even, in responding.

He turned on his side, toward her. "After I'd taken him to the vet clinic, I stopped at the ice cream stand in the Zellers parking lot. I don't know why. I guess I didn't want to face you, and I really didn't want to return and not have him come barrelling toward me the way he always did. It wasn't a hot day, if you remember, but I bought a cone and sat on a bench. The ice cream girl was doing homework–there were no other customers.

"After I'd been sitting a few minutes, I saw a man walking toward me with a dog, a Lab / Shepherd that from a distance looked just like EJ. It was really strange, but then, for whatever reason, I glanced up. The sky was completely blue except for a single cloud, directly above me. I know this sounds crazy, but... it was EJ, in profile. He was running, and from his eye... the most brilliant white light. It was, I think–no, I'm sure–it was a message. He was telling me that he was okay. No pain, only this great light... and joy.

"I thought I might be seeing things, so I asked the ice cream girl to come outside. I pointed up. And she saw it. She saw it, too."

Gil's story was a ghost passing through her. "Why didn't you say anything? Christ, Gil, didn't you think this would help me?

You let me suffer all this time while you kept this... this... *gift* all to yourself?" She was bawling now.

"I promised him. When I saw that... *vision*, or whatever it was... I promised him there'd never be another dog. He could not and *would* not be replaced."

Their baby. Their baby was okay.

She wouldn't say anything yet–she was still mad as hell over what he'd done to Kentucky–but eventually she inched her left arm from the blankets and, after a time, let her cold fingers spider toward his.

§

It was February soon enough. Temperatures plummeted and Kentucky did not appreciate the cold. She'd tried to wrestle him into one of her old turtlenecks. She'd cut the sleeves off, but he'd got hold of it and tore it to strings. Now they were jogging along the Meewasin Trail, although the wind had nearly obliterated what remained of a path, and where drifts subsided grenades of snow and terraced ice made even calculated *walking* a chore.

The snow had been relentless in this new year and it was pelting them again. Kentucky was fully grown now–the puppy defence, flimsy to begin with, no longer worked at all–and on the trail it took every scrap of strength to keep him from running faster than she herself could manage. There were a few others on the trail, bundled and hurrying, like her. They'd already met the woman who walked a boxer and a Saint Bernard: the only two dogs Kentucky truly abhorred. He freaked when he saw them. His lips peeled up and back, and his fur stood as if he'd been electrified. Nadia had taken to pulling him right off the trail whenever she saw them approaching. With other dogs, he'd sit at her signal and let them approach. With all other dogs he could play.

There were, quite amazingly, she thought, a few hearty ducks bobbing on the open, lee side half of the river. Kentucky howled and the birds rose in tandem. This set him off and in the moment he bolted, Nadia hit an icy ridge: she could not hold him; he was gone.

She stayed on the ground, instant tears freezing on her jaw-line. No one around. Her ankle might be crushed. "Kentucky!"

At the river's edge a peninsula of snow jutted over the water, the current lethal beneath it. She pulled herself up and, wincing, limped seventy-five metres, toward the bank where Kentucky was jack-rabbiting between skeletal willow bushes and naked cottonwoods. She would never catch him. She crawled through the looser, knee-deep snow, and, when hidden completely from the trail above, threw her body back into it, like a child making angels.

Kentucky pounded toward her. Just as he neared and she thought she might be able to snatch his leash, he'd take off again. Back and forth, back and forth. He thinks it's a goddamn game, she thought. She would never catch him. Her ankle throbbed like a stupid drum. Let it snow, let her die here and be found in the spring. They say death by freezing is a pleasant experience. You get very warm, she'd heard. "Dreamer... you're nothing but a dreamer...." She sensed something, peripherally. Movement. Five white-tailed deer–a fleet?–lit and disappeared into the scrawl of scrub-brush and beaver-downed trees. The deer were simultaneously airborne; something to behold, she thought.

She fell back again and cried for real, because she loved that damn dog and he showed no loyalty, even to her. She walked him and picked up his shit and paid the vet. She washed the sheets of his dog hair every other day. She played with him and defended him, and it was work, it was so damn much work.

Maybe she *had* been a fool.

It was dusk now. And the cold seeped through her wind pants, her hooded jacket, and leather mitts. Her ankle was keeping time to that painful drumbeat. Her heart? Gong, gong, gone. She could hear the ice cracking above the water. Miniature icebergs carelessly floated by. Her dog. He loved to chase sticks into the river. She dragged herself toward a frayed stump. She twisted and pulled on a red willow branch, and when it didn't release she took the tendons in her teeth and freed it.

"Here boy!"

Kentucky abated his frenetic zigzagging. He hurtled toward her. She winged her arm back, then… "Here, boy." No. She scratched in the snow, and Kentucky snapped onto the stick, jaws closing like a bear trap. He jerked her. She cried out but managed the miracle of grasping the looped end of his leash. It took all of her. The climb back to the trail was a measured and fierce struggle. No one saw. No medals existed for this kind of tenacity, and Nadia thought it was a profound shame. Kentucky kept dropping the stick and retrieving it. Drop, then retrieve. Snow was spiralling now: big, taking-their-time flakes that stuck to her face. The dog jolted her along. She had to ski one foot and drag the other. It took bloody forever.

§

She opened the front door, setting off the bells that had been jingling there since Christmas. "You were gone a long time," Gil called from the belly of the house. "I was just about to put the kettle on. Want tea?"

"Yeah." She unclipped Kentucky, who bolted into the kitchen toward Gil. She could hear the dog hoovering the floor for scraps. "Thanks."

She hopped from the front door to the couch to remove her wet shoes. Her fingers were not working. She carefully peeled back her sock. She would not tell Gil about the twisted ankle, about any of it. She would hide the swelling and discolouration, steady her gait, though she was desperate to slump and wallow for a little lifetime.

"Gil?" she called. "What do you call a pack of deer?"

She was aware of the kettle rocking on the burner. That faraway train sound. What would become of them?

"Don't know," Gil called back. "Maybe a herd."

"Just a *herd*?" It struck her that something so graceful, so spirited, so large and wild yet capable of flight–something so entirely beyond language or human understanding–deserved an elegant descriptor to match.

LIGHT HOUSEKEEPING

Kit will not venture across the lake until she is good and certain it is frozen over and now, a week since her arrival, there is visible proof. Snowmobiles have left long zippered trails across the lake's white shroud, and an ice-fishing shack has popped up overnight, a script of wood-smoke quickly dissipating above it. She has already hiked around the barren campground twice this morning, intrigued, again, by the variety and preponderance of intersecting animal tracks. Deer and rabbit, raccoon and coyote. Other marks record the passing of birds, squirrels, chipmunks. Or so she imagines. Each of these smaller patterns is distinct and perfect–they resemble bicycle chains, the treads left by impossibly narrow wheels. A kind of art, she thinks. A tunnelling animal has puckered the snow's surface, raising it like a cicatrix. Mouse? That's her guess.

She hesitates at the shoreline. It has taken her almost an hour to get here today, though it's not an arduous or particularly long hike from the village. Two kilometres? Not much more. Her husband has found her a light housekeeping room above the beauty parlour on Main; back in the city, her family is getting along just fine without her. Thriving. What nature of gossip might be circulating in this Germanic rural community, house-to-house, over kitchen tables and bitter-strong cups of coffee, alongside fresh-baked cinnamon buns and friendly games of kaiser? Who is this strange woman in their midst? She doesn't dwell. She's in love with the woods that fringe the one-store town. Wizened red chokecherries and saskatoons cling, even now, to their bushes. The circular clearing–halfway point inside the woodland between village and lake–seizes the winter light and cradles it. A generous gift in an offering plate, she thinks. A cradle of gleaming snow. But the elements have done their work. Aspen and birch and willow and hazelnut; the trees form a thatch-work of multi-armed stickmen, falling and fallen, broken and bent. How tangled the woods are. Several trees have snapped at their bases, and trunks lean against each other as if on crutches. Strange geometries. Branches whipped into perfect arcs, like barbwire coiled around prison yards. She envisions a dense and completely different landscape in the height of summer. This is the woods in X-ray, she thinks, I am looking at bones.

Her time alone is ostensibly about paying attention to what is normally ignored and perhaps wringing something like–dare she even suggest it?–something like joy from small discoveries. The curl of a leaf on snow. The textural gradations of bark. And every few minutes today she stopped on the shadow-marbled path to listen. She heard a bird trill, then easily spotted the white bib of an enthused chick-a-dee, tucked inside the frame of a poplar. Behind the bird's rousing song, the intermittent pop of distant gunshots– moose season? Deer? She grew up rural, and knows how hunters file up from the US, or local boys in camouflage attire tear through the bush on ATVs, even on land that is posted *No Hunting*. Beer and shotguns. But surely she is safe in a campground. She listens closely for the next layer of sound–will it be a woodpecker? a lip of snow crashing from a branch? She hears only the airplane-whir of cars on the highway that exists beyond sight.

She steps onto the ice. Across the narrow lake sunlight lathers candy-coloured cottages and executive-style, full-time homes–with trucks and Subarus in the drive, and speedboats protected beneath tarps, and docks she assumes her own children would have great fun diving from. Who could hold their breath the longest? These are the kinds of games she and her own brothers once played. The residences are carefully positioned between lush spruce trees, tall as the species can be. Everything just so. Add the diamond-glistening snow, the light, the ice-fishing shack, and it's a freaking Christmas postcard, she thinks, though the lake itself she likens to a freakishly long tongue. She will cross today. Her mission is to be in the light as quickly as possible.

Without the buffer of trees and snarl of bushes, the snow has whipped into drifts. She deliberately punches through. A challenge. Her hiking boots are not tied tightly enough around her ankles, and a cold crust tips inside her boot, wetting her sock. The rising wind bats her long hair about. She adjusts her scarf bandit-style over her face, and thinks how easily prairie winters can leech the marrow from one's spirit. Or one can follow winter's shifting moods and ride the months along with them. Turban the head in a wool scarf, entomb hands, gird feet and slog through to the other side.

§

"You've become unbearable to live with," Lloyd said on the drive out. He'd been inferring as much for the last year and a half. He sounded sad about it, she thought, and resigned. Poor, good Lloyd. That's what she sensed people would be whispering. "You're up, you're down… we don't know how to live around you anymore."

She was facing the passenger window, her nose almost touching the cool glass. On the city's outskirts ostentatious variations on a multi-garaged, salmon stuccoed theme had risen like new kingdoms. Homes without trees or any other plant life around them. Lifeless. "Hell's half acre," she'd muttered.

"What's that?" Lloyd asked. He lowered the radio's volume, a CBC program about Canadian doctors working in Third World countries. Some people, she thought, made heaps of difference.

"Nothing worth repeating." She studied her husband. After twelve years she could still be surprised at how good he was to look at. He'd grown a goatee, the almost-black hair lightly peppered with grey. His skintone made him appear perpetually tanned and excessively healthy. He almost always was the latter. "I'm cold," she said. "Can we turn the heat up a little?"

One stubble field blurred into the next, the snow deep in ditches and hollows, and no more than a delicate lace over the higher plains. Yes, she knew she was difficult and at times morose; she just couldn't be any other way. It was like the code that most people were born with–the one that served up bliss in at least equal measure with despair–had been scrambled in her ancestral family, perhaps centuries ago. So many casualties. It was not her fault. She was merely a puppet, and this endurance test was merely her life.

They drove past a barn with a spine like a sway-backed horse; then a Ukrainian Orthodox church with conspicuous silver spires built incongruously on a prairie rise. They bumped over railroad tracks.

"Lift your feet," Josiah said, startling Kit. She'd forgotten her son was in the back. Once she was as superstitious as her kids. She can't remember when she stopped lifting her feet before crossing railroad tracks, and holding her breath when passing cemeteries. Things done for luck.

"Frankly, Kit," Lloyd was saying now, his voice lowered to a scratch, "I think the kids are a little afraid of you."

He meant fourteen-year-old Philip, Sandy, their creative seven-year-old, and Josiah, five, the one who loved her best and said he wanted to marry her, but she smiled at the double irony. She was a children's performer. Every week she travelled across the province with her acoustic guitar, a suitcase packed with eye-catching blouses selected to hold children's attention, and a van full of percussion instruments. She entertained and wrote songs for–and sometimes with–elementary school students. The songs were occasionally recorded, depending on school board budgets, arts grants, the success of the visits, her own energy to push a CD project forward.

She was paid well, worked hard at it, and had to be away for one or two nights each week. In the few days before her exile she had presented to sixteen hundred children in one city, zipping between schools while jamming Tim Horton's muffins–lunch–into her mouth with one hand, steering down unfamiliar streets with the other. Crumbs spilled onto the unfolded map on her lap, littered her coat and the floor of the van like large flakes of snow. At the end of the tour she was so exhausted all she could do was cry. Kit Keller, purveyor of giddiness and camp-style sing-a-longs, of affable ditties that had become veritable anthems in the kindergarten to grade three set–*I sneeze when I please and fall down on my knees, my friends call me Madame Achoo!*–was unravelling. There was nothing left after that last. Not even enough energy for that private song she fairly squealed on the highway after difficult gigs: *I'm done I'm done I'm done I'm done I'm done I'm done I'm done.*

Lloyd almost understood. "You just need a holiday," he insisted. "Some time alone in a quiet place. Get back in touch with nature." She did not resist, though she knew a holiday, as he called it, was not the ticket. A hospital would be more pertinent. She packed Ativan: no panacea, but it helped. Two when sleeping pills weren't doing their trick, one for general malaise, three when she no longer gave a flying fuck, and four "little helpers" the day she and her twenty-nine-year-old lover with the old-fashioned name–also married, no children–agreed they loved their respective spouses and would never be truly together. God, what a relief when it was finally articulated and she could quit obsessing. Yes, he'd located her G spot and taught her something called the Screwdriver, but in the end the relationship was just one more thing that sawed away at her already dangerously diminished energy. *Goodbye Harold,* she thought to herself, recalling the title of a Sidney Sheldon book she'd read for the dirty parts when she was a teenager, *Good Luck.*

And now she was here.

There is a grocery store, a restaurant, a bank, a bakery, a bar, a Lutheran Church, and a laundromat that accepts quarters in its two machines. She has a kitchenette, and the hairdresser below is open just three half days a week, so she has solitude. She has the woods to explore, the frozen lake to cross. Sometimes the whiteness of it all makes her eyes water. The sky is almost aggressively blue at times, and at night, through her second-floor window, there's the pox of stars for measuring existential perspective. Lloyd had negotiated the arrangements. "Ten days," he'd said, "take two weeks if you need it." All she'd had to do was pack: one bag full of comfortable clothes and another with books she might just stare at. Her guitar came, too, because old habits died hard. When he delivered her to the village, Lloyd pressed two fifties into her gloved hand. "I have money," she said, but took the bills anyway. She did not know if a single word had been invented to fit the way she felt, but Lessing's "To Room Nineteen" captured the essence of it.

§

She checks her watch: she has been creeping along the edge of the lake for almost twenty minutes—still leery. If she were to go through the ice here, about ten metres from the gravel-and-snow mixed shoreline, she's certain she could make it to safety before hypothermia set in. Her toque is the colour of straw, but surely someone would spot her purple snow pants and jacket against the washed-out palette. Sometimes she hears footsteps and she checks in all directions; no one there, always. Just ice, she expects. Just the frozen crust below settling in.

She counts a dozen cottages fronting the lake. Closest are two shaky-looking structures with masking-taped windows and decks that might shatter if anyone over eighty pounds put weight on them. In another year, she thinks, these modest cabins will be razed, and urbanites desperate for weekend escapes will pour in with their seadoos and trampolines and non-shedding dogs. Maybe a developer will erect condos.

She tramps up the steep bank to the road that winds behind the lakefront cottages, feeling the effort in her calves, and finds a second row of cottages–a loop–the woods surrounding them stealing in, unkempt. Back here, where everything's mostly boarded up–and thus more interesting–few car tracks lead in or out. And the atmosphere has changed. It's not the diminished light, or the temperature: a pall of mystery envelopes this wilder place. She feels privy to something. Secrets, perhaps. Possibilities. Definitely a darker side. Screened porches are sinking. Shingles have blown off. Seasonal places, several decades old, she guesses. They've likely seen multiple generations of families trail sand and pine needles through their rooms. She feels tremulous. Goose-bumped. Ropes knotted between trees serve as clotheslines. An orange beach towel, stiff, on the snow. Woodpiles have tumbled under lean-tos. Wheelbarrows, rakes, and bicycles have not made it into storage before autumn turned to winter. An axe, rusting, in its chopping block stump. Always so much to do. She admires fire-pits ringed in stones the size of human heads, bleached animal skulls nailed over doorways, cutesy birdhouses. The myriad ways owners have individualized their private havens, each an advertisement inferring *Mine* and *Ahhh*. What would it be like to own one? She would write well out here, slung in a hammock beneath leafy trees with her notepad, a peach-flavoured drink and her guitar within reach. Her chest muscles clamp: work, always just below the surface, like a sliver in her finger she can't manage to extract.

But it is helping to walk, the snowy lane nearly blank as a page, the channel of sky between the trees equally unblemished. She's read that walking is beneficial for the emotionally distressed, and she has seen them—the indigents, the weaving, restless-handed addicts, the disfigured, and those who look perfectly *right* from the outside—all over her city. Eyes fixed or heads down, they hike their anxieties and histories across train bridges, along the oblivious miles of river. Regulars. Only in this moment, here in the snow, does she register that she is a regular, too. Those people also see and potentially judge *her*: a woman in eiderdown and hiking boots, a long-strapped purse worn diagonally across her chest, as if it's holding her together. Maybe they note the fervour of her stride, think she's determined, and trying not to be late. For what?

She breathes the raw scent of pine needles and cold air, and listens to the satisfying, stone-like crunch of snow beneath her boots. The road has been gradually sloping up; the effort has warmed her. Before she left her room she'd turned on the radio and learned it was -17. The frigid air amplifies the signature-sound of a blue jay—like a can opener, she thinks, struggling with a difficult can. Great acoustics. And there it is again: ambushing guilt. So much I should be doing, she scolds. I haven't bought the children's gifts yet, haven't written Christmas letters or done any decorating. Baking? Not a chance. She'd promised herself that this Christmas would be better than last, when they took the kids to a downtown hotel with a waterslide, and she didn't even put up a tree. What the hell is she doing here? Who does she think she is? Maybe when Lloyd collects her in another week—sooner, if she calls and asks—she'll be a normal, fully-functioning member of society again, an attentive mother: the fun-loving, quick-to-laugh woman he married as opposed to the basket-case Philip says she's become. The boy has taken to snapping his fingers in front of her face. Once he commanded her to "Walk toward the light."

She stops to pick up a pine cone and examine its scales. She smells it. And realizes she's not alone now. A half-ton truck is approaching, its driver virtually crawling the vehicle over the snow-packed lane, as if he's never heard of acceleration. He lifts his hand off the wheel in an acknowledgement that passes for a wave. Must think I'm an idiot, Kit muses. She has hardly seen anyone since she established her country walking routine—on the edge of the village within minutes, through the woods, across the clearing, invisibly exploring the regional campground. Best is that each day offers something she hadn't seen the day before—wasp nests dangling like rice paper lanterns from treetops; an old swing set, where she pretended to be a girl again until her queasy stomach told her to smarten up; rhyming and misspelled graffiti in the women's change-room on the beach. Best is no human prints save her own.

The driver has stopped on the road. Now he and a big, thick-furred dog are looming toward her. The animal has Siberian husky in him, she guesses. It's straining against the rope leash, as if it wants a good piece of her. She places the man in his late sixties. Bomber-style jacket undone, sleeves frayed, heavy plaid shirt beneath. Canvas, khaki work pants of the sort sold in hardware stores. And rubber shoe covers—what her dad used to call galoshes, and wore over his shining black postmaster shoes. She hasn't seen galoshes for decades, or even tasted that old-fashioned word in her own mouth for as long. Such practical things. Where did they all go? She and the man only nod as they cross paths. So I'm not the only one, she thinks. But it is okay.

She completes the loop of cottages and turns back toward the lake, this time crossing through the middle instead of paralleling the shoreline. Fast. In thirty-five minutes she has shed her winter clothes and is snuggling beneath the heavy duvet—a design of smashed red rose blossoms—brought from home. Sometimes she sees flowers, sometimes bloody fists. She hugs herself beneath the weight, and doesn't do anything else except sleep.

§

For two days she does not speak to anyone—not even *Hello, nice morning*—and by God it's glorious. The real world is waning, but now she is low on food. Bells jingle overhead when she enters the low-ceilinged grocery store, and a man—mid-fifties?—in a blue flannel shirt and black suspenders, materializes in the baking and cereals aisle. In a glance she perceives a golf-ball sized goiter on his neck. Maybe it's always been there, she thinks. Maybe the locals are so used to it they don't even notice. He double-takes; she believes he looks surprised to see her, then is embarrassed at his surprise, so turns to straighten tins of baking soda and cocoa. He looks like an Edgar, she postulates. Maybe a Heintz. Children's music is emanating through an open door near the back of the store. She saunters past, stealing a gander into a living room. TV on. A fair-haired toddler—tied into a highchair with a scarf—is conducting an orchestra of muppets with a spoon.

She selects several oranges and bags a few nearly ripened bananas, a Jersey Milk chocolate bar for a treat. No skim milk in the cooler, so she reaches for a litre of two percent. She has brought her favourite bran cereal, eats some at every meal. She peruses each aisle. More candy than anything else. A twirling stand of warped greeting cards. In the back corner she finds bolts of calico fabric, grey wool socks, mousetraps. Very "Little House on the Prairie," she thinks. A pioneer's general store. Part museum, but there are also reminders of the here and now: long distance phone cards and blank DVDs are available near the till. To stay longer would be conspicuous. She sets her items on the counter's sliding belt.

"Morning," the clerk says. Voice between octaves, like he's had surgery on his larynx. She's learned that sometimes people with unusual speaking voices make exceptional singers, and she hopes this is true of him. As a rule, she wishes the best for people.

"Good morning."

The man punches prices into the till and doesn't look at her. "Just visiting?"

He pares speech down to the essentials, Kit notes. "Yes, I'm only here for a week or so. Ten days. How much are these?" She lifts a local newspaper off the stack at the end of the counter.

"Free. Not much in there. Not much happens around here."

She can almost hear the *We like it that way.* Maybe he is an exile, too. He and his goiter, she thinks. He finishes bagging her groceries. In the city one is expected to bring his or her own shopping bags; there's a charge for plastic. Not here. "Well, thank you. See you."

She briskly crosses the wide centre street. The hairdresser, whom she received her keys from, is in her own barber chair, arm poised over her head, curling iron in hand. Well. Maybe she should have her hair cut while she's on this *holiday.* Get it zipped off to shoulder-length, or above her ears. She'd have to be more conscientious about earrings then. She's had the same easy-care style–long hair and bangs–since she was in high school; a change might be cathartic. Or not.

She unpacks her few groceries and throws the newspaper on the floral duvet. Fists or roses? A little of both today, she decides. Only the bedding, her taunting guitar in its hard case–taking up the space of a Josiah-sized child in the corner–and the books on the dresser are familiar. If she stays in she might be inspired to do something productive–write a few seasonal ditties, consider spring touring possibilities–but she's already half-dressed for the weather, and knows that when she arrives at the campground and sees the tree-lined trail, she'll be glad of her effort. Oh, yes, she will walk. Productivity is in part what derailed her in the first place.

She bunches her double-gloved hands up inside her coat sleeves: her fingertips tingle. No sun today. She questions the logic of it being so cold under an overcast sky: this is not the way the weather's supposed to work. She hustles through the village, past the shovelled walks and reindeer displays and evergreen wreaths. Christmas Eve Service at the Lutheran Church, 7:00 p.m. All welcome. She's soon in the regional park, spotting new tracks, though the wind has almost completely erased her own bootprints from yesterday's trek. An abbreviated hike would make sense today, but she finds herself stepping onto the lake again. A Ford F-150 is parked near the ice-fishing shack, the same thin exhalation from the stovepipe.

Before long she is marching up the road between the two rows of cabins. And there is the man from the other day. Same pants. Same happy-faced but potentially aggressive dog. Today she'll have to talk. "Hello," she says, facing the lunging animal as if it, not the man, will respond. The dog has one blue eye, one brown; she bets it's mixed with something wild.

He strains against his collar, tail spinning. His master jerks on the leash, elbows high. Worn leather work gloves. Cigarette package poking out of upper right pocket. "He wants to get close to you and jump up."

She does not step back. "Is he old?"

"Don't know.... Punk Dawson gave him to me. Part husky, part wolf." The man rubs his grey-stubbled chin, turns his head to the side, spits into the snow. Tobacco. "Needs to be walked every day... comes everywhere with me, else he cries."

Kit thinks about this. Until he was three, Josiah would not let her out of his sight, as if he knew he'd only have her for a short time. When she was on the phone he climbed her legs. He wailed when she left the house without him. It was irritating and exhausting, and she'd written in her journal that the dependency enraged her. Was she a terrible mother if she swatted the boy's hands off her when he only needed to be held? It was like both her love and energy had run out before this third and most tender-hearted child was born. He cried more than the other two put together. She was unprepared.

"The dog's lucky to have you," she says, and pats its head. "Well, have a nice day." She continues on, allowing a few moments to collect before she checks to see if they're following. No. They've turned in at a small trailer with a dirty yellow tarp stretched over the roof, a deep freezer outside the door. He wouldn't need to plug it in, she thinks. But could he live there year round? So cold.

A white rabbit with black ears bounds under a cottage on cement blocks. Someone is burning wood. The fragrance transports her to the disparate campgrounds of her childhood: Waterton, Grand Beach, Cypress Hills, Jasper, Waskesiu. Her parents had been keen on camping holidays. For two weeks every summer they hitched the tent trailer behind the wood-panelled station wagon, filled the thermos with Kool-Aid, scooted Kit and her brothers into the back–*sans* seatbelts–and set out for a new destination with the windows wide open. Everyone camped back then; the first time she stayed in a hotel was on her wedding night.

Back in her sparse room she uses her nail to scrape away the ice crystal design on the window. Four trucks and a snowmobile are parked at the restaurant. Am I getting better? she wonders. She mummies inside the duvet. Tough to tell.

§

The local paper covers the events of five rural communities and she scours every line. Someone has lost a toque in the school yard. Millie's sister Bess had a nice time in Palm Springs. Craft sale on Saturday at the Pioneer Lodge.

There are other diversions: a colour TV, a VCR, one untitled movie. She plugs it into the machine. "Cat on a Hot Tin Roof." The picture is washed out, characters and sets cast in varying degrees of white, as if overexposed. And the sound is not right. She struggles to make out Elizabeth Taylor's dialogue but it's work, like listening for familiar words in a foreign language.

She sleeps the afternoon away, then–for a change–decides to have dinner in the restaurant; no need to throw a coat on to cross the street. She drags her fingers through her hair, tries to lock the door behind her but has trouble with the catch. It doesn't matter.

The café is called Mabel's. Light-faded hunting and fishing scenes balance in cheap frames on the walls, and Kit sees that Gordie Howe made an appearance here: his autograph is scrawled across his forehead in a black and white photograph beside a fridge filled with pop. A pre-teenaged girl sits cross-legged at the table nearest the kitchen, a diaphanous pearl-coloured skirt over her jeans, frizzy hair done up in a knot like a synchronized swimmer. An open text and mess of papers tell the story of homework. She is the only person in the room.

Kit sits beneath a *No Smoking* sign and opens the plastic-wrapped menu. Anything will do; food hasn't interested her in months. A woman swings out the bi-fold doors with a carafe. She's on the thin side of the scale, thirty-five or so birthdays, Kit presumes, the muscles in her forearms well-developed, and she's wearing pink slippers. Prettier from a distance. When the woman's directly before her, Kit notes large pores and shiny skin beneath the fluorescent lighting. The waitress unsuccessfully stifles a yawn. Her knuckles are enlarged; Kit's warned Sandy that cracking one's knuckles will do this. Sandy doesn't care. Is this dim café where the waitress imagined life would take her? Is this enough for anyone? Kit studies the menu. Specials handwritten on a slip of paper and stapled in–Salisbury steak, pork cutlets–nothing is over eight dollars. She envisions the scores of villagers who've gathered here. Farmers with waning Old Country accents in the same chairs at the same tables talking about the sorry state of crop prices, the high cost of inputs, and how global warming might ruin it all before their grandsons are old enough to drive combine. Men who had to leave school to help their fathers seed and harvest. They had been hungry as children. They sported wide fingers, thumbs half-missing or gone. They made better grandfathers than fathers, appreciated a good dirty joke and a warm raisin pie. They did not swim or golf. They'd bitch when the cost of a cup of coffee was increased by ten cents, and they served as church elders. They favoured one or two shirts and were married to a single brand of jeans. They could get an extra five or seven years out of a swather far past its prime and could work miracles on an engine with a length of old pantyhose and the salvaged whatnots only they knew how to find in the dingy, greasy-smelling minefield they called *the shop*. They wiped up after themselves at the sink in the porch and called their wives *Mother*. Salt of the freaking earth, Kit thinks, and wonders whose chair she's taken.

The waitress slides Kit's cup across the table and fills it. "Man, I'm beat. How's it going for you today?"

"Not so bad," Kit says, looking into the woman's gap-toothed smile. It appears genuine; lately it takes so little kindness to mist Kit's eyes. She returns to the menu. Words swim. Two of the dessert choices have been eliminated with black marker, but ice *creme* remains an option.

"Sorry, I don't even ask no more. Coffee to start?"

Kit reaches for the creamer. "Thanks. It smells good."

The woman says she'll be back in five. She swings into a chair across from the girl and lights a cigarette. A slipper hangs off her foot, then drops. Kit does not think about her own kids, nor the thousands of others she meets each year. *Children, we have a very special guest visiting our school today.* She concentrates on how it feels to be alone in that creaky bed above the hairdressing shop, free to collapse into and out of sleepless dreams all through the day and night. The unpronounceable country. She could get used to it. She would be thrilled never to set foot in another school gymnasium, apply for another grant, write another goofy fucking song.

She orders a turkey sandwich and fries. A huge meal, smothered in a lake of gravy, and she makes herself swallow every bit of it. She also orders a milkshake, an old-style vanilla served right in the tin it was mixed in, and fabricates headlines for the local paper: *Hollow woman fills up. Local café owner last to see city woman.* She finishes her meal and imagines no one's tipped like she has since Gordie Howe and his elbows blew through town.

Back in her room she turns to the news; it's white noise more than information she craves. She knows this insincere weatherman with the bleached teeth and immaculate wheat-coloured hair; he also has a radio talk show. He's interviewed her three times and on each awkward occasion acted like he'd never seen her before. What to do with that? During the weather forecast she counts the number of times he says, "We can tell you that…." Eight. Does no one monitor this stuff, she wonders?

She turns off the TV and tucks in. In her dreams: sirens. Who is hurt? Josiah? Philip? She's confidant Sandy can take care of herself. She tries to wake up. Can't.

In the morning her head feels plugged. She thinks of gauze, and the way a dentist stops up blood after an extraction. The tranquilizers. She must try to cut back. How's that for a small step? Not *I must* cut back, but *I must try* to. She tentatively lifts the blinds; more snow has settled on the village. She is reminded of Christmas, of family, her failure, her frailty. And she sinks. So easy to succumb to it. No, that's not it: she does not have a choice. It's like being dragged beneath murky water. A slough. She's flailing and kicking but keeps dropping until there is no light at all and finally, when the last of her air has been spent and her lungs surrender, a heavy rock's set on her chest. This is the way she drowns. Was it the same heaviness for her grandfather, who took his life in a tool shed? Her aunt? Her brother who attempted but did not succeed?

She reaches for her pills and dials home. She does not know the hour or the day. Philip answers and acts like nothing is unusual, like it is any other week and she is just out on the road, calling from a hotel to say howdy. Everyone's fine, Sandy got an award in her art class.

"Can you put Dad on?"

"Sure," the boy says. But no goodbye.

Lloyd asks: "Are you ready, Kit Kat?"

He hasn't called her that in years; the sweetness devastates her further.

"Not yet."

§

She wipes the skiff of snow off a picnic table and sits. Not cold: if she were inclined, she could stay here all day. Listening. Just breathing. She pushes her hood back, unzips a few inches of jacket. A ruckus in the trees: a snowy owl. It lights on a branch, then trapezes to the next tree, and the next. When she can't see it anymore she walks again. Snow-prints like horses' hooves. A squirrel's close and sudden chatter. *Pop*. A hunter's gun, making her jump.

She meets the man and his dog in the dead centre of the lake. He seems to her like someone who might accept the jobs no one else wants to do—work at the dump, play Santa at the town party, bury the dead. He would do these things, she bets, without complaint or expectation of payment. He points out a huddle of geese at the far end: the tip of the tongue. "Hanging around," he says, as though airing out private thoughts.

"Huh. I never noticed them before," she says.

"Open water there. You can't see it from here, but there's sticks around it... so nobody gets too close. Shoulda seen in the fall. Thirty thousand snow geese on the lake. Sounded like a freeway."

She is close enough to smell him. Pee and loneliness. She tentatively offers her palm to the dog, and when he doesn't take her hand off, she strokes his thick pelt.

"He's okay," the man says. She notices he has no bottom teeth. "He's friendly."

She and the stranger regard each other, then–as if reflexively–they both turn toward the soldiering spruce trees. Late in the day; the giants are in silhouette against a mauve sky. *Up,* they point. And she sees it is the only way. The trees. Her thoughts turn again toward Christmas. Lloyd would have the house lights strung now, perhaps not in a straight line, but close, and there'd be mistletoe hung in the vestibule. The family's deflated stockings would be nailed to the fireplace mantle. Mandarin oranges... magazines... chocolate... a scratch lottery ticket for Lloyd....

"Well," the stranger says, "I guess."

She recognizes this as the transitory moment when either could ask: *What got you here?* "Yes," she says. Yes. She takes an inventory of all that is required–a good head, a receptive heart–and for the next few seconds she has nothing to fear. "I guess so."

JOHNNY DEAD BED

Before this, my semi-final move (*semi,* because the final is the one we're all inevitably being sucked toward, and perhaps even that move is not *el fin*), came the proverbial escape to the country, the suburban split-level, the inner city two-storey brick, a rotating barrage of dilapidated, upscale and standard apartments, the ninth-floor college dorm, and, before that, the many rooms of my youth.

This story concerns the inner city brick. The real estate agent was a ferret with too many small, clicking teeth, and it was love at first bite. He was too fond of the phrase "most probably." "You'll want the extra room for when that little one is born, most probably." His eyes slid (hungrily?) to my eighth-month belly, like I was storing a huge egg he couldn't wait to devour with his ferret tongue. "Most probably," I said back, and Brander smiled at me with his eyes. Later he remarked on the unusual syntax. "It came out like 'the little one will most probably be born'... as if there's some doubt."

Brander lectured to bored eighteen-year-olds at the University of Saskatchewan when he wasn't working on His Thesis. He put too much of himself into his lectures, which were, ultimately, unappreciated by the flippant kids. Try as he might, he was never nominated for one of those "Outstanding Professor" awards. He put even more into The Thesis. The pie should have been sliced into three equal pieces, but mine was only a polite sliver. I forgave his imperious idiosyncrasies, like correcting poor grammar. I would put up with it for some time to come.

When we bought the house we were little more than kids ourselves; we didn't have the income or the connections we would later gain. Like us, our friends and associates were mostly renting, but Brander's parents believed that with a baby on the way we required more permanent surroundings. Fences would become increasingly important. A crib at the end of the bed wouldn't do: a proper nursery was in order.

Tom and Edith frowned on our musty apartment near the university, with its oven-like hallways and communal laundry room. Mostly Tom, Brander's father, frowned. Edith's streamlined lips were cast in a permanent scowl; one could never judge her moods by her expressions. Clearly, however, she disapproved. In all honesty, I was not very charitable when it came to Edith. But tit for tat and *quid pro quo*. She always made me feel nowhere near good enough for Brander, and insinuated that my father's work–as the regional manager of a chain of retail stores–ranked several shelves below Tom's holier-than-thou vocation: Law.

It wasn't so much the things Edith said–or didn't say–that were meant to diminish me; it was the way she watched and waited for me to flounder, to expose myself, to flop on shore like a screwed-up fish. Our first meeting was at a pretentious restaurant where everything that wasn't crystal was silver or linen. I survived the initial, detached hug from Tom and took the cold slender hand Edith offered. My own father would have known better, about the hug. Wine was ordered, swirled, sniffed and approved. Our small talk had the same sort of perfunctory air to it. "… and you have two sisters? Younger and older?" "Yes. Holly married an electrician from Hudson Bay. My younger sister, Camille, lives in Sooke. Near Whiffen Spit." I was hoping I wouldn't have to get into more details, and I didn't.

It was only a minor interrogation. The food arrived. Brander ordered for me: he knew the ropes. What arrived looked less like food and more like a centerpiece. Tiny cabbages, a shellacked piece of roast, brown rice topped with a sprig of some weed or another.

Edith's vulture eye caught my split second of indecision over which fork to begin with, and she nudged me, gently, with an elbow, and tapped the correct fork beside her own plate. It was pretty much a toboggan ride after that.

My mother-in-law's one virtue, as far as I could see, was that she'd instilled a zealous work ethic in Brander. Instilled, or demanded. Either way, he was a roll-up-the-shirt-sleeves-kind-of-guy, whether marking papers, raking the leaves from our masticated lawn, or making love. The way he tackled the latter confused me; at first I thought it was lust. I also gave Edith points for Brander's name. At a time when the big names of the day were veritable bookends like Robert, Michael, and David, she bucked the trend with her only child. Brander. Shades out of the ordinary. It fit.

Although Tom "hrumphed" and "hmm hmmmed" more than most, I did not consider him a threat. He was a jellyfish with brown age spots on his high forehead and plump hands. A pipe-smoking jellyfish that Edith moulded into whatever shape she needed.

After the wedding–a surprisingly small affair with all the best matrimonial accoutrements–we had a few months for settling in, and, for me, time to adjust to my new family. Then came the positive pregnancy test–surprise!–and the search for the house.

Edith wanted to get her grubbing paws in on the action, but I was determined to find our first home ourselves. Think pre-internet: we dug up an agent in the Yellow Pages. I lived by the Yellow Pages. From pizza parlours to chimney sweeps, all were as close as my fingertips. *Let your fingers do the walking,* they used to say. An indispensable book back then: the contact information for all those people with all that diverse knowledge–or, more appropriately, *know-how*–slid into my kitchen drawer beneath the oven mitts. Knowledge is different from know-how. I understand know-how. It, and the now redundant

Yellow Pages, were much more useful than any of the *knowledge* or 19th Century classics Brander intravenously fed to his students; they would take it no other way. I poured over the real estate companies, recognizing some because I'd seen their signs, their hot-air balloons in the early morning sky while Brander showered. I mined the newspaper for agents. Who had the most open houses? Who won the sales awards? One phone call, one awkward explanation of what I was after, and we were hooked up with Graham, our skittish agent.

If I were in the market now, I would employ the services of any one of the agents I consider close friends. I'm a Luddite: their business cards are alphabetically filed in a gold box–an antique store find–atop my desk. I would spread the cards on the polished oak and choose on some arbitrary basis, like who had the most appealing business card. The shiny black embossed on white? The silver script and filigreed border?

I was four months pregnant when we began our search. By my six month we'd traipsed through an entire flotilla of houses, some of which still remain lockboxed in my mind: the corner dollhouse with arched doorways that led into other rooms; the grey stucco with its mysterious star-shaped stain on the basement wall; the yellow barn with the purple linoleum; the 1950s bungalow with the rusted fridge that emitted toxic fumes and sent us bolting for fresh air. The lonely ones, the discarded ones, the well-loved ones that left me feeling as inadequate as any new parent. The ones that didn't feel right, or look right, or–as in the one with the squeaky floorboards and wind whistling through the attic–*sound* right. The divorce houses, the promotion houses, the recent death houses, where the air was palpable with funereal grief.

How I despised viewing occupied homes, knowing that the owners hated it even more: cleaning until the rooms were impeccable, having the private guts of their lives–photographs, bed linens, toiletries–readily displayed (and therefore judged) behind something as penetrable as a closet door.

We settled for the two-storey brick. It was within walking distance to the university, city centre, the river, a school, and a hospital. Who knew when one might need one or the other? It was in one of those eclectic neighbourhoods favoured by poets and painters, students, the unsuspecting elderly (who would never have guessed that their neighbourhood might be considered chic, and would probably never have moved there in the first place if they *had* suspected), a few riffraff, a grab bag of professionals, and some, like the little man who shuffled past at 5:00 p.m.–whispering obscenities, squeezing his privates, and making karate chopping motions–who defied definition.

The house was affordable; the downpayment thanks to Brander's parents. *Los padres de Brander.* It was what those in real estate deem a Carpenter's Special. I expect it is still standing, or, rather, *squatting,* with its shoulders hunched like one of those collectable British bulldogs. After us a retiring psychology professor bought it. After that, I heard it had been broken into suites and regressed into a place that nice girls avoid.

Graham informed us that that the previous owner, a Mr. Kovach, was an elderly widower who had wallpapered over most of the windows. The man had died and relatives were eager to get their hands on some capital. What Graham didn't impart was that Mr. Kovach had died there. In the house. Tumbled off the cellar steps to the concrete floor, and his demise.

The house–with its white shutters, maple hardwood, pantry, four bedrooms, clawfoot bathtub, red brick fireplace, garage, and reasonably generous yard with great garden potential–screamed *Buy Me.* We did. I had five keys cut and tried them all. Brander carried the one hundred and seventy pounds of eight month's pregnant me across the threshold. We also acquired the old man's wrought-iron bed, a seven foot dresser that must have been built in the room, a plum couch, various curtains (which we immediately shredded and replaced with venetians), a winter's supply of firewood, a pee pot, and one wooden crutch.

The true story about Johnny (aka John J. Kovach) came from Wendy, one half of the the only couple in the neighbourhood who didn't fit: too normal. She delivered an apple pie shortly after we moved in, and gave us the goods on Johnny. The pastry was a nice touch, a rural touch, reminiscent of my childhood. I liked Wendy immediately. *Immediatamente.* She and Ken and their pre-teens lived in the pink clapboard behind us. Wendy hinted that Shyla and Erick would be excellent babysitters, when the time came. Ken worked at Canadian Tire; the hardware department. My father would have liked him. "Funny," I said to Brander, after Wendy left, "it doesn't smell like a death house."

We burned Johnny's wood and hacked up the dresser but kept the bed. Once I'd touched up the ornate Victorian frame with black paint and threw a handmade quilt on it, it passed even the Edith test. "But you must do something about those carpets," she urged, referring to the once fashionable but now dowdy and worn patterned rugs in the upper rooms. "We're going to lift and replace them as soon as Brander has time," I reassured her, but he never had time and I rather liked the tattered things, mouldy as they were.

After Brander left in the mornings, I'd wipe his breakfast dishes, then clamber back into that old bed under inches of blankets and the lumpy quilt. The room stayed dark with the blinds closed, and there was rarely noise from the street below. I'd safely drift in and out of dreams. The bed felt–as beds often do–like a giant womb.

The baby in my own womb was restless: it was getting close. I chose the room with the slanted ceiling for a nursery. It had a window seat and faced the back yard, where rusty leaves covered the consequences of neighbourhood dogs. The room next to ours had more light, but I felt it might be startling to newborn eyes. Also, Brander had hinted that it would make a fine study.

The house contained an ample washroom, and a sunroom I couldn't wait to fill with plants, with green, with life–but I'd have to wait. It wasn't insulated, and already it was too cold in the evenings to watch the sun set through those one-pane windows. I added "Buy Boston Fern" to my mental To Do list.

I wallowed in the space and quiet. The apartment block had rocked with music and voices, sometimes deep into the night. There were several students in the building, doing everything but studying. When we'd learned that I was expecting, it was decided, by consensus, that I'd not return for my final year of university. The baby needed me at home, and besides, it was only an arts degree, and what would I do with it anyway? One needed a well-considered plan before he or she entered into higher education, or so one of Tom's diatribes went, and I'd had only a half-hearted desire to do something other than work in retail for the rest of my life. The tuition and time were not lost, however, for I met Brander in those hallowed halls, and he was everything I wasn't.

I spent hours trundling around the house, investigating like a little girl might each room of her newly-acquired dollhouse. Except this was better. I pressed my palm against the cold brick fireplace. "Mine." The stained glass above the bay window. "Mine." The battered, oak banister; the lazy-susan; the failing back steps. Mine. Mine. Mine. I forced my feet into the cellar. There was no sign of an accident, not a hint of blood, but I felt better after, knowing what wasn't there.

Those long afternoons, while my baby performed slow-motion summersaults inside me, I sat in the solitary stillness of my new brick house. There were occasional visits with Wendy and a persistent Avon Lady, but mostly I was alone. I half-heartedly tried to conjure the ghost of John Kovach, but there was nothing there. Apparently he'd had Alzheimer's; perhaps he didn't remember where he lived. It would be wrong to say his presence had vanished completely, however, for each night we slept in his bed: the bed of a dead man. You don't forget that. We laughed about it, even made jokes to disguise any discomfort we suspected the other might be feeling. Brander was much better at wordplay; he was the one who came up with "Johnny Dead Bed."

One of those afternoons, a day in late October when the snow dusted everything and contemplated whether or not to stay, I was sitting in Brander's study; it doubled as our library. A fringe benefit of being a student (Brander was in his fifth year, I'd completed three and some) was that we'd accumulated an impressive collection of books. I'd slogged through geography and sociology texts brightened with colourful photographs to hold students' attention. They'd rarely held mine. Brander's contribution to the library was more impressive: all the literary greats were in attendance. As well, pushed into an invisible corner, all the *Coles Notes*.

I came across a text from the previous year. Spanish. My high school French teacher, Monsieur Robichard—an old man whom the boys mooned and tormented—told me I had an aptitude for languages. It was offhand compliments like that, morsels, really, which stuck in my brain and saw me off on unlikely tangents. Spanish fit into my degree requirements and I thought the language romantic, so I registered and flourished. When I found the book again I blew a dead fly off it and decided to brush up, or rather, to keep brushing, because one year of textbook Spanish had not made me fluent.

After rediscovering the book it was never far from my reach. I was consumed by the language, basking in it for hours on end. "Brander, you're home already? *¡Qué sorpresa!* Where did the time go?"

I began to think in Spanish. When the phone rang I had to check myself to be sure I answered *hello* and not *bueno* or *hola*. Numbers became *números*. Groceries: *comestibles*. I'd always skipped from passion to passion; this was nothing new.

"Natasha, where are you?" Brander often asked. I rocked in the bentwood rocker, rubbing my burgeoning belly. *Natasha no está. Regresa más tarde.*

We'd eat late, sometimes in front of the fire, then he'd lead me up the carpeted stairs, down the hall with the faded runner and into our bedroom, where the pearlescent moon was framed in our window, and we'd crawl into Johnny Dead Bed, though sex was now too much effort for us both.

The nights grew longer and colder. The house's woodchip insulation was insufficient, especially upstairs. "Brander, let me call someone about the insulation," I tried. "It's going to be too cold for the baby."

"We can't afford it right now," he'd say. He almost always had his nose–in fact the better part of his face–buried in a book. The tips of his ears were red. *Rojo.*

"Your parents will help."

He looked up from his book, set it down, the spine arching in protest. "My parents. Why is it always *my* parents? The crib, the high chair, the downpayment... now the insulation. They're shit to you unless you need something from them."

"I'm sorry. It's just... the baby... any day now...."

He returned to his book with a *hrumph*.

§

Jameson was born on a winter-like morning in autumn. The sun chiselled jewels into the snow. The same hour of the same day an Earthquake in Mexico killed hundreds and the dead were laid out in schoolyards. People were hacking up their brothers and sisters–even babies–all over the world. There was a gas war. It was also the birthday of Fernando Valenzuela, the famous baseball pitcher. Later I called the newspaper to get an extra copy–fresh, no coffee rings–from the momentous day. I folded the paper and placed it in a box labelled "Jameson's Treasures." The Jeane Dixon horoscope proclaimed: "Today's children are good at keeping secrets–both yours and their own. They have a lot of faith in their own judgment and rarely ask for advice. Luckily, their instincts are excellent. Do not expect these deep thinkers to be the life of the party: chances are they may not even *attend* the party. Content with their own company, these Scorpios prefer solitary nature walks to crowded gatherings." What more could I ask for?

I'd suffered through hard labour all night but still couldn't sleep. Brander was present for the whole thing, spooning me ice chips, mopping my head. When the pain ripped me apart and I begged for drugs, he squeezed my hand and said, "You don't need them, you can do this." He was wrong. I needed them, but did not get them. Trying not to push until I was told to was the worst part; like stopping a runaway train. But I did it. And the doctor called it a classic birth. After delivery I was rolled into the recovery room where an ochre-haired nurse brought tea and plain toast. I'd never been closer to God in my life, and expect I will never be that close again. I was blessed with a healthy child: a son for Brander, a grandchild for his parents, and mine.

I kept Jameson in my room–a ward, with three other new mothers. I'm certain I glowed when one of the nurses, behind my pulled curtain, held my baby and said: "I like this one best." Brander's parents wanted to pay for a private room, but I was glad I'd opted for the ward. The embarrassment in having episiotomy stitches examined, of receiving an enema or having one's breasts (big and hard as coconuts) kneaded were far less severe knowing that three feet away another mother was enduring exactly the same indignities.

We brought Jameson home, where the heart should be, but Brander's never was. It was my house–it had always been mine–and Brander seemed to sense this, as if the walls had a will of their own and the furnace conked out to spite him.

There was a baby shower, held at Edith's. I didn't know many of the silver-haired women with painted-on lips and cheeks. They cooed over my baby and wanted to see his little feet. They brought layettes, bunting bags, and a curious mobile with heavy pieces of copper shaped like stars, the moon and sun. I disliked the idea of a shower–a tradition I associated with a bygone era, back when women wore aprons and were allocated a little pocket money from their husbands–but tried to be gracious and appear amazed as I unwrapped each offering and tried not to destroy the crepe wrapping paper, all those pretty pastels.

Brander carved a week out of his schedule and offered it to us, and it was the best gift he could have given, although not the only one. He also presented me with a ring–a sapphire, blue like his eyes–and thanked me for our spectacular son. He did not receive a present from me in return. I wasn't one to fall into the commercial trap of a card for every occasion (St. Patrick's Day?), a gift for every reason. Besides, at that time I believed that every day and every good thing on God's green earth was a gift.

Life settled down. Jameson proved a good baby, which meant little except that he slept and ate well, and occasionally, by coincidence, turned up the corners of his pink lips at the right time so that Brander, Tom or Edith thought he was smiling. Brander was at immediate ease with the baby, adept at clipping the tiny fingernails and swabbing Jameson's ugly navel. He'd been the one to go in during the circumcision, while I cried into my hospital pillow. He was a natural at bathing our son in the plastic tub, at burping him over his shoulder.

I frequently bundled Jameson and stuffed him into a Snuggly, walking the wet sidewalks of our neighbourhood. Wendy said motherhood looked good on me; another morsel for my jar.

Within two weeks after the birth my stitches had healed and I was eager to resume our "nightlife." Early on we'd adopted a strange habit of using euphemisms for sex. Brander referred to orgasms as "birthdays" or "happy endings." "It's too soon," he said, "You should have a check-up first." I had the check-up, received the physician's all-clear, and we fumbled through, but it was not like before. It pinched. I was still bleeding, and my breasts leaked milk onto the sheets, leaving them clammy. Time. *Necesitamos tiempo,* I said to the baby. Lovemaking had been a regular and integral part of our pre-baby life. We'd each come to the marriage with some experience in that area, but never swapped particulars, which was just as well. Judging from his ability to know when, where and how, I assumed Brander's coital résumé was more impressive than mine.

Spring arrived, as it always does, even after those wretched winter days when the sky's uniformly grey and you don't expect to ever see the sun again—it comes. I started tomato plants from seed and each morning set flats in the sunroom. In the evening I ferried them back to the bay window in the front room. The seasons were in transition; nights were cool in the unheated sunroom, and it was too early to trust the wispy seedlings—tender things—entirely to nature.

Jameson bounced in a jolly jumper. When he grew too heavy for that it was into the walker. We had an excellent arrangement: while he bumped from table to couch, I cleaned windows, polished wood, scrubbed, painted, filled holes in plaster, changed wallpaper, tiled the washroom, and made the house my own. Sometimes I'd dust off my hands and read to my son. Jack *y el* Beanstalk. Snow White *y los siete* Dwarves. I measured the quality of each day by the number of ticks I made on my To Do list. Usually, life measured up pretty well.

In the summer Brander and I moved Jameson's playpen outside. He marvelled at the cabbage and monarch butterflies, and stuffed grass in his mouth while we attacked the previously pet-plagued yard. We dug a small garden plot. There would be radishes, and both Romaine and butter lettuce–if the bugs didn't get it first. Beets for borscht. Peas, yellow beans, and my spindly tomatoes. Brander constructed a fence along the back lane. His parents brought an anniversary gift: a barbecue. They didn't buy it from Wendy's husband, Ken. We picked up a patio table and chairs at a yard sale, and a paddling pool–from Ken–for future years. We often looked out our back window to see what we'd become.

But day and night were just that. Night and day. "Is it me?" I'd ask, after Brander'd rolled away yet again, mumbling about an early morning. I'd pull the quilt to my chin.

"No. It's no one," he'd say, his chest glowing in the moonlight. "I'm just tired."

"You've been tired for three weeks. This isn't natural."

"Who says?"

"*I* say."

"Look, our sex life was bound to drop off a bit," he said, without taking a moment to think about it. "We've been married almost two years. We can't go on like rabbits, at each other several times a day. It happens to everyone."

I knew this was untrue. Wendy told me, and other women I'd known over the years. I was aware that Tom and Edith slept in separate beds and I couldn't fathom ever ending up like that. I'd come to depend upon Brander's warm body at night. If he was up late working in the room next door, I'd watch the moon and check for satellites and falling stars and maybe something else up there, something unexplainable, until he joined me. He emanated heat, and more than that, he embodied a quality I couldn't name, although perhaps *sanctuary* came close. I'd curl into him. Then, and only then, would I sleep.

In late August I suggested counselling. Brander suggested a party. We'd string patio lanterns along the clothesline, send witty invitations to his colleagues, and spend too much money on alcohol. This wasn't like a college party, where everyone was expected to BYOB. We were homeowners now. Parents. Responsible. Brander was an academic and we were not throwing a party, we were *entertaining*.

It wasn't a huge crowd, but there were several strange faces. We barbecued steaks and ate caesar salad with massive croutons that never did soften up. I'd baked Irish soda bread and had used too much buttermilk, so the loaves were the size and shape of cow pies. Someone brought a cheese plate. Someone else brought a spinach salad, with strawberries and flaked almonds that looked like excised fingernails. We'd bought mid-grade wine glasses for the occasion, and beautiful paper napkins: like Monet's Giverny watergarden battered with rain. The weather co-operated—one of those soft-aired evenings when the light seems elastic and stretches on and on. I worried about the food, about the weeds I hadn't had time to address, about all the ways in which I might misrepresent myself, and how that might negatively reflect upon Brander.

I was relieved that Wendy and Ken agreed to come; Shyla had recently passed her Babysitting Course, and Jameson was happy to spend the evening pulling at her long hair and dangly earrings. My good neighbours and I hovered near the barbecue and made ourselves look busy. Useful. "Would you like more sauce on that? Maybe some onions?" This was where we fit: with the barbecue tools and lighter fluid. The animated conversations about dead English poets and postmodernism were conducted in another language, much further out there than Spanish. Once the barbecue cooled we gravitated toward the punch bowl. *¿Tienes sed? ¿Tienes hambre?*

After the meal there was an uncomfortable pall. *Incómodo.* People worked harder at conversation without the scrape of plates, the jangle of cutlery to fill in the gaps. I knew I was expected to aid this process, and I waltzed from conversation to conversation, adding little more than a presence, an affirmation, and an occasional chuckle. I knew enough to laugh at the right times, a lesson learned with Tom and Edith. But mine was just a temporary task; as soon as the spiked punch, beer, wine, and scotch mercifully took effect, no one noticed whether I laughed at their jokes or not.

Hours after the meal–when everyone was well-lubricated, the music was louder, and the lawn chairs had picked up and deserted their original positions–another guest arrived. Her shimmery hair, also dark, appeared to float just above her shoulders. Nondescript black turtleneck. A short skirt emphasized tanned, dancer's legs, and black Grecian sandals that crisscrossed up and over her ankles. She held a jean jacket, and her trim handbag was slung sideways across her chest, as was the fashion. If she'd had breasts this would have emphasized them. It would have emphasized mine. Something was concealed in the jean jacket. A bottle of red wine.

"Hi," I said, extending my hand. "I'm Natasha. Brander's wife."

The latecomer's gaze left me cold. She panned the other guests. "Hi. God, I'm so late." She took my hand and shook my fingers. Bracelets jingled. "Roxanne. Roxanne Bodner."

"Can I get you a glass of punch?"

"I'd like that." She handed me the wine, which I set on the makeshift bar and left unopened. She might have been twenty.

Brander hadn't noticed the late arrival yet; I pounced. "So are you in the English department, Roxanne?"

The girl seemed to gather up her shoulders and pay attention then. "No, well not really. I'm in my second year. I had Brander last year–" A strange, even comic choice of words. Brander would have been amused. "–for English. I've also been working at the university this summer. Just filing and stuff."

Wendy was suddenly beside me, crunching potato chips. I introduced the two women, then Wendy ducked out, insisting, "We need to fill the pretzel bowls."

Roxanne and I watched her disappear into the bright lights inside. "Great house," the girl said. "Would you mind giving me a tour?"

I was pleased to show off my house at every opportunity, and took her in through the back, narrating as we walked room to room. "Of course it wasn't like this when we bought it. We've had to do a lot of work."

"Was the mantle like this?" Roxanne asked, stroking the carved oak; *my* wood.

"Yes, but it was painted over and I stripped it."

She was impressed with the nursery, with the blue striped wallpaper and border of green trains. I wasn't particularly crafty but had managed to stitch the letters of Jameson's name together, stuffed them with batting and pinned them to the wall. I felt they spelled other things, too, like *contentment, family, life as it should be.*

"And last but definitely not least," I said, swinging the door wide, "the master bedroom." I followed her in, so couldn't gauge her initial reaction. A sudden intake of breath? A giveaway sigh?

"It's all antiques," she said, studying her reflection in the standing oval mirror. She skimmed over the slippers on either side of the bed, the framed photos of Brander and me, and the two of us with the baby. I'm sure she would have liked to skim over the bed, too, but she couldn't, and I knew what that was like, thinking something so hard, so secret, that you're afraid you'll say it out loud, and then you horrify yourself by doing exactly that. "Johnny Dead Bed."

§

If I were less of this world and more of the world of spirits and other good ghosts, I might say that it was the house looking after me that night. Or maybe old Johnny himself. Of course, all that dirty laundry came out in the months to follow, complete with all the hollow promises, the suspicions, the threats. In spite of everything, Brander continued to be a wonderful father. His thesis was accepted, and he taught even more classes to even more unappreciative students. Jameson—like the lilacs, the delphiniums, the undemanding pink and purple petunias that bordered our home—bloomed.

I realized the night of the party that my life had neither begun nor would it end in the two-storey brick. I also came to realize that some of Brander's knowledge—which I'd so often scorned—had rubbed off on me, and that knowledge and know-how *can* hold hands, fleetingly, like young lovers trying not to get caught.

I buried myself in books and found many Canadian authors to my liking. I wrote them fan letters. I copied and taped favourite lines of prose into a scrapbook. Among my treasures was W. D. Valgardson's adage: "In life there are no real beginnings or endings. There are so many moments where one can say 'that's where it started,' and, in most cases, it is both true and false. Life is nothing if not untidy."

And so, with the poets and painters, the accountants and drug addicts, the lewd karate chopper and the rest, I accepted my untidy life. My passions would turn, and turn again.

NATURAL DISASTERS

My wife says that dream interpretation authorities—I hesitate to use the word *experts*—claim that repeated dreams of tidal waves are the subconscious mind's way of processing a traumatic event. A rape, for example. A fatal accident. Some situation involving violence. Dreaming *contextualizes*—one of their pet words—a dominant emotion or concern. The dreams are really about fear, terror, vulnerability. Their (ahem) *research* indicates all dreams, and particularly recurring dreams, contain relevant messages for the dreamer.

Or so they say.

Though we live twelve hundred miles from any ocean, my wife has been dreaming of tidal waves and has been swept up (ha!) in a laborious mission to reveal the nature and meaning of these dreams, somewhat in the way a particularly keen grade eight student might approach a report on the same subject. Each morning as I leave to battle the hounds of high risk investment hell, she packs her own briefcase (an old one of mine) with lists containing the names of books she must borrow, articles she must read—really, anything written on the subject within the last twenty or more years—and takes the no. 2 bus to the public library.

She peppers discussions with phrases like "nets of the mind" and "day residue." We've been married eight years—my second, her first. I am a patient man. I humour her.

The first question any psychoanalyst would ask is whether or not she dies in these tidal waves. She does not. She invariably wakes just as the monster wave is about to strike—sometimes it has even begun to curl over her, though she thinks, she *believes,* she will make it to safety. In these dreams, regardless of whomever else appears in them—including, on occasion, yours truly—she is consistently the only person who appreciates the disastrous potential of hurricane winds and the increasingly disturbed sea. The waves quickly escalate. Often she is watching this impending calamity from behind glass, as in a restaurant, say. She says she perceives the imminent danger like an ancient heartache, or a mallet in the gut, long before the threat is made public, and begins planning hours before anyone else even sees fit to pull on a slicker, much less head for the hills.

My wife has become what she calls a "self-psychologist." Bunk. Her week days are spent in the downtown library among the homeless, the oozing addicts, and the mentally ill, collecting so-called facts, compiling figures: *By age 60 the average human will sleep 175,000 hours, dream 87,000 hours with 197,000 dreams. Although a significant majority of us remember our dreams, less than ten percent understand their meaning.*

Babble. I don't dream at all, although she disputes this, too, insisting everyone does, even old ghouls like myself. I've tested her, asking how dreams can possibly be worthy of serious study when most are either misremembered or altogether forgotten. She came back with this: "Remembering the individual dream is not the important part–though any remembered fragments can be critical in learning about oneself, or even in producing a work of art"–she's dabbled with pastels. "What's most important is making cross-connections, which can occur even when the actual dream is forgotten."

As I said: bunk.

These are her days. Her nights are spent tossing–or not–with waves that will end the world. Of course, upon waking, spared once again from being obliterated, she cannot return to sleep, and the lack thereof is making her jittery. Tonight she's turned into a rare and veritable bear. She snapped at an unidentified telephone caller. I agree that among the most annoying of modern telephone options is the Call Display feature, whereupon the name and number of the dialer are revealed, thus allowing the recipient to screen incoming calls. We don't subscribe to this technology ourselves, and I, too, have been driven into a white rage when a complete stranger rings up and says, "Hello this is _____. Did you call here?" No, I assure him or her, I did not. "Well, perhaps your wife, or you, dialed a wrong number, or your children... do you have teenagers, by any chance?"

This was precisely the type of conversation my wife found herself engaged in this evening as she was approaching her desk with the day's mail and a cup of sugared tea. "I did *not* call you. My husband did *not* call you. Our children definitely did *not* call you." (We don't have children.) "My great aunt Sophie did not call you. My sister-in-law, Bette, in Sudbury, did not call you. No one in this house at the present or in the past has ever, or *will* ever, call you. How my name and number appeared on your GD telephone Call Display will just have to go down as one of life's great unsolved mysteries."

"Dear," I said, taking the phone from her cool, trembling hand. "Perhaps a nap would be beneficial." I tucked her into bed, pulled the blind and soundlessly closed the door.

My wife is a mystery, and as delicate as a wrist. I like to stay on top of things, for her protection. I easily locate her journal and take it into the window-light to read her latest scribbles:

Understanding the messages given by the subconscious mind enlightens the conscious mind to what exists beyond what we experience in the five physical senses, thereby enriching inner life. As individuals learn to respond to this inner communication, they acquire a co-operative relationship with their own souls.

A co-operative relationship with their own souls! It's difficult not to bleat with laughter. There's a fool born every minute; what galls is that these sheisters actually publish books, hold retreats, and gain cult-like followings from innocents like my wife. I close and replace the journal in the drawer where we keep maps and address books, and am drawn to the rambunctiousness of the neighbourhood children, carelessly stamping in puddles behind my car. I call out the door: "Hey, go make a mess in front of your own house! My wife's not well and she's trying to sleep!" The children gawk at each other and I am anticipating defiance, but then the tallest of the trio–an ungainly kid with exceedingly large feet and no eyelashes; one knows he will never amount to more than a community college diploma in Food Services–leads them away, and soon they're producing noise pollution a little further away from my Mercedes.

I don't expect my wife is getting any rest. Wakes at the tiniest noise, that one. I swear she can hear the socks slide off my feet those nights I arrive home late. But is there something else going on here? Should I worry? Has something recently occurred–a mugging at the sketchy central bus stop, perhaps–that I know nothing of? Surely she would tell me. We keep very few secrets, my wife and I. Personally I think her agitation and sleeplessness is hormonal. I've witnessed great and sweeping changes in her since–well, it has to be said–since her emergency hysterectomy last year. This forced change of life, this radical menopause, has sent her spinning in so many different directions hardly anything surprises anymore.

The first time I took the smallest peek into her journal I found such strange things there. She wants to begin dressing like the women in the Sears catalogue on the pages between thirty-four and fifty. She is going to make a conscious effort to slip words she never uses–*disingenuous, fastidiously, mother fucker*–into everyday conversations. The profanity is most shocking. She is going to keep her fingernails in tiptop shape, and learn to recognize the music of three major composers–Schumann, Rachmaninoff, and Vivaldi: the Red Priest. And there are the expected entries concerning her tidal wave dreams, rated on a scale that only she could ever comprehend.

There are other things, too. Sex things. She's been writing about stag party scenarios, and double penetrations. *Bukkake* scenes. Fantasies? It's ludicrous! And not in any way titillating. My wife is, shall we say, *conservative,* behind the closed doors of our bedroom. She had wanted children, and before we realized this was biologically impossible in our case, she had, if not welcomed, at least tolerated–even, on two occasions, *initiated*–"the act," as she refers to it. You see then why her journal writings come as a disturbing shock. *Tempora mutantur.* How times have changed. In short, I believe she's decided to shrug off the metaphorical skin of her old self and become–at least within the safety of her diarizing–someone other. I fear schizophrenia. In her handwritten pages–the script elegant, and so small it's scarcely legible–I further look for clues.

Some dreamworkers believe there are twelve universal dreams, including dreams of writing high school exams and not being able to find the classroom; of being naked in public; of flying; missing a plane; and running from tidal waves. Variations on these universal dreams have existed from before history was recorded and within every world culture and class. Those who experience recurring tidal wave dreams may witness themselves or another character–known or unknown to the dreamer–drowning. Because dreams offer insights into the state of one's own awareness (communicated in the Universal Language of Mind), it is essential to keep two universally true principles in mind: Every dream is about the dreamer. Every person, place and thing in the dream represents the dreamer.

As I said, I am a patient man, and I know that this, too, shall pass. I do not profess to be perfect: once a week I visit a lissome (she laughs when I use this word) young woman named Katya in her north end apartment with a view of a tennis court. We've established a certain rhythm, just as my wife and I, after years of marriage, have established a predictable rhythm. I hardly notice the monthly transfers of several hundred dollars from my account into Katya's. I'm helping her through college. Well, we both know there is no college, that the texts she leaves open with passages highlighted in yellow are merely props. She's very good at what she does. We are, it goes without saying, extremely discrete. There is no Call Display.

§

Today I learned that the earth is 75% water and the physical body is over 70% water. Physical beings can't survive without it. In the dream world, water reflects how we exist in the everyday world. Dreams of being deluged by water in any form—but most notably in a tsunami—indicate the dreamer's waking sense of being overwhelmed by life and daily experiences. Working with a dream therapist can alter the course of these dreams and bring not only understanding but also much needed peace to everyday life. By setting ideals for Self and consciously acting upon them, the dreamer begins managing control of Self in everyday experiences. Clinical research studies demonstrate that if/when the tidal wave dreamer/victim feels overwhelmed, he or she must move individual ideals to the forefront of the mind and act upon them. This practice has proven effective with a large majority of test subjects, who report that they no longer feel a need to escape from life. Water remains predominate in their dreams, but they learn to overcome the tidal wave by transferring the scene into something pleasant and safe. They might now dream of floating in a backyard pool on an inflatable mattress, or wading through a stream, hand in hand with a child. They are, in the transference, very much in control of their existence.

§

Tomorrow her twin sister—fraternal, I assure you—arrives for an extended visit. I have never been fond of the woman. An ostentatious dame, confident as a television talk-show host or a female judge. Drapes herself in bright colours and gauzy materials, somewhat like a peacock. The scarves do not always conceal her long wrinkled neck. And she thumps around the house as though stomping red ants. She's always squinting at me behind her thick, black, masculine glasses. Plus, she's a vegan. A vegan! "What the hell is that," I asked my wife, "an extraterrestrial?" For years the sister was just a vegetarian—hard enough to take—but now she's dived right over the edge. "You might have given me more warning that she was coming, Alice. An entire week?"

My wife is cocooned in a white fleece blanket by the window, doing nothing more, it would appear, than watching the first snow fall. How like a chrysalis she is. "But I did tell you," she says, "last week. She'll be in a seminar almost every day, and you'll be at work, mostly. By the time you realize she's here, she'll be gone."

I could hardly argue the fact. The sister is all that's left of my wife's immediate family, and Alice is not a woman who needs to surround herself with hordes of friends for validation, or company, or whatever it is so many women seem to require. There's a lady from the church whom she sometimes has tea with. She considered joining a quilting group, but doubted her abilities and never went to the first bee.

I imagine if I walked toward her and picked her up, I would not feel a thing in my arms. There is so little there. But the journal: that interests. She's not leaving it in the drawer with the maps now. Discovering where she's left it, devising situations so she'll not disturb me as I glimpse snatches: this is the new game.

§

It is often possible for dream therapists to detect a dominant emotional concern from the content of the dream without knowing much else about the dreamer. Concerning a tidal wave—one gargantuan wave greater than all the others—it logically follows that there is one clear "storm" at work in the dreamer's waking life.

Under this formal passage, she has written in pencil: *Yes. Oh, indeed.*

§

The sister is in the house. I hear them, in the study before the gas fireplace, my wife tittering like a mouse, her sister chortling and cursing like an old sailor. Such unlikely siblings–much less twins–in every manner, it's a phenomenon that they're biologically related at all. I haven't said as much to my wife, but I do have my suspicions about her sister, especially since on this visit she's stormed in with her straight hair scissored off above her ears: she might be a lesbian. Regardless of her sexual persuasion, her gastronomical idiosyncrasies–flatulence right at the table... how vulgar!–and garrulous behaviour, I have been nothing but hospitable toward the wretched woman, yet we both know the air between us is disturbed. Our tacit agreement is one of tolerance: we are even pleasant, but smiles are forced (as if on strings) and there is a weight to even the smallest of gestures, such as passing the steamed carrots across the dining table, or saying "Good morning." I think she's abominable. And I number the hours.

After dinner I excuse them from helping with dishes. "You two must have much to catch up on. Please, it doesn't hurt me to do the washing up. Go!" I brush them back in the direction of my study, then I clear and rinse the plates, serving dishes, cutlery and water glasses. Expensive items, but I risk chipping and leave them to lean on each other in the drying rack. I trace past the study door–French, installed after we purchased the house–and stand just out of the light: their gaiety has subsided; nothing now but the rise and fall of voices that beg not to be overheard. I knock quietly before I enter. "Well, the pair of you are certainly having a serious chat. I've just popped in for my reading glasses. Have you seen them, Dear? I thought I'd left them on the desk."

My wife unfolds her stockinged legs and joins me at the desk. Together we lift papers, shuffle folders, open drawers and stir the contents. The missing glasses are the weight of an egg in my jacket's left pocket. "When did you have them last?" she asks, and I try to recall, even scratching my head for effect.

"This morning, I think. Going over the morning's headlines. S&P–" I look at the sister, "–sorry, that's Standard & Poor, downgraded France, Austria, Italy and Spain's AAA status. Moody's still has France on an AAA rating."

The sister sits heavily on the sofa, watching with an unattractive, downward slant to her thin lips. Not a peacock. Not even an ostrich; she is a nearsighted toad of a woman. "I can't imagine...." I mumble, and settle into a chair beside the quiet fire. "I'm awfully forgetful these days." An unsettling pall follows; I hear my blood pulsing. No, it's the ticking clock.

"Shall I fetch you a cup?" Alice asks, her eyes nervously darting. "There's still tea in the pot."

"Certainly, Darling. That would be lovely. If you don't mind my company, that is. I know you two must be like a pair of ripe melons, bursting with hometown gossip."

"Not at all. I'll be right back." And she rises, almost floats to the kitchen, slip of a thing that she is, even less of her now that she hasn't been sleeping well.

I ask the sister: "Well, then, how are things with you?" It's shadowy in the study at this hour, the fire and a small banker's lamp on my desk offering the only light. I like it this way. Tonight I would prefer to hide in the shadows, become the proverbial housefly on the wall.

"We were discussing Alice's tidal wave dreams. I find it most interesting that she should keep having variations on the same dream... and keep surviving it."

"Quite," I say, and realize I'm fingering the outline of my pocketed glasses.

"I'm encouraging her to continue to try to unlock its meaning. The studies are good for her. Of course journaling really helps, too. A bit like having your own therapist, journaling. But I am concerned–"

"You're her sister. That's natural. But I shouldn't think you need seriously concern yourself. I take good care–"

She shoots a look meant to cleaver me. "There's something underneath all this," she says in a stern, finger-wagging tone. "And she really doesn't look well, not at all. Have you any idea what might be troubling her?"

"None whatsoever, but frankly I don't put much stock in this 'dreams as explanatory metaphor' rubbish she's so taken with."

"No," the sister says resolutely. She crosses her arms and I see that on each wrist she's wearing those copper bracelets that purportedly reduce one's arthritic pains. Another crank idea. "I don't suppose you do."

§

Last night's dream: I was on a wide, curving beach. A bay. I was alone among various other parties who were doing what people ordinarily do on a beach... sunbathe, build sandcastles, stroll, try to finish ice cream before it melts. Everything seemed normal, but soon I could hear something like a train in the distance. I was aware of the wind scattering sand over my bare legs. Soon the others were shaking their towels and gathering sand pails. Mothers were dragging reluctant children from the water. "Hurry now. I don't like the looks of that sky. Let's get your brother and go." *The train sound was growing. The beach emptied. The last man was having trouble closing his sun umbrella. He conceded defeat, left it, and fled. A wave broke with a crushing thud, and the wake reached my feet. It was like being immersed in ice. The train was roaring now, and I could see a vast* brassiere with one hand twisted behind her back, and sliding the garment off while simultaneously pulling her flannel nightgown down over her shoulders. It is, I imagine, how a nun might undress.

Sometime during the wee godless hours of the night, my wife clicks on the bedside lamp and awakens me with a stark question: "What were you dreaming about?" She is sitting upright, her slept-on hair a cornucopia of tangles. The light is no less offensive than a blaring horn; I feel a brief pain in my eyes, fear it may develop into a headache by morning.

"I wasn't, for goodness sake. Turn off that blessed light. I've told you, I don't dream."

"Oh yes," she says, "you do."

§

Transformational dreams are major dreams that tell us profound truths and have the ability to steer us on a course of our choosing. These dreams occur in our lives when it's necessary to see past any lies, distortions and other blinders we've put in place to avoid pain.

My dream: I am standing waist deep in the ocean. In the distance an enormous tidal wave is bearing toward me, growing in height and force as it moves ever closer. I will certainly be killed but am helpless to move. With sheer moments between myself and the wave, I make a decision. I meet the wave head-on, plunging through its swell. I come out the other side, breathing.

§

It's been a devilish day. Barret Capital Management is being investigated for manipulating client accounts and issuing false statements in what's being alleged as an elaborate trade allocation scheme. I was stamping out fires at the office every time the bloody phone rang.

And where is my wife? I've arrived home and she is not at her usual post at the window. She did not have a glass of sherry ready for me, nor was I greeted with the pleasing domestic fragrance of the seven-layer casserole I'd been expecting. Her clothes hang in the closet, bathrobe's behind the door, her shoes and boots are lined up like sentries. Everything else is in place, but not my wife. I consult the message board by the telephone where we often leave notes for each other–*please pick up milk, don't forget to pay the power bill,* or brief endearments like *Have a great afternoon*: nothing there. She has, quite simply, vanished, as if–forgive me this metaphor–one of her monstrous waves has finally come and plucked her off her child-like feet, folded her, at last, into the great, green, broiling sea and delivered her from this world without leaving so much as a fingerprint or a pale brown eyelash in remembrance.

The sister? Oh, I expect so. Such a negative influence. Alice hasn't been quite right since the visit. Anyway, I'm certain my wife will be back soon, with sincere apologies for her tardiness. She really is as reliable as the tide. I check the window again for her car lights. The snow's lashing down now, I see, and she'd be afraid to drive in it. Yes, she'd be in quite a flap about this first little storm. She's like that, my Alice.

LISTEN, HONEY

The telephone rings while he's tearing blankets off his mattress. He had a woman there last night. Twelve years older and said she has three kids: "Maria, Freddy, and the little one. His real name is William, but we call him Bear. Want to know why we call him Bear?" The woman had skinny legs and a pot belly, and she'd come out of his bathroom wearing only a beige push-up bra. She had his Bic razor in one hand, and shaving cream dripping off her pubic mound. It was no sight to see. He thinks about bears, how they do it out there in the woods and how that *would* be something to see, and how he'd done her hard–though he didn't stick it where she'd asked. He would have kicked her out last night but they were both wasted and fell asleep. This morning she wanted him to take her to Denny's for something to eat. He thought fast, said he had to get ready for a job interview, and maybe she should giddy up on home and have breakfast with her kids. She didn't like that much. Now it is afternoon and his head is splitting. The phone is no longer ringing and he is looking at his sheets. Goddamn it, he'll have to wash them.

He is in the basement laundry room when the next call comes in. He returns to his apartment, sees the red light on his answering machine blinking like a heart monitor. Two messages now.

"Oh, shoot, you're not home. Three months is too long for a mother and son not to exchange words. Sure wish you were in. Guess I'll just leave a message–"

He pushes stop and makes his way to the kitchen to pour a shot. Easy does it. Nowhere to go today, no one to answer to. He sits on the couch with his knees open, bare feet splayed beneath the coffee table. Looks like he had a party last night. Dead soldiers on the table and a few taco chips left in a bowl. An open jar of salsa. DVDs on the floor beside his hardhat. He listens to the beginning of his mother's message again and lets it play through.

"That thing you were saying last time we talked, about hating your job and your boring life. The 'great big void,' I think you called it. Well, you're still a young man and you've got time to change things. At some point everyone feels that void in their life. After your father died I felt like I'd fallen into a crater. Remember that time we went to the Grand Canyon in that little station wagon we had, and you kept wanting to look over the edge and we kept pulling you back, and I was screaming so much your dad finally took off his belt and tied it around your waist? Oh my god that was scary. You were just a tyke... probably don't remem–oops, sorry... I think I just said 'your father died.' Of course he's not dead, he's alive and well, isn't he. Well, you would know better than me, as–"

The machine cuts her off.

The young man thinks about his father, who has his own business now. He rents out canoes and kayaks in summer, and snowmobiles in the winter. They see each other every week. Or even more often. Sometimes they take the kayaks out and camp overnight on the riverbank. Sleeping bags, and beef stew straight from a can. Orion in all his pinpoint glory gawking down at them. Sometimes they meet in a sports bar, have burgers and beer, watch a basketball game. His dad's a tall man–taller than him, and he's almost six feet. He always thought he'd catch up to him, even pass him. He thought he'd be a bigger man–wasn't that the way evolution worked? Each generation a little "more" than the last? Hell, he doesn't know. Maybe he's getting one of those nature shows he watches mixed up with a dream or something. He wonders, if they ever got into it, if he could take his dad. He wouldn't put money on it. Not yet.

The red light flashes in time with the thumping inside his head. He shouldn't mix. He's learned that. What was it last night? Beer, vodka. Some weed for good measure. Harsh. He'd been transporting, like there was a little chemical somethin'-somethin' in the mix. And his dreams last night. Standing on a new planet and looking up at Earth. Seeing logs and people fall off and go spinning into space. Human satellites. Totally apocalyptic. He should find out more about that Mayan end of the world shit. Nostra what's-his-nuts. Nostradamus. This is supposed to be the big year. And he's turning thirty. Man, that's going to be hard to take. When his mom was this age he was already twelve-years-old. Crazy. Last time she called she was seriously out there–sobbing and sniffing one minute, belting out laughter the next. He couldn't tell if she was nervous or jacked. Maybe she's taking his advice now. Getting some white jacket help.

She wasn't always like this. He remembers crawling into her lap in a rocking chair. Waving to her from the Kinsmen Park train. She used to leave rhyming notes on the fridge to remind him about his homework and chores. No chastising the first time he came home drunk, or the day he got suspended for beating the crap out of that deserving bastard who stole his shoes. Once upon a time, she was this mom with a cape. Super Mom. Jesus. That was a long time ago.

He stabs the play button again. His mother continues, her voice low and far away. "Anyway, that valley, well I'm not sure I'm quite out of it yet, even three years later so, well, I'm just saying.... I don't know what I'm saying. I'm just talking."

Pause.

He wonders what she looks like these days. She could appear fifteen years younger or older than her true age, depending on her mood and whether she got any sleep the night before. And how she wore her hair made a difference. Long was best. She used to say that lap swimming–fifteen hundred metres, two thousand in one seamless go–took a few years off. She was not like his friends' mothers, and a guy could kind of respect that. For a while she got into body building, even entered a few competitions. Didn't win. When he was fourteen he had a buddy tell him his mom was buff. His dad was buff, too, but his mom was buffer.

He shakes a cigarette out of a pack, lights it and holds the match upside down to see how close it can burn to his fingertips until he has to shake the flame out. Close. There's more on the machine. He listens.

"Hey, you know how you told me you smoke dope sometimes but it doesn't do that much for you? Well, I didn't want to say anything, but I've smoked too. Recently. Jay–I told you about him, right?–he pretty much always has some, and normally I don't partake, but this time I thought, what the hell, maybe it'll make me laugh. Or maybe it'll numb me for a few hours. Mellow me out. But it didn't work. It didn't do anything except taste bad, and I burned my finger. My pointer. It's still tender, which makes typing hard. Not the best thing when you're a secretary, eh? Anyway, I didn't get a buzz. About a week later I was thinking maybe it didn't take because I hadn't done it for so long, so when Jay lit up again, I took a couple of hits. Still nothing. Is that what it's like for you?"

Machine cuts her off again.

At one time his father would have freaked if he'd known his mother'd used drugs. Now he wouldn't care. Well, *he* wouldn't say anything about it. They've got this unspoken agreement, he and his dad. Since his parents split, they sold the big house, and his mother flocked off to the coast, they don't discuss her. She is off the map of the world. It doesn't bother him; she screwed around with his dad's best friend... whatever happens now, man, she has it coming.

The phone jangles. His mother's number. Is it slightly sadistic to let her go on like this, when clearly she's lonely as hell? He drags his body back to the galley kitchen. Opens a fresh bottle. Well, he's been waiting for an occasion. Smashes the ice cube tray on the counter. Glass. Frosty ice. Rye. Coke.

"Me again. Anyway, if you're not one hundred percent happy now, I'm sorry. But maybe this'll cheer you... you don't have to pay back that money you owe me until you can afford it, okay? I'm doing all right. Well, at least I'm not worrying about where the rent's coming from. Sure is different, living in this city, but you know what? I get to see the ocean everyday. Today I watched a seal and a surfbird play like friends. Well, maybe they weren't playing. Maybe they were actually tormenting each other, but it was neat to take a break and watch. I don't do that a lot, you know. Maybe you remember, I was always busy, always working. Even when I wasn't working, I was mentally preoccupied. I think I missed a lot. I'd do things differently if I had another–"

He smacks the pause button. It pleases him, having this control. What if he never played the end of the message and she died? He could complete her sentence, finish her off any way he wanted. Maybe one day he'll be a dad, and this recording is what he'll share with his kids. *Listen to this. This is your grandma. Too bad you never got to meet her.* What was she about to say? That she was sorry? She's never said that. And now it's too late to make a difference.

The asshole in the apartment above cranks his music. Wouldn't be so annoying if the guy had any taste, but buddy plays girl music. When they hit the high notes it's like a cloud of rhapsodizing mosquitoes. Usually he chucks a shoe at the ceiling, or grabs a broom and whacks it, but what the hell... guy probably heard a shitload from down here last night. The cougar was a howler. When she was on top he could see a nasty bruise on the underside of her tit. He didn't put it there; he knows that for sure.

The phone rings four times. He stares at it, wondering how it could make so damn much noise and not even move. His head is seriously killing him. Jesus. Did he have any Tylenol? Foreman at the jobsite swears by raw eggs. Crack 'em into a glass, suck 'em back, health restored. But he can't do that. Plus: no eggs. Maybe some water. If he could get off the couch again. He hears his voice message: "Hey, Trev here... if I owe you money, I know already. You owe *me* money, let's talk."

"Sorry about that, son.... I forget what I was saying. Anyway, watching that seal and bird, it took me outside of myself, which was a good thing. I spend way too much time in my own head, and it's a dark place sometimes... well, *most* of the time. These last few years.... Hey, I forgot to ask if there's anyone special in your life at the moment. Bet there is. I know I'm your mother so I'm prejudiced and all, but who wouldn't want to be your girl? You're so handsome and funny and athletic. And you're smart, too, but you don't know it yet. I don't think you even suspect it. I wish you'd give university a try. You'll soon think you're too old to begin, but that's not true, it's just not. I wonder where you are. I wonder what kinds of things you think about when you're alone, those moments before you fall asleep. Hey, remember how I used to read to you in bed? You had that book about Louis Pasteur, and every time I'd start reading I'd slip into an English accent, and you'd make me start over again from the beginning. Or those nights we'd talk for hours in bed, you, me, and your brother, laughing about Mrs. Cartwright, she couldn't fart right, her ass was airtight–"

Click.

He was a man already when she'd left. His own place, a decent job delivering Pepsi to convenience stores, a car he could trust on the highway, and it still felt like he'd had the shit kicked out of him. Sometimes, even now, he'd look at his father with his new family and that feeling rushed back. It just seemed wrong. Like when you're watching a movie and the actors do something completely out of character and there's no more credibility, the movie's ruined, you can't believe it, you're done. Gravel in his stomach instead of guts. No one warns you when you're an eight-year-old at Cub Scouts earning your Map Reader Activity Badge, or when you're fifteen on the soccer field, your parents in lawn chairs on the sidelines beneath a plaid blanket, that it's all going to end up in a reeking pile of shit. Christ. What was the point of anything?

His mother wasn't always like this. She used to pull him from class for spontaneous picnics and mountain biking in the valley trails. He got to skip class for ice cream. She taught him how to fillet fish and drive a stick shift. He recalls a lot of laughter in the big house. Then she blew everything up. Efficient as a suicide bomber. Why did she blow everything up? Nothing means anything anymore. He considers friends now married–or even strangers holding hands in a theatre line-up, or hanging out in malls with their arms chained around each other–and he can't be happy for them. Suckers. Love is a frickin' joke. That's what he knows for sure. That woman last night. He bets she doesn't believe in love either.

His cigarette has burned down. He stabs what's left into the lid of the salsa jar. He should make an effort today. Clean this shithole up. If he has to get sick he's going to do it in a bucket. The thought of getting his head near the filthy toilet worms bile up his throat. Water, yes. Ice water. That's where he'll start. He sits there, envisioning ice in a glass. Clear, cold water flushing out the poison he's fed into his body. He's got a chill. There's something on the floor, half visible beneath the couch. Purple. He hooks it with his foot and drags it out. Huh. A fleece jacket. Definitely not his. He puts it on. The sleeves end at his forearms, and it pulls across his back. Can't zip it up, but he feels warmer.

"Hello, Mother," he says to the walls, the next time the phone rings. Four rings, his message, then hers.

"Day off today. I watched Oprah, then built a fire in the woodstove and started into a big bag of peanuts I've been saving for a rainy day. Just sat there, on a blanket on the floor, eating peanuts and watching the flames. See? I'm different now. The next time you talk to your dad, you should tell him that. I hear he's getting married in September. And no, I don't want to know a thing about it. Not a thing."

The wedding will be in Fernie, at a resort. He and his brother are standing up for the groom. They're expecting a ton of guests. His mom's sister will be there. And her parents, but nobody's supposed to say. Could set her off big time. He doesn't want to think about it right now. Frickin' head. Frickin' woman with a low-cut top and sparkly earrings, grinding into him on the dance floor beneath the DJ's booth.

"Jay's been good to me, in case you're wondering, but even when he's here, sitting across from me, I sometimes still feel like I'm alone. To tell you the truth, I suspect he's seeing someone on the side, and I don't even care. I don't care enough about myself *to* care, I guess."

There's an extended pause, a sound like birds hitting the window. Then she hangs up. Well, he's been wondering when she'd go off the rails again. Doesn't seem like she's been drinking; he'll give her that, at least. Other times he hasn't even been able to understand her. And what about this Jay guy? He imagines a weasel. Probably wears his hair long and turns up the George Thorogood in his jacked up 4 × 4, playboy bunnies on the mudflaps. Jesus. This was his mother. Maybe he should take a week, head out to the coast. See how far she's fallen. Pick her up if he can.

He deletes all messages. Thinks he can manage to stand again. Slowly, slowly. Molasses. Turtles. Paint drying slowness. Pain hammering his skull. Dizzy, too. Steady. Couch to wall to kitchen counter. Breathe. Open cupboard, one clean glass left. Run water. The ringing. She's freaking relentless.

"Honey, I'm going to tell you something and I don't want you to get worried, but sometimes I wonder if the life I lived really was the life I lived. I mean, sometimes I don't know if I really *did* give birth to you and your brother, and live in that big house for all those years as a family. Did it happen? I need to hear that it happened. God I wish you were home. I know there are pictures and letters and all that to prove the past, but when your dad eradi–oh, never mind *that* sad old song, but it's like he was the other half of me, and now I can't even figure out how to breathe. Some days... well, at least I still have you, right? I know you're closer to your father and you like his girlfriend and her kids, but I hope you've saved a little bit of room in your heart for me."

Oh, fuck! Break out the violins. He hoped this wouldn't be like that time she'd called his dad and she kept saying "I'm not going to make it, I'm not going to make it," until his dad had to call the cops. She was hospitalized for a month. No one, as far as he knew, went to visit.

"I suppose the tape's going to run out again soon. First, though I want to tell you about what I'm looking at right now... I'm looking at the rainforest, and I can see an owl out there in a dead tree. It's big as a breadbox. Think it's a Great Horned Owl. I've got *The Sibley Guide to Birds,* and Jay gave me a set of binoculars for Christmas. I like to take them down to the shore. I always figure I'm going to see a whale, or maybe a shark's fin. I keep hoping for it, you know?"

He remembers the time they watched "Jaws," and how excited she'd been. She said the movie was an institution, and watching it with him felt like participating in a rite of passage. It actually was pretty good. Maybe he'd rent it this week, see if it held up.

"Listen, honey, I–"

The recording clicks off. Should he just pick up? Otherwise who knows how long she'll carry on. And this bloody ringing. Like being stabbed in the head. He could unplug the phone. Yes, she's his mother, but she's also a whack job. And she brings him down. Last time she told him that she'd just bought a new scarf at the thrift store. After she'd washed it and taken it out of the dryer, she put it on and said it felt like a hug. Brushed acrylic, she'd said, but as soft as cashmere. She felt so alone, she said. So she kept doing it, she kept warming that scarf and wearing it until it cooled, and then she realized it was easier just to microwave it.

His laundry. According to the building's schedule it's not his "day," but screw that sideways. He counts his remaining quarters. Nine. That should get his sheets about halfway dry. He'll have to hang them around the apartment again, over doorways and such. Big ghosts. If he had a balcony he could at least give them a little air. His apartment is a dump. He's not holding his breath, but if he ever did meet someone nice, someone he'd like to spend a few months with maybe, he couldn't bring her back here. He doesn't have a bed, for one. Just a mattress on the floor. His clothes are heaped into a corner, and towels drape across his weight bench. One gander at his stupid table, his couch with a pioneering scene, his mismatched plates and cups, and the chick would know they're Sally Ann specials. It's hard, man. And he works! This last gig, cleaning construction sites. Been steady now for two months.

He's nearly ready to go downstairs and rotate his laundry when the phone rings again. She isn't talked out yet? Or maybe she senses he's there, hiding in plain sight. Women have intuition, eh. Maybe she knows.

"Listen, honey, I hope you'll think about coming to visit some time. I put all my gas and groceries on Mastercard, and I'm pretty sure I've got enough Airmiles to fly you out. Just for a weekend or something. You'd love the coast. I know you would. Do you still watch those nature shows? Well, we're in the thick of it here. You should see the salmon runs. There's bald eagles and these cute round birds called dark-eyed juncos. And hey, we've even got rats! Tree rats, they call them, or roof rats. They run through the beams and it sounds like they're dragging bodies around up there. I'd take you down to Beach Drive and Dallas Road. God it's pretty. I was there last week, walking along the edge of the cliff–super steep, but there are steps down to the beach. Mostly I just go to smell the salty surf–it's still so foreign and, well, delicious. So I was on the edge of the cliff and I saw this dog, a black dog, out in the ocean. It was treading water like a hu–"

She's gone again. But she has his attention now. He wants to know what's next. He hopes she'll call back, finish her story. He won't even throw his clothes into the dryer until she does. He lies on the mat beside the front door. A runner, really. His dad's girlfriend gave it to him. She's always giving him things. A coffee pot. A harmonica. What the hell is he going to do with a harmonica? She tries too hard. Talks too much. His brother says the old man could have done better.

He's too tall to fit on the mat. His feet and head stick off the ends, but it's okay. The cold floor feels good against his face. Grit under his cheek. Hair and lint and what is that–a beetle?–trucking along the baseboard. How long do beetles live? Do they feel pain? Desire? Love? *Call back,* he thinks. A wave of nausea tumbles his guts. He could make it to the cabinet beneath the sink. Grab the bucket. He'd feel better after.

She calls.

"Honey, I don't even know if you're getting these. This will be my last message. I was telling you about the dog. I'm a terrible guesser, but it was maybe seventy-five or a hundred yards out. You could swim that far, easy, though no one would want to go in this time of year. In fact, they tell me the water's cold all year round. A woman was standing on the beach calling it in. She had a smaller dog running around her legs and barking. One of those little white things you often see old men walking. She kept calling the big dog but it wouldn't paddle in. It stayed in the same place, and I thought maybe it was caught in something, and I wondered how long a dog could tread water."

He thinks of "Jaws." Imagines the dog as it might be photographed by an underwater camera. Legs moving as if on a treadmill.

"I stood there and watched for fifteen minutes. The woman was yelling and waving her arms–really beginning to freak out–and I wondered if she might actually kick off her boots and go in, or if someone else would help. Other people were watching the spectacle, too. And anyone could see the danger. I couldn't believe that dog. Sometimes he'd sink a little then pop back up again. It was really something. But he wasn't getting any closer to shore. The woman started screaming. You don't hear that very often, a grown woman, screaming in public. And then I noticed the rings around the dog... the rings in the water, from his splashing... they weren't as big anymore. I waited another five minutes or so. Then I had to go."

She pauses. He's been holding his breath, and when he gulps the air he realizes his ribs hurt. The woman last night? He rolls onto his other side and tries to pull the fleece jacket closed. The movement ignites a wide strip of rhythmic pain from the base of his neck up across the top of his head and down to the space between his eyebrows. A mohawk of pain, he thinks. The best thing in his life right now is the cold dirty floor. He's feverish, and sick, and a little itchy down there. Jesus—he hopes she was clean. Bear, she'd said. She called her kid Bear.

"Well, it's been nice talking to you, or *sort* of talking to you. I love you, Sweetheart. Goodbye."

After a time he crawls on his elbows to his bedroom. The blankets—hand-me-downs, from the time they all lived together in the big house—are jumbled into a soft nest. Jesus. Why'd she have to tell him that dog story? He rolls his blankets up and holds them like a baby. Yes, he'll be washing them, too. He only has the one set.

PARAPLEGIC SEX

After her lover leaves—on excellent terms, though it's highly probable she'll never see him again—Joelle untangles sheets, flits across the unlit room to the kitchen, grabs a bag of extra salty salt and vinegar chips and brings them back to bed. This urge to put something else immediately in. What's up with *that*? Her lover. A phrase with a most welcome ring to it, something she could get used to, drop into conversations with... absolutely no one. Her lover, Matt—whom she was amused to learn had sported a blue mohawk only a few years earlier—has forgotten two packaged condoms by her bedside table. *Her* bedside table, for God's sake. Adjacent to the marital mattress she's shared for the last two decades, conceived all three of her children on: Billy, Andrew, Harper. BAH. She opens the foil wrappers with her canines, sets one condom over each eye, like monocles. She wishes she would have thought to ask Matt about his brushes with venereal disease *before* they'd been intimate. Genital warts and epididymitis. "But only men can get that last one," he'd said. "Women just pass it on."

Might she die? The thought entertains her. She will certainly not be donating blood anymore—something she and her husband enjoy doing together every six weeks, their only regular date. They compare heart rates, blood pressure, see who can win the race to the post-donation Coke and donuts. Neil often wins. She won't get past the inquisition now: *In the last twelve months have you slept with a man who has accepted money or drugs for sex? In the last twelve months have you slept with a man whose sexual history you're unfamiliar with?*

She decides to allow herself the benefit of a full three nights—what's left before her family returns from visiting paternal grandparents—in the stained sheets that smell of her lover's hair and the final cigarette he'd smoked beside her. She really doesn't know Matt from Adam, and after the rum kicked in and he kept kissing her, smiling all the while with the gap between his teeth clearly visible, she'd wondered, briefly, if he was a lunatic, an escapee. One hand on her bare hip, the other gripping a machete? Then they'd done it, and she came twice, and she just may have seen God. It was so easy. After, the boy tweezed a cigarette from the pack with his teeth and leaned on one elbow to stare and stare into her eyes. "This is fucking Utopia," he'd said, smoke pouring brilliantly between his syllables.

She could smell herself on his lips.

§

Joelle is a professional planner. Companies, organizations and individuals hire her to orchestrate social and trade show events. On her desk an old style Rolodex is stocked with recipe cards; she is apprehensive of technology. She owns a computer, of course, but was slow to sign up for highspeed and wireless, and she does not believe in Facebook or Twitter. Who has time? She also distrusts microwaves, but acquiesced so her kids might devour the same high-fat, zero-nutrient, cheesy after-school snacks as their friends.

Spin the Rolodex and boom: the name and number of a symphony cellist who can be hired on a few day's notice. The caterer as adept at concocting Szechuan smoked tofu with wasabi cream cheese sauce as she is at pear vichyssoise. Want quail eggs? Got 'em. One hundred saskatoon berry pies with melt-in-your-mouth crusts? Piece of proverbial cake. Joelle's no less talented herself. She can whip up couture gift bags in a jiff, transform an ordinary room into a Polynesian luau, or a barnyard with rented goats, the Parthenon. Her gregarious personality and almost machine-like ability to organize have earned her both a diverse circle of friends and much success across the calendars that add up to her life.

She is a doer. In the early years—before her firstborn discovered the white lie of a Sunday morning stomach-ache that is often the beginning of the end of all-in-the-family churchgoing—Joelle both taught the junior class and was also the most efficient Sunday School superintendent Zion Lutheran had ever known. When she worked as an executive secretary for a mid-sized Alberta oil company she was the team member relied upon to get the job done *yesterday.* Companies wooed her; up the ladder she shimmied in her just-above-the-knee-length skirts. At the top, something like vertigo struck: it seemed only reasonable to hang out her shingle. Joelle C. Williamson. Event Coordinator.

Business booms.

Why then, is she unhappy? She thinks of her heart as an old leather shoe, tossed from a car, left to the highway and beaten by rain. It hasn't happened overnight. She tracks the emotional slide through her unhung gallery of wall hangings; it's a little like viewing self-portraits. Her mother, in her occasional wisdom, passed over the birds and bees homily and told each of her daughters that every woman needs an artistic outlet. "Take up clarinet," she suggested. "Try origami." Joelle dabbled in pottery—too messy—and for years lugged a boxy Pentax K1000 around in her handbag, never once in all of her surreptitious snapping even coming close to capturing the way a vagrant's eloquent scowl or a plastic bag flagging from a branch can seem to hold the secret to the meaning of life. The camera was so hefty it kept smashing her cigarettes, and it was a bitch to focus. She gave it up long before digital became the norm.

Fabric, however, is another story. She loves the colours, designs, the textures. She's a tactile lass: to walk into a fabric shop and trill her fingers over the velvets, silks, brocades—even the corduroys—is no less titillating than touching skin. Fabricland is her Louvre. She chooses plain canvas for backing, then cuts and stitches visual narratives for her own amusement–or therapy, though she didn't recognize that for some time. The pieces on her collapsible wooden banquet tables illustrate her tailspin: in the last few years, her colours have tended to emulate stagnant ponds and oil slicks. She is inspired by images from the news–the starving child, guerrilla warfare. Pestilence. Sometimes she adds juxtaposing text. Astonishing, the things people say. *Perfection gets old on a long drive. He poured water with a flourish. Water and ketchup…? More ketchup! I flew kites semi-professionally.* She keeps her creations private. The kids have come to accept that when Mom is in her craft room, she's to be left alone. Neil isn't bothered: he has a room (aka the garage) of his own. He calls it his Man Cave; a phrase she freaking abhors.

But now she is glowing. Glowing! Someone has thought her beautiful, has lifted her hair and bitten the back of her neck. He has cupped her foot as if it were porcelain. Perhaps today she'll begin a new collage. Yes, it's high time for something completely original, and nuanced. Clearly, it must be a nature piece. Dried roses and poppy seeds. Leaf rubbings. She'll incorporate feathers. She'll soak the canvas in a lavender-scented bath before she begins, and look for pansy prints at Fabricland. She'll call this one "Garden." Or better yet, *"Le Jardin."*

§

When he calls a week later she experiences an electro-erotic surge through the phone: hand, to shoulder, to heart, to groin. Instantly wet.

"Can we meet?" She regards even his breath over the line as sexy.

Her youngest, the girl, is within earshot. "Sure, if you'd like to discuss the details, I can meet you at Donahues. You know the diner… in Mount Royal? Say, one o'clock?" Trembling. "Perfect.

Can't wait to see you." He makes a sound like a small motor into the phone; her vertebrae vibrate.

Harper is packing her lunch. Her children learned to be self-reliant at an early age out of necessity: their mother was a whirling dervish. Billy still complains that he was the only kid in grade one who had to make his own sandwiches; a fact Joelle is proud of. Harper adds a Golden apple to her insulated lunch bag and has difficulty zipping it up. "Hey, this bulges like a tumour. New client, Mamacita?"

"Yes. It's a small office party for a team of landscape architects. They're tired of the same old. I'm thinking belly dancers."

"Cool." Harper cocks her right hip. Her left arm flies up, fingers poised like a flamenco dancer. She does a slow, seductive rotation.

Oh. Joelle backs against the countertop for support. "Sweetheart, you're eleven. Where did you learn that?"

"Shakira," Harper says, looping her backpack over her arms. "YouTube."

§

She spots him at a back table and knows immediately that they will–they *must*–be intimate again. He could take her right now. In her minivan, behind a large rock on the Bow River, some low-end joint in Motel Village with cigarette burns on the carpet and no free pens.

He kisses her mouth and gives her shoulders a promising squeeze. He's the tallest man she's ever been with. She beams up into his wide-apart eyes and feels the parts of her shake like a Mexican marionette. She snaps her knees into lock mode, sees how truly young he is, how his jeans hanger on the hard angles of his hipbones. Silver thumb ring. Leather laced around his wrist. Tight T-shirt and underneath it a muscled stomach not unlike a marimba. Shoulders from there to there. He sits and says, "I lost my job."

"What?"

A long-jawed waitress appears and requests their order with seemingly personalized aloofness. Joelle reads off the first thing on the menu. "And coffee, please. No sugar."

"Down-sizing. Jesus fuck." He rakes his fingers through his jet-black dye job. His hair is thick as a pelt, and long enough to pull into a ponytail, but she likes it this way. It begs to be touched. To be wound between her fingers, and yanked. "Calgary's booming, we hire twenty new employees a month, and–" He pauses to light a cigarette, tilting his head as if protecting the flame from wind. "It's this guy in Finance, close pal of the manager. I was out with friends last weekend at Twisted Element, and he was there… in little more than chaps and nipple rings. I honestly didn't know he was gay."

She so wants to ask: are you?

"I'm standing beside the bar and he asks me to dance. I say no thanks. 'Come on,' he says, 'be brave,' and he pushes his groin into me. I fucking lost it. I grabbed his arm and yanked it behind his back. Then this Liza Minnelli queen gets his panties in a knot and calls the bouncer. I was… ejected." He sips his coffee. "Come to work Monday and there's a letter on my desk. Corporate assholes didn't even have the balls to tell me in person."

She clams his hand across the table. "I'm so sorry. What will you do?" The door opens, setting off jingle bells. She snaps her hands back. Her friends come here. Clients. "Can you… *live*? I mean, were you given severance pay?"

The meals arrive before he can respond. She sees that she's ordered a stack of blueberry pancakes under a profound dollop of whip cream. Could be messy eating. Matt has a reasonable clubhouse. The layers are stabbed together with a toothpick that hoists a tiny green triangular flag. Were it pink, she thinks, it would be a sign.

"I'm good for a few weeks." He removes the flag and grazes the sharp end across his tongue. "Maybe a month."

Oh. Is this what it's about? There's no fool like an old fool, her father or Archie Bunker—she often confuses references—used to say. But then Matt's eyes majestically change. Worry-lines evaporate and he studies her most intently. It's possible, she thinks, that his eyes have become larger, richer, browner, more interesting since the night his work and hers brought them together and she decided, for once, to be selfish. His eyes are like cookies she could pluck off his face and swallow. And he has lips like a baby, with that extra nub of flesh in the middle of his upper lip.

"Now," he says, and beneath the table his foot rides up her inner calf, "let's talk about *you*."

§

She thanks Jesus for her work. There is a dinner party for the directors of the Calgary Public School Board, a retirement deal for one of her former bosses. That she can still keep her head on, get through the necessary arrangements, is what most amazes. Her hands are shaking all the time. She smokes more to steady them, which doesn't work. Little puddles smack at the back of her knees. Neil doesn't bat a blond lash, and BAH are fine. She's imperceptibly trained them to hardly need her; perhaps it was training for *this*.

They mostly go to Matt's, when his roommate is away. Her lithe sweetheart's walls are Oriental red, and he's hung her wallhanging—*"Le Jardin"*—where the three o'clock sun throws a spotlight on it. His bedroom's modest, but if he had more money and possessed the materialist mindset to spend it, she believes he would exhibit excellent taste. Travel, he says, is where most of his income's funnelled, and a large, thread-worn backpack—*sans* Canadian flag sewn on the back, which she's sure means something—validates this claim. His futon bed's dressed with a brown and navy plaid duvet that reminds her of humbug candies. There's a tall espresso-coloured IKEA dresser with slim silver pulls, a Queen Anne chair covered in moss green velvet, his ubiquitous black military boots–super sexy–with impeccably scuffed toes, a square glass ashtray containing long butts, a wooden trunk with a battered latch that belonged to his maritime grandfather (and looks like it might contain gold coins), a bronze standing lamp with a goose neck (over which he's looped belts and a black hoody), a tin-framed mirror–a pattern of red-centred yellow daisies on a royal blue background, like one haggles over in a Third World market. Several hardcover classics she's always meant to read are omnipresent on the floor. *Anna Karenina. Ulysses. Moby Dick. The Shining.* Along with these books is a coffee-stained copy of *The Hobbit,* which she will never read; she tried after her Billy raved about it, but she couldn't keep all the dwarves, trolls, elves and hobbits straight, and she couldn't give a smaller damn: reading fantasy ranked up there with filing her income tax return and having underarm hair lasered off.

The first few times at Matt's she feared his roommate would walk in on them. They had stolen a half dozen late afternoons, hours regretfully not yet dark enough to hide her abdominal scar, the pendulous breasts (one slightly longer) and dimpled thighs. How could he desire this? He claimed he couldn't get enough of anything about her.

And she needs to know everything about him. One evening– the visits are stretching along with their shadows–when he steps out to buy another bottle of merlot and smokes and her family thinks she's arranging a corporate hootenanny in Canmore, she takes an inventory of his window sill to get to know him better. She's touched by the five orange nasturtiums in a blue clay pot and fresh dill suspended from a hook via shoelace. A watercolour paintbrush. An ornate metal font–for holy water?–with a carved ivory Mary. One link from a dog's choker collar. Coral and thumb-sized shells from beaches she knows nothing about, and this pains her. At either end of the window ledge, two Chinatown-type tea cups with lettering that may mean *Long life*. One cup holds a pair of brass hinges, a Canada Flag stick-on tattoo, a squashed wasp's nest, two dimes, a nickel, and a Swiss franc; the other hosts a Triple A battery, a paperclip, a white thumb-tack, an anonymous screw, and a rolling paper–he's invited her to smoke weed with him; she prides herself that she's not stooped *that* low. Three empty seed packages rest behind tea cup no. 2: Sweet Peas [Giant Spencer Mixed Colours, Lindenberg Seeds Ltd., $1.50]; Jumbo Sweet Pea [Spencer Giant Mixture, McKenzie, $2.99]; and Morning Glory [Early Call Mixed, McKenzie, $1.79]. She makes a note to engage him in a discussion about flowers. She sees the bleached skull of a small mammal with all teeth intact; scary. One bobby-pin? *Don't think about it.* One black elastic band. *Little sister?* A souvenir coin from Notre Dame. A handful of striated sea rocks and more shells, like touchstones. She pockets two of them. There's a Canadian flag pin. Three teak monkeys connected by tails and arms. *Bali?* A rustic metal bicycle on a chain with four miniature cowbells attached. A colour photograph of autumn trees. One dead fly. Beneath all else, the wood-carved word "Shalom" hangs from a nail, just above the kitchen sink. Shalom. Shalom! She is falling in love with this boy.

"Back with provisions," he calls from the doorway. She rushes into the bedroom again, fluffing her hair for a foxy impression.

"You've been missed," she says, turning slowly from the unkempt bed. She takes the brown bag, removes the wine bottle and slides her palm up and down the neck in what she hopes is an obscenely suggestive manner. Her turn to up the ante. How far would she go? She doesn't know herself. "I almost started again without you."

§

They keep at it for months. She feels like the heroine in her own *film noir*: the moody, obscure music he plays; the sneaking and cryptic notes and whispered phone calls. She speaks little of her family, rarely implies there are children. BAH.

He notes her interest in his books and it's fantastic that she doesn't even need to articulate that she wants him to read to her, that he intrinsically knows being read to in bed by a deep-voiced man is near the top of her long–and growing–list of turn-ons. He parts *The Fountainhead* and reads the part where Roark encourages Mallory to talk about the things that matter, the things he really wants said–not stuff about family and childhood and friends–the things he *thinks*.

This is the backbeat to what they have together. He does not know her age or if she cheats on her taxes; she does not know his middle name or whether he eats with his mother on Sundays. Sometimes when they make love it's like losing her virginity again. Nothing is said. They keep their eyes open and breathe. She spends hours touching and kissing his feet. She eases him to sleep by drawing invisible circles around his eyes, purring her new vocabulary of French endearments, her lips grazing the miraculous folds of his ear.

Sometimes in bed he asks her to hurt him. "I've been with men," he confesses during one session, and knowing this makes her want him more. He helps her into the leather strap-on, guides the dildo into his lubricated ass. She weighs his balls like she's testing fruit. She shows him how best to touch her, has him tie her legs apart in the chair, tells him dirty stories while wearing her professorial glasses, the skirt of a power suit hiked above her thighs. "Thank you," he says, "thank you." His voice could melt butter, she thinks. It could liquidate the Arctic ice cap.

"No," she says, "thank *you*."

§

At home she hugs her husband's naked back, slides her knee between his legs and flushes with guilt, but not its stronger cousin: remorse. Does she not deserve at least a fleeting measure of happiness?

"Good night, Mom. Good night, Dad," Andrew calls as he passes their door en route to his own room. Except Billy, who's created a laird in the basement–for his angst and shit, Neil says–they're all on one floor. She likes having them close by. Likes to hear their sounds... Andrew singing pop songs in the shower, Harper on the phone with her mélange of BFFs.

"Night, Sonny Boy," Neil says. "Sweet dreams." He clasps Joelle's hand and pulls it around to his sternum. They both sleep best this way.

If it's wrong, why has God made her like this? She requires two lives, at least. The warm blanket of knowing that she possesses this long-time, stable connection, this anchor who would never do a thing to hurt her. If she admits nothing, she will never be alone. And the other life, the part that jackhammer's her heart and confirms that she is absolutely alive. This *thing*–how can she christen it?–has nothing to do with the kids, her everyday life, the unqualified interconnectedness with Neil that she feels in her very marrow; their history has been miles from unpleasant. She has scrutinized this from all angles, pieced it together with fabric, dye and thread–though mostly Matt is her new artistic outlet. So why not tell? It would eradicate the marriage, but why not grab the last vestige of passion she might ever know and truly run with it? Because. When the pendulum stops swinging, her straight up fear of growing old and ugly and sick and poor and alone keeps her from irrevocably leaping off the cliff.

But this thing. This *gift*. She has no control over it, and it is beginning to consume her. She finds herself appropriating personal pronouns–*our* bed, she's said–and there have even been the perilous first whisperings of love. So many sweet moments when she's almost confessed: "I'd give it all up for even a few years with you, Matt." Yesterday she tied his tattooed arms behind his back with her hair scarf, then laughed because he was so difficult to position on top of her. A torso, sliding sideways off her body, off the bed. "I feel like I'm having sex with a paraplegic," she'd said, struggling to pull him up and keep from banging his head on the floor. They couldn't stop laughing and finally tore the nuisance scarf off. Three minutes later she was on all fours and he was riding her from behind.

"Now that," she said, pointing out the finger-trails in the carpet, "would make a damn fine photo."

And she's slipping up: she's called Billy by Matt's name. "A client," she says, fervently apologizing and fast-shuffling the subject. "Billy, you doing okay for spending money?" She slides him a twenty from her wallet. Her missteps now add up to eighty dollars.

Of all her children, it is the eldest, Billy, the bad boy, that Joelle loves best. The girl, Harper, is a tenderheart, and winsome. The wheaten-haired apple of her father and grandparents' eyes. Joelle can't believe that she's turned out anyone so well-adjusted. Harper forever has a cornucopia of friends tugging at the ends of her sleeves, just as Joelle did. "Want to go to the mall, Harper?" "Can you come to my sleepover?" "I can bring one friend to Disneyland, Harps. Mom says it's okay to ask you." Andrew, two years older, is slightly bookish and quiet. He chooses two or three friends and devotes himself utterly to them. Their obsessions follow a seasonal rotation: fishing, cycling, snowboarding, games. And he loves her deeply. Even now he will curl into her lap like a toddler, his head fitting into the dip beneath her collarbone, just above the swell of her breast. It melts her, this loving. He was the one who announced he wanted to marry her. He brought the fistfuls of dandelions, the breakfasts in bed. She fears that his first doomed love affair will destroy him and he'll never recover. She's seen it happen this way sometimes: a boy is crossed by some beauty and soon he's forty and living alone with his frozen meat pies and shabby towels, forgetting to shave on the weekends.

But Billy–oldest by a decade, the child who stumbles home if he shows up at all–is the reason she doesn't sleep, his story a litany of detentions, suspensions, flirtations with drugs and petty crime. He has stolen from her. He is, she is almost certain, the mastermind behind the break-in at his grandparents' house, the theft of his auntie's new car stereo. He is the phone call at odd hours, the silent but not-so-anonymous presence on the other end of the line. She discovers him on the back step at dawn, a topography of vomit caked on his jean jacket and dried in his hair. He was thirteen the first time they found a quarter ounce of marijuana in his pocket, and Neil wouldn't accept it for what it was. "You think this is herbal tea?" she'd cried, shaking the bag at his face.

She writes long desperate letters Billy laughs at, or, worse, leaves unopened on his pillow. He should have been her abortion, he says. He hopes he gets cancer and dies. On one of a hundred similar nights–after six hours of elbows-on-the-sill staring at the street-facing window, counting the accumulating minutes like a pulse, willing him a moment of discernment so he'd recognize how his self-destruction was a bacterial virus working its way through all of them, and praying that God grant her boy Guardian Angels so he'd not get knifed in a gang initiation or jump off a bridge–she'd finally collapsed into an exhausted sleep on his bed. An hour later, his footsteps. She lurched down the dark stairs, palming the walls. The eerily quiet house, her agonizing, the lack of sleep: she felt she was swimming through fog. "Billy." Her son was jumpy, sores oozing around his mouth. She could see this was her boy but his eyes were pinballing. All wrong. "I love you more than anyone," she'd cried, and crawled like a penitent toward him, begging that he let her help him. Billy shook her off his legs like a snake.

§

It is late, and insipid moths are hurling themselves against the window. An obnoxious sound, like some little bastard throwing rocks at her tent in the overflow section of an unsupervised campground. It doesn't matter that his roommate is in the next room. *Paul* knows. It doesn't matter that she was supposed to be home two hours ago to cut the grass and return a half dozen business calls. Something reckless has come over her heart. Must be how terrorists feel, she thinks. The adrenaline charge. She could take down a plane with her energy. It is enough to sit across a room and study him. Just now he is reading in bed with three pillows propped behind him, bare ankles crossed. She could weep! It is unbearable how he languidly brings his cigarette to his lips. When he inhales, closing his eyes, she wants to be that cigarette. When his sister phones from across the country and he speaks to her as if Joelle's not even in the room, as if his "I love you, 'Nita," isn't the most extraordinary phrase she's ever heard, she wants to be his sister.

When she is not desiring to be the boots on his feet, the molecule of dirt beneath his fingernails, she sometimes steps back and regards him as a portrait for privilege: his parents paid his way through grad school, he never worried about money, even during the month he was unemployed. A new opportunity quickly arose. He is among that rare class of people for whom a safety net would always be stretched in place. She loves him profoundly.

And she is getting careless.

"Let's get something to eat," she hears herself say, and what she means is I want to walk around a grocery store with you pushing the cart. I want to throw in a brick of cheese, peanut butter, laundry detergent, a last-minute bouquet of carnations and baby's-breath because I am *feeling* all flowers. I want people to look upon us and see how happy we are. I want to skip across a parking lot in the rain, leaping puddles and swinging hands. I want to share a red umbrella. I want old married couples to smile at us. This is too big now, she means, and I want to let it out.

"Okay."

They slink out of his room. Paul glances from the TV before expediently flipping through channels. A sonic wall, she thinks. *Deus ex machina.* "We're going to get something to eat," Matt tells him, knotting the long black laces around the tops of his boots. T-shirt half untucked. A few minutes ago her lips were on that particularly fine portion of skin. "Want anything?"

"I'm good," Paul says. "I might not be around later, so if Trace calls please take a message." Trace, Paul's girlfriend, is twenty-six and writing her Masters thesis on bio-art. Not a line on her face. Joelle has met her exactly once, and the experience made her feel minute. Matt, Paul and Trace, all talking and being clever and witty, the way the young and well-educated do. They wear sloppy clothes–T-shirts with slogans that showcase leftwing persuasions, slightly dirty jeans–and make them look *über* fashionable, make *her* feel underdressed. None of them eat enough. They know just enough about old art and more about new. The girls forego make-up and wouldn't dream of perfume. They all listen to independently-produced music, choose films by their directors, possess well-used passports, and mock anything popular. In their kitchens: *wasabi, edamame,* soy beans, and *naan.* They're big on pottery and tea. They have a special way of dancing and entering a room. She is outside of it. *Persona non grata.* A razor-wire fence has been erected to keep her type out.

"Bye, Paul." She has the decency to feel ridiculous.

§

Next time they get a hotel room in south Calgary. It is 2:30 in the afternoon, and Matt has just stepped from the shower. Joelle feels how tenuous it is–how tenuous it has always been–and expects the wind could pick him up at any moment and whisk him, a bone kite, to the blue beyond. He moves through the suite in a white towel, and when it falls, he backs against the couch, watches her watching him stroke his sublime cock. He is always taking his clothes off, this young man. But look at him, she thinks. His pubic hair is neatly trimmed. A sacred heart tattoo is healing on his chest.

Her cell-phone rings and stops. Rings and stops. She makes no move toward it. The third time the ringing does not end, and he says: "Are you going to answer that?"

He is so lean, she thinks, his thighs only slightly bigger than her own. There's no muscle definition in his lanky legs, no scars anywhere. He is white, and seamless. "No," she says, turning and lifting her skirt, brushing her buttocks against him.

"It might be important."

"Probably my son." She flops on the bed, parts her legs. She is ready.

"Your son?"

He knows there are children, why, she wonders, does he suddenly look so perplexed? "Don't worry, he's not six."

Matt stops touching himself. His penis falls against his thigh. "How old–"

"Twenty-three."

He is gracious enough to avoid an audible gasp.

§

What is going on with Neil? He has started taking better care of himself. He's all but cut fat out of his diet–no more hand in the potato chip bag while watching the late-night talk shows–and he has, quite irrationally, she thinks, taken up long distance running. Shouldn't he have a doctor's blessing? There are heart issues on his side of the family. She almost trips over him as he's crouched in the dawn light, slipping into his new and expensive "stability" sneakers, which he says accommodate for his flat feet; apparently he is an over-pronator. "Just going to get a fast eight K in before work," he says, moronically cheerful. He talks like this now. He uses phrases she's never heard of: negative splits, ten and ones. And that ludicrous word–fartleks–that makes the children screech with laughter.

"Isn't it great that dad's training for a marathon?" Harper says, coming upon them in the entry where no one ever orders their shoes or even scrapes the mud off. My daughter's wearing a bra now, Joelle notes. "*I* think it's the coolest."

Joelle didn't know about the marathon, didn't realize he'd become that dedicated. He's never been athletic. What's happening beneath her own roof has become nearly as surreal as what goes on in those other rooms, across the city. She's in some kind of limbo. And why is her daughter of the new underwear up this early? She follows Harper into the kitchen and watches her pour cereal into an astonishingly yellow bowl. New? Old?

"Mom, you slept in," Andrew says, joining them. Getting so tall, she notices. He can look her right in the eyes now. "You're driving us to school today, remember? Harp, save some for me!" He snatches the cereal box from his sister. Special K. Maybe her kids are on a health kick, too. Harper snaps the box back.

"Sure," Joelle says, "just takes a minute to change." She plods upstairs, feeling like she's done hard time. Is Neil having an affair too? She tries to discern how that makes her feel and comes up blank. Over the years they've had the discussion about monogamy, her stance–even when there was no Matt in the landscape–that it's unnatural: "People will always be attracted to other people," and her husband's insistence that he wouldn't have their relationship any other way, and if she had a mind to, if she had even a fleeting *thought* about fooling around, she'd best pack her things and say *sayonara* to the kid-lets; she'd only be seeing them weekends and every other Christmas.

She hopes he's involved. Then again, she hopes he's not.

§

"Tell me about the font." Neil's taken the younger two to Sunshine for the weekend, and she has stayed the night at Matt's apartment. She needed to experience a morning with him. Wake together in his bed. To open her eyes to white light creeping between the blind slats and find him beside her would, she hoped, make it more real. Something has to. Well, she'll keep trying.

She's brought him a demitasse of espresso in bed. He cups his hands to receive it from her. "The font?"

Endearing how he wakes suddenly and completely, unlike Neil, who takes his time surfacing from sleep and always gets out of bed last but rarely makes the bed. "Or whatever you call it. That Catholic thing in your kitchen. Are you Catholic?" She kneels on the floor beside his head. "Never figured you for one." She touches his forearm. Lovely shocks pass through her skin.

"No, I'm not Catholic. I like to think of myself as spiritual, but–"

She finishes for him: "–but not religious." A common sentiment, she thinks. Politically correct. It's the first unoriginal thing he's ever said.

"Yes, something like that." She sees a wave of irritation cross his face. Maybe he's still tired; busy night. "I collect Catholic iconography–small pieces, of course. I find it interesting. Occasionally quaint. I've got a large painting of Jesus in a clawfoot tub back at my parents' house. Our Lady of Guadalupe–'that Catholic thing'– comes from a village north of Mazatlán. El Quelite... it's just across the Tropic of Cancer. You know where *that* is, right?"

She twitches. Is she being taught a lesson? Maybe she's not to notice what he has on his shelves, or perhaps she's not allowed to question what she sees. They're making the rules up as they go. She takes a drink from his cup to avoid having to say anything, and feels she swallows too loudly.

"You haven't travelled much," he says, sitting up. Not a question. And no, except for tropical resort vacations, she hasn't. She's been busy raising her family, spending gruelling days in corporate offices, and in these last few years, coordinating luncheons and parties for people who get to travel all over God's green acre and collect whatever they bloody well find quaint. She considers the backpack in his room. If she told him about her all-inclusive trips to Varadero and Puerto Vallarta it would slide another kind of wedge between them. He probably has a diatribe about the ethical evils of all-inclusives–foreign owned, the devastating impact on local business, the pittance they pay their over-worked employees. And the issue of North American gluttony: she's certain he could wax poetic about that atrocity, too. He stayed in hostels and camped on beaches. That was his way, and his kind.

"Listen, I've got to get going. Billy's having problems at school, and I need to spend extra time with him." She won't say that it's an alternative school. Kids who should have graduated years ago but didn't make it in the mainstream. Let him ask if he's interested.

"Do I get a kiss?"

He sounds sullen, she thinks, but yes, he gets one kiss, and then another.

§

The Sunshine trip was a success. "Mom, you should have been there," Andrew says, new ski-lift tags on his jacket. He is at the age where soon it will no longer be considered cool to get excited about family excursions; she misses him already. Adolescent girls detach sooner–Harper is a case in point. "Dad says I'm getting really good at carving," Andrew continues. He is radiant, she sees, and wind-burnt below his eyes where the goggles didn't reach.

"There were *tons* of hot guys there, Mom," Harper says, loudly. "*Totally* hot. Like Justin Bieber hot. I'm adding them on Facebook. Want to see photos?" She pushes her phone at Joelle. It's pink. Joelle has no idea what all the buttons are for, or what apps her daughter has downloaded. The girl's obsessed with her phone. All of present society, it seems, is obsessed with phones.

"Yes, Love, I do want to see them," Joelle says, "just not right now. You've got to get to school, and I've got a meeting in half an hour."

She's out all morning, scoping out prospective venues for a new radio station's kick-off party. She's considering enlisting some of the Calgary Stampeders for a literal "kick-off" at McMahon Stadium. Another option is to stage an event at the Planetarium. A space odyssey theme. The radio station's program director is her contact and he's leaving it up to her. At the Planetarium she has to deal with an assistant who spends more time texting than she does answering Joelle's questions about liquor licensing and extra parking.

Back home the house is blissfully quiet again. Even Billy, it seems, must have crawled out of bed and gone to class. Neil's at work. She finds it rather sweet that he phones home once a day to "touch base."

She slings her jacket on the coat rack. Her clothes are like accessories in all this deceit–only they know about her parallel life. She's compelled to check her pockets, and finds the shells she'd taken from Matt's place months before. Beautiful. She slips out of her shoes and pads across the hardwood, sees that breakfast dishes have made it to the sink–Harper's chore this week–but not the dishwasher.

Upstairs she runs a bath and balances the shells on the tub ledge. What the devil kind are they? She slips on her robe, grabs the shells, and logs into the family room computer. It takes her an hour and forty-five minutes, but there they are: an Atlantic Dogwinkle–or Frilled Dogwinkle–and a Bullia.

"Hey."

Billy. Usually she can sense if she's being watched. She can sense *Billy*.

"What are you doing home? You startled me. No school?" She makes sure she's not falling out of her robe, belts it tighter.

"Teacher's got pneumonia." His arms hang at his sides, and she sees how skeletal he's becoming. "Or something." He whips his bangs back. People have always commented on the mother-son resemblance. Now his face is so drawn and still, she thinks of her descendents, a great great grandfather in a sepia photo. That back-breaking rural life. Her son looks so much older than he should.

"Oh," she says. "Well, it's nice to see you. I'm just surfing here. Procrastinating, really. I'm supposed to be working." She follows his gaze to the pretty shells.

"What are those?"

"I'm doing ocean-themed centrepieces for a seafood dinner at the faculty club. Thought I'd do a little research, and it seems I've wasted half the morning."

"Uh." He turns around. A skull and crossbones are black-markered onto his jean jacket. "I'm going back to school."

She hesitates to press him. Together they are a fragile thing; a reef best left untouched. "Guess they got a sub, hey?"

He whips around. "And I guess you had car trouble Saturday night and couldn't make it home." He slams the door, and the stained glass parrot in the window rattles precariously against the pane.

Sick. That's what she feels.

§

Billy goes AWOL and now it's day ten.

"This is the first time we've experienced calm in months," Neil says, beside her in the ensuite bathroom. He's shaving, and she's clipping her fingernails at their separate sinks. At one time she joked with her Zion Lutheran friends that his-and-hers sinks were the secret of a happy marriage. "Tough love, Jo. I'm sure you've heard of it."

Yes. Last year they tried an intervention, like on reality TV. Two months of rehab and he was back on the street, couch surfing, living under bridges. Festering. She's already tried the numbers of friends he had when he was in regular high school. No one has seen him. "We don't really hang out any more," they tell her, all those boys he used to innocuously skateboard and ride bikes with. "I haven't seen him in a few years." She doesn't know the names of the kids in his new gang. Doesn't have numbers, doesn't know what their parents do. Has she facilitated her son's decline by not caring enough? But she loves him so! It would help if she could discuss this with Matt, but they haven't gone there.

"But Neil he's our son, and he's barely out of his teens. You can't tell me that you wouldn't be elated if he walked in the door right now." She herds her clippings into a pile and scoots them off the counter into the wastepaper basket.

"Not until he steps up. We've done everything we can for him, and he just won't step up. You think it's not killing me, too, knowing what he's doing out there? Knowing how dangerous it is?" He rinses his razor and taps it against the sink. Then he unzips and pees.

She looks at her reflection. Ordinary round face, slightly moonish; ears tucked neatly against her head. Long neck she never draws attention to with jewellery. Nose a little too perky, perhaps, but that tricks people into thinking she's younger. Her right eyelid seems to be drooping. She winches it with her thumb. Maybe she'll have a lid lift. If she can persuade her doctor that it's hampering her vision, she could get the procedure for free. What she looks is tired, she decides. Loving in all these directions has made her feel ancient. "But we can't give up–"

"Listen, we've got two other kids who are not yet fucked up. Let's give them some time and attention, too." He catches her eyes in the mirror. "I'm off to work. Oh, and could we have pasta tonight? I've got a craving for lasagna, and the kids love it. Andrew, especially."

"Sure. I'll get some garlic bread when I'm out. Want a Greek salad, too?"

"Only if they have them marked down," he says. "Extra Foods might."

They kiss and he's gone. She understands his specific anguish regarding their firstborn; he'd pulled strings to get Billy a job with Calgary Parks and Rec, and their son blew it. By the end of the first week he was coming in late. Middle of the second week he didn't show at all. And she knew it wasn't the potentially negative reflection on Neil that rankled, it was the inconceivable hurt that Billy didn't care enough about his own father to even try. Neil said it was like being thwacked under the ribs with a tire iron and taking a steel-toed boot in the chin as you dropped.

§

Line-ups at every check-out. She should have gone to IGA. Further away, and she really didn't feel present enough to manoeuvre through freeway traffic, but Extra Foods was always maniacally busy. All she needed was the bread and lasagna; the ready-made salads were not on sale, and she was not up to preparing one from scratch. She evaluates which line might move the quickest, and stands behind a senior with a basket of mostly large items that will quickly scan. He's waiting for the woman in front of him, and oh, God, now she can't find her coupons. Joelle lifts a crafting magazine off the stand. A long time, she thinks, since she spent any time on her wall hangings. And no one's noticed, or at least they haven't mentioned it.

"Joelle!"

She starts. Matt is coming toward her on his long legs. Navy pea jacket she hasn't seen before. "Well look at jaunty you," she says, thrilled to see him out in the open. She feels like they've been stage actors, and have hardly spoken outside of the set that's his bedroom. "What a surprise!" They hold each other and she doesn't think about where they are or fluorescent lighting, the proximity to home.

"Is this where you usually shop?" He steps back, his hands still warm on her arms, and again she can't believe that she knows this young effervescent intellectual, let alone that she knows him in the Biblical sense. The lines she's crossed. It's been almost one year of her life. The man ahead of her is having his lettuce weighed. She's thankful when the cashier has to pick up the phone to question a price.

"Not usually," she says, "but I'm not far from home. What about you? You're miles from your place." Somewhere in the backdrop a child is pleading for licorice. A grey-bearded man in a turban and kurta has pushed his cart in behind them. Toilet paper. Crackers. Dog food.

"My parents live in this area," he says. "I'm going for dinner. Mom said to pick up whipped cream." They both smile, and she feels suddenly shy. Whipped cream. Indeed.

They are standing there–closely, affectionately familiar, unable to refrain from touching–when someone whistles loudly, as if purposely calling attention. The whistle pierces through the market clatter and silences the impudent kid wanting candy. Time is temporarily suspended. People spontaneously cover their ears and turn to the source of the irreverent whistle. Jesus fuck! Billy is five bed length's away, staring her down. She looks for one second. He bolts toward the door, as if caught stealing. He knocks over a potato chip display. Someone gasps. There's his jacket. Skull and crossbones. Matted hair. Billy the hangdog, her heartache, her boy.

"Meth head," Matt says, derisively, and snorts. "Nice jacket."

She will not see her young lover again.

§

There is a Christmas pageant; and Neil's first spring marathon–Woody's, in Red Deer, with its course along the river; and a summer camping trip to the west coast; and then the kids' autumn activities–hip hop for Harper, and Andrew's surprised them with an interest in wrestling. He's good. Her father-in-law survives a heart attack. Her rolodex spins and spins. She plants a garden and makes borscht for the first time in her life. They consistently do not win the lottery. They get a grey cat. Someone rear-ends Neil on the Deerfoot. There's another Christmas pageant. Joelle sits solo in the pew her family used to occupy, and she mouths the words to the hymns. No one asks her to volunteer anymore. There are many new people whose names she says once then immediately forgets.

Time simultaneously passes quickly and the hands of the clock never move at all, and what she does mostly is sit in her craft room with the lights off. And what she does mostly is think. She tells herself until she almost believes it that Billy's melancholy and rage are elemental, not borne from some wound she may have inadvertently ignited. It began so long ago.

Sometimes, rarely, her son still phones and breathes at her, but she never sees him, not even a shadow of him, and perhaps would not even know if she passed him on the street–another one of those crazy-eyed kids who eats his own scabs and sits with a cardboard sign and a cup for donations at his feet. They had the same feet, her Billy and Matt. Smooth, like alabaster. Well-proportioned. Feet for washing. For worship. Her boys had feet like Christ.

RABUN COUNTY

The school bell rings, the exodus occurs. Emma remains seated and imagines the heaviest element leeching up from the floorboards, soaking through shoes and skin and invading her circuitry of veins: the lethargic climb through well-muscled calves, along the supple thighs, inside her complicated middle parts, navigating the twisty intestines, colouring the tendrils in her chest, weighting each arm... bangled wrists... hands, until it reaches the restless fingertips on the black-lined page of her notebook. What is the heaviest naturally occurring element? Ah, yes. Uranium. Atomic number 92. And a trick question she is prepared for: the heaviest man-made element, Ununoctium. Element 118. That should impress him.

Chemistry's the last hard class before she graduates, thank you Jesus. She would pass without the extra tutoring, but she's asked especially for it, and didn't teacher seem pleased? She thought so. She nudges a pen off the desk and–aware that he's furtively watching from his own desk–bends so slowly to recover it one might believe she's suffered a trauma to her back or neck. Outside buses pull away with their raucous charges and nose toward the Blue Ridge Mountains. Someone's car alarm is bleating. Closer still, one fly has mounted another in the corner of the window; the female's hind legs steadily twitch. Emma is hyper-aware. And soon teacher's shoes–oxblood, leather–are drumming down the aisle toward her.

He stops three desks away and asks: "Would you prefer to come to the front, or shall I slide a chair over?"

She considers the angular shape of him. Tall enough to hunt geese with a rake. Brown eyes a hue lighter and less intent than her own, a scar like a miniature witching rod beneath the right eye. Neat black brows. Newly sunburned throat. Pressed shirt, sleeves rolled above slender forearms, moons of perspiration. A book reader, nothing like the men around here. He's closer to her age than her father's, she decides. Someone who'd take dance lessons before his wedding. Write a sappy song for his wife and croon it at the reception, nervous fingers plucking the guitar chords too quickly, his voice suddenly boyish and shy, as if even *it* is unprepared to make the commitment. "Your desk will be fine." She's taken to playing up her southern vowels.

She zips a pencil into its case, flutters through her notes. Stares at him with the intensity of one boring a hole in wood. Mr. Hamilton turns away first, and she understands. This is the beginning. It's begun.

§

There's Emma again, roaring up the back steps, expertly missing the gap where a board punched through years ago. The screen door opens with a sound like a child saying *Whee*. She wings her books—"I'm home, Varlene!"—and checks beneath the oil-clothed table, inside the pantry. She removes the rag rug that covers the cellar's trap door and calls down: "Where's my big sister hiding?"

But Varlene's not playing today. Emma finds her on the sofa, calico skirt flipped back, deer legs splayed, eyes grid-locked on the copper-coloured ceiling stains as if some happily-ever-after is cinematically playing out between the rough beams and cobwebs. "What did I say about that, Leenie?" She claps above her sister's vacant face to break the trance. "Get your fingers out of your business."

Varlene adjusts her skirt and arranges herself against the arm of the couch like a starlet. Emma collapses at the other end. Another night of twisting up in the sheets. Crazy dreams—her dad's diagnosed with cancer, and the doctor's making *her* responsible for telling him—and waking with her jaws sore from tooth-grinding.

She'd give her eye teeth for some real sleep. Her sister thunks her bare feet–too swollen now for anything but flip-flops–into her lap. Shoot. The girl's tried painting her toenails with Wite-Out, and she's smeared it onto her dirty toes. *Shouldn't have left it out,* Emma chides herself.

Varlene rolls up and sits on her knees, her face close to her sister's. "Know what I haven't had for a long time, Em?"

Her breath's like sour apples, Emma thinks, and wonders if this can be blamed on changing hormones. Teacher would know. "What's that?" she asks, kneading her own temples.

"An ice cream sandwich. Hup, hup. Can we go to town? Pretty please with a cherry on top?"

Varlene bounces on the sofa and the springs protest. A mouse family inside, Emma thinks. Least that's what it sounds like. "Not before supper... you know the rules. Daddy'll be home soon. I'll make something to eat, then we'll see. Maybe he'd like ice cream, too." The ribbed upholstery has impressed a pattern on Varlene's cheek. Like a tribal scar, Emma thinks, or a birthmark.

"Chocolate or maple walnut... them's his special favourites."

"*Those.* Those *are* his favourites." The clock chimes. Emma stands and hauls her sister up by an elbow. "Come on. Time to start supper." The girls are the same height when the blades of their backs meet and they gaze sideways at the bathroom mirror; people say they could be twins. Not true, Emma thinks, it's just the hair. If not swept into an elastic or twisted into a single braid like a show horse tail, their board-straight locks graze their waistbands. She's grateful her hair's a reasonable brown; Varlene's is as white-blonde as the day she took her sweet time being born. Toddlers and old women can't resist touching it.

"Got to pee first," Varlene says, holding herself. She clumsily runs toward the bathroom and does not close the door.

"And then what?" Emma calls after her. She consciously straightens as she returns to the darkening kitchen, walks as if balancing her chemistry text on her head. Poor posture's repulsive. The woman who birthed them—an unsolicited ghost who infrequently strobes across her thoughts—habitually drew her shoulders in. She was, Emma recalls, beginning to resemble a question mark. "Varlene? What do you do after using the toilet?"

The girl shouts back: "Wash my hands real good!"

Emma watches transient shadows creep across the stacked plates and mugs cupped inside each other, the three good pots and cast iron pan, the brown Betty tea pot with the lid that doesn't fit right. She sniffs the air, notes the trash is right to the top of the can. Must dump it, she thinks, and presses her forehead to the window. She doesn't put much stock in Christian prayer, but if she did, this would be the hour for a little help from on high. The worst thing has happened. No, *death* would be worse. Varlene's, their dad's. But this was close. The second worst thing.

She nudges the window open to maximum height and secures it with the stick they keep on the sill. Fresh air in great gulps. That's better. The woods are alive, undulating. Chattering squirrels animate sycamores, maples, and hemlock, scattering brushwood in irregular showers onto the thick mulch of leaves. Sunlight bleeds through wherever able. Pretty, she thinks. The woods often beckon. She likes to gather snapped branches from the understory and weave rustic grids and asymmetrical sculptures. She binds them with string or panel nails. They are not lanterns, or lobster traps, or bird cages. Just shapes, nothing more. She tacks them around the house in ways she considers artful. When her dad's had enough of the *clutter*, he plucks these pieces off the walls and tables and pitches them back into the woods. Ready-made playgrounds for snakes.

She hears the toilet, the water tap, footfalls. "Come help peel potatoes, Leenie. Before long–"

"Daddy'll be home." Varlene rubs her belly, head bobbing. "Hup, hup."

Emma's fingers thrum against her own heart. She imagines wire encasing that fragile organ, a cage growing smaller as the weeks pass. Almost eight since her sister's last period; the luxury of time does not exist.

Varlene crowds in beside Emma's elbow. "Can we have sausages in a chain?"

The myriad creatures her sister evokes: a sea turtle. A duck, with her flat, expanding feet. "Sure we can, Kiddo." She passes Varlene the peeler and a pan of grenade-sized potatoes, saving the smaller ones for herself. "Be really careful with that… we're not in any race here. And try to keep the peels on the paper."

Varlene begins a tuneless song about bees and buttercups. When she stops mid-verse, Emma knows she's unable to recall the words.

"We're big girls now, right Em?"

"Practically women."

"Practically women," Varlene repeats.

Emma opens the fridge and a sour milk smell assaults her. "Ooh. Smell this." She holds the carton beneath Varlene's nose.

"It's like throw-up," the girl says, and pinches her nostrils.

Emma dumps the curdling milk. "I'm almost done school now, and soon you'll be working full days at the Opportunity Shop."

"Hup."

"Steady there." Emma trains an eye on her sister's hands. She'll never control a pencil with them, Emma thinks, beyond the fist-drawn scrawls she considers her name. She'll never shift a gear, or lace a shoe without struggle, or appropriately count coins to pay for a lemonade. "We don't want another accident." The family recently celebrated Varlene's nineteenth birthday with a red velvet cake, foil-wrapped quarters baked inside. Varlene nicked her finger cutting the first slice–why had they let her try?–and the resultant caterwauling had Emma scrambling for the locked stash of feel-better sweets. After a Mars bar and a kiss on the Disney-bandaged wound, Varlene was impatient to blow out her candles. "Look, Em, I've still got three boyfriends!" Emma excused herself. It was getting too damn hard to keep it all in.

"Like this, right?" Varlene conscientiously peels the warts off a potato. The skin curls and drops across an obituary in the *Clayton Tribune*.

"That's right, Leenie-girl. Just like that."

The windows rattle. A quarter-ton truck shivers before its engine subsides. "Daddy's home! Hup, Daddy, hup." Varlene knocks the peelings off the counter.

Ten steps on gravel and Cy's at the threshold with his tin lunch pail and thermos, asking: "How's my girls?"

"Great, Daddy! Kisses?" Varlene drapes around him. Like a 1950s wife, Emma thinks. She studies her father, figures he's shrinking. A wick slowly burning down. The chemical process of combustion. She knows the mill's been chewing him up since he was seventeen and eager to prove himself in his brother's outgrown overalls, knees already patched twice over. "Hi, Pop. Supper won't be long."

"Smells mighty fine," he says, and kicks off his work boots. He hangs his hat on the nail by the door and slings gloves over the rungs of a stool. His hair is thick with sawdust.

Varlene methodically retrieves the bottle that lives in the cupboard with the cooking oil, baking soda, a ten pound bag of white flour, and grits. Emma sees how her sister's hair is much like a flame in this light. Varlene fills a coffee mug, handle long gone, and passes it. "Your medicine, Daddy."

§

The year Emma turned five and Varlene seven, their mama packed up her suitcase, wrapped it in binder twine, and drove off with a flea market junker from Bristol, Virginia without even stopping for a goodbye squeeze. Far as they know she's living in some barn-board shack in Tennessee now, or gone over Alabama way. That summer their father took the girls to the swimming hole down from Betty's Creek Road, and on long picnics with barbecued chicken sandwiches and jars of sweet tea one could stand spoons in.

The county circus arrived in Clayton. Trapeze artists with ample bosoms, Emma recalls, and holes the size of cooking apples in pink netted tights. The barking ringleader: "And now, ladies and gentleman, boys and girls… a special treat for one lucky audience member. Who would like to be the first, the one, and the only to ride Indhira, the Indian elephant?" Emma'd joined the crowd of rural Baptists in raising the roof. The ringleader marched toward her on his white boots: "I reckon this little lady will do just fine." He extended a ruby-ringed hand, but his small eyes and foreignness were terrifying, and she'd clung to her father, reaching for the fold of skin where a power saw had sheared his thumb at the knuckle. She'd made a habit of rubbing her own thumb across the smoothness, believing it a charm.

§

Five tutoring sessions, and she knows some things now.

Aside from his teaching position and desire to have his family experience another part of America, it was trees that brought Mr. Hamilton all the way from the west coast. Georgia pines. He's conducting *a layman's study which may become a paper on the southern pine beetle's cyclical and seemingly arbitrary nature.* She has that memorized now, like she's memorized the periodic table of elements, and the Second Law of Thermodynamics: *entropy increases over time. Heat cannot flow on its own from an area of cold to an area of hot.* Her teacher's researching how to anticipate the pine beetle's movement, *and thus suppress outbreaks and pine decimation.* Teaching chemistry is something he fell into, he explains. Biology–that's where his true passion lies.

She knows about his wife, a potter and Midwest governor's daughter. Emma studies the framed photo on her teacher's desk. Defined cheekbones, pointy chin, hair ordered back except for one long strand licked by wind. In another frame, the three of them–the daughter might be six–in white and navy, keeling on a sailboat like celebrities. California. Land of dazzling teeth, magazine fashions, flawless skin: attributes reserved for the well-off and people who win total makeovers on TV. Out here there's a lot of what folks call *summer teeth*: some are here, some are there. She's tried not to gawk at his family's images, or to imagine his sporty wife unbuttoning his shirt, sliding the sleeves down arms that have never, she guesses, fed a log into a saw, over hands that might not even know how to change a tire. *'Bout as useful as gooseshit on a pumphandle.* That's what the good ol' boys would say about a high-collared man like this.

It's like syrup, she thinks. Their relationship's sugared into a slow pouring out of personal details ingeniously woven into the rich language of protons and electrons, chemiluminescence. Chemistry, for sure. They sit surrounded by the practicality of beakers, funnels, an autoclave. Fingers have touched across pages, and knees have met beneath his desk. At first he jerked away like he'd been electrocuted, but now: lingering. It's so easy, she thinks. And when it happens–and it must happen soon–it'll be a far cry from the saliva-drenched marathons with Judson and his cousin from Lexington, who claw at her like drowning men.

Will he whisper *Emmaline,* as the name appears on her school records? She's a long road from romantic, but she wonders all the same. He and his perfect wife probably say *thank you* after having sex, and read Wallace Stevens' poetry before clicking off the energy-saving lights. No backseats. No cleaning up with a dirty sock, or stumbling out of the woods to rejoin the party and shotgun the next can of beer.

"Emma, are you following? The difference between ionic and covalent chemical bonds...."

Science. Equations. Enigmatic symbols floating up from the review he's prepared. No, she's not following. She still needs everything explained three times. "Let's go over it again, please," she says, and looks up at him through her wispy bangs. "I'm still not quite getting it."

§

"Tell me the circus story," Varlene orders. "Hup!" Emma's finished washing her sister's hair and is now combing it out on the bedside. The circus story. Varlene's *bestest*. Emma reshapes the memory according to whim, adding a carnival, fireworks, sometimes an organ grinder, an imaginary trombonist, knock-kneed giraffes, tap-dancing, three-legged men, deformed babies pickled in mason jars.

In reality it went like this: "Come on, Emma," her father'd said, his hand in the small of her back. "It'll be fun. I'll come up with you." He and the small-eyed man escorted her to the platform and lifted her onto the animal's huge tasselled back. *I must not fall.* She'd not been afraid of slamming the ground, nor the inevitable crush beneath the elephant's plate-sized feet, but of the pain she might inflict were her daddy to lose her so soon after her mama's mutiny. Emma recalls being led around the ring. The rocking motion. Her embarrassment when the animal dropped a load and the crowd exploded in laughter. The stench of manure. A clown with red shoes dashing out with a shovel and pail. She dared a quick wave at Varlene–alone, and panic-eyed in the bleachers, cotton candy making glue in her hair.

"And fortune tellers?" Varlene asks, eyes round with expectation.

"Ouch. You're pulling, Emma."

"There surely were," Emma says, lifting her sister's hair and letting it slither through the comb's teeth, "with smoky crystal balls. Also an alligator-skinned family, and the fattest woman in the world, wearing a crown like the queen."

"And polar bears?" Varlene asks.

"You got that right," she says. "Six of them!"

"How 'bout Elvis Presley?"

Emma can't help smiling; this is what her sister is good at. "Sitting right behind us."

§

The preacher came by for a time. They listened while he made pronouncements from her mother's kitchen chair, over raisin pie and pots of honeyed tea.

Blame of oneself or others is a worm that festers in the soul.

His metaphor, Emma knows, was meant to speed Cy's healing, but the message never took. When she was fourteen her dad confided how it'd ripped him to ribbons the way she'd tried filling the house with the sounds and spaces only a mother makes. "My baby girl, barely able to see over the stove, and there you were, making a kind of stew."

§

Time's a rigorous science; Emma adds up the weeks on her fingers. Two more have passed. *Molecules,* she thinks. *Evaporation.* She's on Betty's Creek Road and ancient Charlie Dockens–kin on her mama's side–is offering a ride. "Almost home," she says, and waves him on, though the heat's now something to swim through. She'd love to stop at the swimming hole where the preacher baptizes believers and they break out in tongues. But there are water moccasins, copperheads, rattlers. And she's seen black rat snakes stretch clear across the road. She plucks her blouse, quivers the damp cotton for relief. The humidity's made a ballast of her hair.

She checks her watch. Five o'clock, which means Varlene's had two hours of independence already. Near about an hour too long, she calculates.

Blame is a worm that festers in the soul.

She damns her mama, who spoke too loudly and brayed like a goat, her legs long and usually bare. All the other Baptist women knew how to dress proper for church. They wore nylons, even days you could fry an egg on a rock. Her mama wasn't invited to study the gospels or swap recipes in kitchens. She returned from church picnics with most of her potato salad going sour in the bowl. On the edge of everything, Emma thinks, kicking a stone from her path. That's where they existed. Edge of poverty. Edge of the state. On the goddamned edge of decency. She's heard talk that her mama needed it like an animal, or a man. Would've been better if she'd died, like Mary Louise's mother, struck dead by a semi on the interstate. *She'd* been elevated to the high status reserved only for those whose loved ones have suffered a tragic and too-early death. It also helps, Emma knows, if the lost are beautiful. Well, even in soiled lace and hair slip-sliding from bobby pins, her mama was undeniably that.

She shifts her backpack and squints up at the mountain, marvelling at how the trees completely swallow houses and the dirt roads that wind through them. Georgia's so thick and green, especially with the spring rains. Ferns up to her armpits. Spanish moss jumping from oak to oak, sheltering bats and rat snakes and jumping spiders. Back in the day, women used the moss to stuff mattresses. Or so they say. And the trillium is in bloom. She'll collect some, float a few crimson blossoms in a bowl to cheer the kitchen.

Strangers in a van speed past. Too close. They honk and throw a beer can out the window, nailing a sign. She runs a finger inside her sneakers where her bare heels rub. There'll be blisters, she guesses.

§

She inhales and holds it as long as she can. Some days he smells of rain, some days ginger. More like a woman than a man. Today's smell: Dentyne gum. "Would you like one?" He pushes the pack toward her with his fingernails. Cuticles meet. She thinks about human chemistry, a science unchanged since Adam and Eve fled the garden wearing nothing but heart-shaped leaves. She removes a stick and places it on her tongue.

"Listen, Em–"

The increasing familiarity: Emma, Emmy, Em. She feels weightless. "Yes, Sir?"

Words trembling like leaves: "... flying to California... spending time with her sister... first baby... the weekend... wide open... and go over the ninth chapter again."

What she'd give to experience *his* perceptions. First day of class, someone asked if he'd ever been to the South before. Nope. He called it *quaint* and *exotic*. "But Georgia's divided," he quickly added. "Like every place, it's many worlds." Emma's knows this is true. At flea markets one can still buy Nazi candlestick holders, T-shirts addressing the "War of Northern Aggression," and Confederate flag belt-buckles that disguise knives which could gut a man in one swipe. A few miles away the same sun beats on international private schools, country clubs. Estate homes with elaborate gardens and picture-perfect verandahs sit next to shacks where piss-stained mattresses pile up outside yards like layers of a cake gone wrong. Garbage festers in the oppressive heat, and mangy hound dogs fight for the best bits. "Y'all better not touch the back of that one," warns neighbour Danny, the nine-year-old who chases after anyone who happens by. The boy has shingles, and like she and Varlene, no mama to love him proper.

"Of course, if you're already studied out...."

"No, let's do that," she says in her new, measured way. "That'd be absolutely fine."

"Great. And Em... you're almost a high school graduate now. I think–when we're alone–I'd like it if you called me Owen."

He's closing books, and smiling in what seems to her a careful way. Were the janitor to walk in and sight them among the test tubes and graduated cylinders, she believes he'd not sense a dang thing.

§

I couldn't be everywhere all the time. She consoles herself as she butters bread for Varlene's brown bag sandwiches, and again while she boils water in a saucepan for tea. She tells herself this in the night, her sister mumbling in the neighbouring twin bed, below gossip magazine photos of Brad Pitt.

Blame is a worm. I couldn't be everywhere.

She repeats it walking home from another tutoring session; and at the kitchen table, the small family clasping hands through the blessing out of habit more than belief; and as the sun slips behind the mist-wrapped mountains. Somewhere someone's mowing a lawn.

And she's learned something new again: teacher's sheets are the colour of marzipan, and softer than human skin.

§

Trees hem in the interstate; she can't see beyond them. There's another crush of clouds above. Nine consecutive nocturnal rains. She loves listening to the force of nature, wondering if the house's foundation will hold or if they'll be pitched into the gap, like a canoe down the Chattooga River.

Her sister fidgets with the radio; Owen's car, lent for this day, finally here. "Where we going, Em? Hup!"

Sometimes she thinks Varlene's faking. "Atlanta, you already know that. We'll see a movie, and eat in a restaurant... any one you want. How 'bout a real pizzeria?"

"But why we going to the doctor? I ain't sick."

Emma digs in her bag. Yes. There. A Find-A-Word puzzle book. "Here... I've started this. There's a pen in my purse somewhere. Want to try? You find the same letters in the puzzle that make the words on the list... see how many you can get. Easy as sliding off a greasy log backward."

She passes a jeep and gets well ahead before she returns to the right lane. She's not been this far from home since the eighth grade trip to Florida; every few miles, real estate signs and billboards—new hotels, condominiums, golf courses, and restaurants—punctuate the green. It's not progress, she thinks, only change. Traffic's diverted near Tallulah Falls. Crews of migrant Mexicans curl over shovels and jackhammers, T-shirts soaked through as they widen the interstate. She slows enough to see brown eyes beneath hardhats. Judging her? Seems so. Emma intuits the immigrants' secret: this is not who they are.

Owen's right: the South *is* divided. Across the state line, artists and writers have poured into Asheville. The Greenwich Village of the South, the papers call it. She's heard doctors and such are constructing multi-million dollar homes up in Highlands. Richy-richies who buy million dollar lake properties, tear them down, build again. A shitload of money's flooding into the mountains. You can buy fancy furniture and designer clothes right in Clayton now. And the change has come fast, like night sometimes sneaks up, she thinks, or sorrow.

§

Teacher surprises her.

He has disparate passions–collecting antique tools, fly-fishing–and speaks to her like a long-time friend. Like a lover. Easy to lose themselves in the kudzu vines that run wild in the wooded acres behind the school. They forget their real lives. She picks a small leaf from his hair and blows on it. He clasps her hand and brings it to his chest.

"I got in trouble today," he says. "The principal's warned me about propagating anti-Republican politics and anti-gun ideals. He's even come down on me about a Dr. Phil rant in the staff room." He laughs. They are beginning to laugh a lot together. "Hey, look! A pine warbler."

Emma rolls onto her back. Birds dart between the treetops. Yellow breasts. Cardinal red. Merry songs. "You've got something against Dr. Phil?"

Her teacher hooks his leg over hers, the hair on his shins a soft carpet. "I do. He's a moral entrepreneur on a mission to cure the ails of middle America with his right wing ideologies, one televised family crisis at a time."

Now there's a theory, Emma thinks. "Keep talking," she says. "I like the way you sound and the thoughts you think." He's already told her that when locals–*your people,* he'd said–cock their ears to his flat intonation and ask where he hails from, he's found it's easier to answer *Virginia.*

§

The doctor is black, and a woman to boot. Owen, Emma thinks, would be pleased. The stranger takes Varlene's hand and leads her down a white hall, the girl's single braid swinging like a pendulum across her back.

For a long time, Emma will remember this: her sister does not even turn around.

§

Homebound. The speed and multi-laned traffic, her unfamiliarity with the city; Emma grips the wheel like a life-raft. It would not do to have to explain an accident. *That* would be trouble with a tail on it. Varlene's pale and unnervingly quiet, her palms flattened against the air vents.

"See that?" Emma motions toward Turner Field. "That's where the Atlanta Braves play. Would you like to see a game some day? We'd eat corndogs and sing 'Take me out to the ball game.'"

No response. The doctor promised she'd be back to herself in a day or two. Good as new short of a week. "Well, everyone says it's super fun, Leenie. Almost better than the circus."

Emma studies the interstate trees: they look entirely different from this direction. They continue north, passing Gwinnett County, Hall, Habersham. She reads signs aloud: *Dulcimers. Guns and Pawn. Homemade Jams and Jellies.* Traffic's still held up near Tallulah Gorge: more Mexicans working the clay.

On the radio, the opening fiddle strains of The Doobie Brothers' "Black Water."

"Turn it off. Em."

They drive a long time, the miles burning in silence.

Mountain people have set up a roadside stand for quilts and vegetables outside Clayton. Someone's painted *Isaiah 53* on a board and tacked it to a post. Five miles later, simply *Jesus*.

From Los Angeles to *this*? Owen must feel like he's stumbled onto a movie set, Emma thinks. Baptist revivals and Moses slabs pronouncing the Ten Commandments, and this part of the peach state's tarnished by that scene from "Deliverance" it'll never live down. Tourists from as far away as Germany show up with cameras for a gander at Billy Redden. No longer a homely, backward, banjo-playing kid–he's all grown up now, and cooks at the Coffee Jar Café on Highway 441.

§

Thirty minutes today, time enough to spread the blanket on a moss bed. He trails his fingers up her inner arm and down between her breasts, making her shiver. She says: "That feels like a spider."

He stops then, and she senses it's going to get serious again.

"Em, you've got to tell your father, and talk to the police–"

She contemplates the tricks of light through the pines. A cardinal swoops between branches, as if on a string. "My favourite bird."

"Find out who, and where… how long it'd been going on." He holds her chin between his thumb and forefinger; she can't look away. "They should be charged."

He's talked about procuring an attorney, finding Varlene a safe place. A *home,* if that's what's required. It would kill her dad. Owen's paid for everything, and she's grateful as hell, but it doesn't follow that he should get some say.

"For all you know, Emma, it's still happening."

She sits up, reaches for her top. She speaks the native truth: "It's not how we do things here."

§

She does not attend her prom.

And then the school bell rings for the last time. Summer, and she has a job. Her official title is *Research Assistant.* Much to learn about the southern pine beetle, and, she's finds most of it fascinating. *Dendroctonus frontalis* Zimmermann. The most destructive insect pest of pine forests in thirteen southeastern states and in parts of Mexico and Central America. Its name, she thinks, makes a pleasant little song. Owen says he thinks so, too.

§

A moon pie in its wrapper on the bedside table. Varlene's inert on her patchwork quilt beside a magazine spread open but upside down. Emma dusts the white-blonde hair off her sister's face, hovers a hand over her belly. A month behind them now, but heat comes through her palm as if it's rising off an element. Scarcely visible blue veins–no something smaller than veins, she thinks, *capillaries*–run like crazy maps beneath her sister's translucent eyelids. *You have such pretty hair. You're our best girlfriend, Varlene.* Was that the way? Two or three of them, taking turns? She imagines a well, lowers a pail of suspicions back into its depths. There is that, or the other thing. She can hear him out there now, crossing the wood floor, dead tired of his life, of breathing sawdust, of trying to pretend it all doesn't hurt bad as a snakebite. By his steps she knows he'll be at the window now, staring out, hurting and thinking, drinking whisky from a cup that no longer bears a handle.

Emma takes the magazine off the bed. "Okay, scooch over, Leenie-girl. Just five more minutes before lights out." She'll bring in the circus now, unfold the old story like a tent. She'll make each word weightless, swinging. Even the elephant, positively trapeze.

SCENES FROM A FAMILY ON FIRE

1.

There's a good son, a bad son, and an absentee sister who lives in Temecula, California with a real estate developer named Ender who deals *Exclusively in Nine Figure Properties*. In their Christmas photo the remote in-laws are staged in tan-coloured golf shorts beside a blue-tiled swimming pool. Within the frame of their professionally landscaped garden, they appear, Shannon feels, only slightly less glum than the couple in "American Gothic."

"Hanging things," Andy's remarked. "They've got hanging things. Vines and such."

We have hanging things, too, Shannon's mused. Cobwebs from light fixtures. My blouses slung from a pipe above the dryer.

Five years earlier, when Ender was making a killing in Seattle's sizzling real estate market, he and Charlotte sent a cheque for the amount of one plane ticket. "We'd love to have you both visit," the attached card read. The way of the rich, Shannon thinks. This subterfuge of generosity.

What most impressed during that visit was not the Spanish-styled house overlooking Puget Sound or the meal at the Marrakesh Moroccan Restaurant–where they'd sat cross-legged on the floor beneath velvet tapestries and ate couscous with their fingers–but her in-laws' plastic cutting board with *Good Morning* imprinted on it at least a hundred times, mantra-like, or as if ordering its users: *You* will *have a good morning, goddamn it.*

Charlotte phones on Christmas day, sometimes at Easter, and entirely rarely throughout the year. The nonreligious-holiday calls feel anachronistic to Shannon; it's easy to forget that Andy has an older sister. When the phone rings today and Charlotte's number's displayed, her heart gives its usual twig: she wishes Andy'd hurry up with the shovelling and get in here. She could simply let it ring, but no, she isn't like that: if a phone rings or a doorbell dongs, she responds with politesse.

"I picked up the most wonderful modern roses at the Pike Place Market today," Charlotte asserts. "They're almost blue."

Minutes later Andy hastens winter in through the back door. "Your sister," Shannon stage whispers, "on the phone." He steps into the kitchen without removing his boots and grabs the cordless. The siblings are soon debating which is less desirable: Saskatchewan's snow or Seattle's rain.

Shannon keeps the landline phone jammed to her ear as she looks out: slow-motion snow. An arabesque of white flies. Andy makes noises into the phone as necessary. What would it be like if she left? Who then to regularly punctuate the silence since the kids left, utter pleasantries to a faraway sister? "We're going to see Jackson this summer," she interjects.

Charlotte stops. "Really? That's nice. How's the little guy doing?"

"He plays soccer–" Andy says.

"He's fine," Shannon adds, her voice sliding over Andy's. She hopes this is true, but knows the odds are heartily stacked against their nephew. "His mother–Kerry–says he does well in school."

"Good speller," Andy interjects.

"They've moved, you know. To Kamloops." Shannon's certain this is news to Charlotte; she's eradicated both her own mother and youngest brother from her life.

"Well you say hi from Auntie, okay? Give him a great big hug from Auntie."

"We will," Andy says, and then it's goodbye.

Shannon wipes the puddles his Sorels have left on the linoleum. Moon boots, she thinks. One large step. "Did you hear it?"

"What?"

"Her rapture at having escaped. It freaking reverberates," she says, borrowing her daughter's second favourite F-word, which satisfies, Shannon feels, in the way a knock-off cola does: sufficient, but nothing like the real thing.

2.

Shannon and Andy are eating salami and French mustard sandwiches at a picnic table beside the Columbia River in Revelstoke, BC. Their children grown up and out, they hardly know what to do with their freedom, though Shannon's ached for it since she brought her firstborn home from the hospital, laid her in the crib, looked at the fists balled like nautili and said, "Now what?" She'd wanted to be a mother, yes, but learned that sometimes if you wish too hard for something, you don't recognize it when it arrives, don't have any idea what to *do* with it. She'd entered her twenties a free-spirit who dressed like a gypsy—hoop earrings, rather garish head scarves, dark, flowing skirts from which jack boots with scuffed toes kicked out. The bangles on her wrists made a kind of winsome music—small bells above a door. She had little to do with classmates, preferring the company of her professors. Where'd *that* girl go? she wonders. Who is this woman with all these petty needs?

They'd married relatively late: she was thirty, Andy thirty-three. Her kids say late marriages are the new norm. When *they* get married, *if*—"and it's a *huge* if"—they get married, they'll already have educations, careers and maybe even mortgages *in the can*. Well, their mother's not as traditional as they think. She's had a few experiences herself. And she didn't take Andy's last name, even when that was an unpopular move. Her daughter, when she's teasing, calls her a trailblazer. Now that Tegan's pursuing a degree in environmental studies at Trent and Brock's seeking his fortune via the cliché of oil-rich Alberta–she and Andy drive a smaller vehicle–a Volvo wagon–but suffer the same shortage of room for their tent, disassembled bikes, suitcases, and food as always. They buy deli meat and bakery buns, bottles of apple juice, bricks of tart cheddar cheese Andy slices with his Swiss Army Knife, and fresh bags of ice in highway towns. They drain the cooler's pungent water in Superstore parking lots, juggle the new supplies in with the ice, use the cooler's lid as a counter for preparing sandwiches, and eat at picnic tables beside scenic sights: exactly what they did when the kids travelled with them.

"Wonder what he'll do when he sees us," Andy says, stretching his bare legs, the muscles slack in repose. "It's been almost two years."

The sun's white–a slightly stained tooth in a blue handkerchief, Shannon thinks–and not sharing much heat yet, but it's still early. They like to get an early start. She strokes the wide-logged picnic table top. It's well-scarred: profanities and the names of lovers knifed into the blonde wood. Several letters look like a deliberate font: modified Hebrew characters. She traces the grooves, feels a shiver of something like complicity between her shoulders, as if gleaning insight into the lives of strangers. She reads such scrawls with the same interest she reads bathroom graffiti. What kind of character would write "Pee Happy" beside a 1970s happy face? She's told her mother that she prefers the company of strangers. "And dogs," she added. "I much prefer the company of dogs." Her mother, a high school art teacher who never did get around to becoming an artist– her portfolio of pink and blue watercolours of the temperamental prairie sky abandoned to a corner of the basement where moisture and black mould are destroying them–answered: "Who doesn't?"

"It's been closer to three years, and he's just turning seven." A bluebottle lands on her straw and she flags it away. "He won't remember us well, if at all."

"Maybe not." Andy's eyes are closed, laugh-lines toward the sun. Despite the greying hair, with that spray of freckles just beneath his eyes he'll look young forever, she thinks, and touches his hand. All these years. This tenderness.

"The river sounds like a landing jet," she says. What would it be like to live mountain-surrounded, above this river, robbed now of its colossal salmon and steelhead runs by the Grand Coulee Dam, but still a prodigious force and a natural glory? Bears strolling Main Street. Tourist money. Occasional avalanches. So unlike their small city's landscape which, she feels, can be summed up in the monosyllabic *flat* and *bare*. Weyburn. Lately, every time she travels she conceives a supplanted life. "Should we pack up?"

Andy pitches an apple's remains into the nearby garbage bin. "Two points." She can always count on him to narrate the obvious– "There's a deer in the ditch," "This radio station has played three Paul Simon songs in a row"–and sometimes he even makes her laugh, though he's generally laconic and serious. The kids have fun with his solemnity, consider it a victory when one or the other is first to crack the veneer. "There's at least another two hour drive ahead. Let's fly."

3.
Destination: an acre of land somewhere on the north shore of Shuswap Lake. They have sketchy directions, and the street names she'd scribbled on the back of a Home Depot receipt sound make-believe–Pottery, Elm, Clay.

The closer Shannon gets to the reunion, the more she boils. Jackson's father is a drug-addicted deadbeat who left the boy and his mother for a genital-pierced Fort McMurray stripper. Over the years, Cam's hit them all up: pleading, even *crying* from a gas station in Dawson City; a jail cell in Peace River. *I lost my cheque. Some guy stole my truck*. He has a propensity for drinking and finding trouble, takes itinerant positions as a bar bouncer or construction worker in rough northern towns where rundown houses, interesting fences, and new trucks–pimped so as to disturb the peace to greatest effect–proliferate.

He could be anywhere now, Shannon knows. His mother hasn't even heard from him for months. He could be dead.

And they are Jackson's godparents.

4.

Shannon has periodically ranted to friend Monica–a divorced RCMP officer who does border patrol at the Estevan-Noonan crossing and brews coffee on the strong side. Last time was the fall before the winter of the snowflakes like white flies.

"We get late night calls from bartenders: *Pick your mother up*. But I shouldn't be surprised," Shannon said over coffee at her friend's new condo. "By the time I came onto Andy's scene, his mom was already well down the highway to the skids."

Monica nods. "Weyburn's small enough… in a larger place she'd be sleeping in alleys."

Had Eleanor really once worked as a medical secretary, paid her bills, prepared chop suey and lasagne for her family? Shannon can't fathom it. The only Eleanor she's known is a coarse, chemical blonde with perpetual dark roots; a tragic story who wears her rye-drinking, chain-smoking lifestyle on her face, and spends her government cheques on what she can least afford: lottery tickets, gel nails, and satellite TV. "She squeezes into tight jeans and tops designed for women born thirty years earlier."

"Oh, I've seen her. They're more costume than clothing on her frame," Monica says. She's outfitted her condo in a black and white scheme that Shannon does not find comforting. Brazen geometric designs on the throw pills. Black and white photos of lilies in budget frames on the wall. "Refill? Oreos?" Monica pours before Shannon answers.

"That woman," Shannon says, "hooks up with men she considers upwardly mobile if they own a running vehicle."

Monica laughs, and pushes the plate of cookies toward Shannon. She is filling her emptiness with food, Shannon thinks. Some women do it with exercise, a new car, out-of-town flings. Divorced and alone. Even now, there's a stigma.

"I'm serious. Before you moved here… you wouldn't believe the sorry parade over the years." She recalls Eleanor hanging on a man with a perm and cowboy boots which, perhaps because of the fit, inflicted him with a gait Shannon associated with childhood polio. "This is Darwin. He's a sanitary engineer." Was Eleanor so stupid she didn't recognize the euphemism? Three weeks later the woman'd be at their door again with her latest: "This is Mr. Foster." She'd beam up at a too-thin, scruff-bearded character with catastrophic teeth and a pock where an earring had once existed. "He works at the library," she'd boast, and pinch a speck off his natty sweater with long silver fingernails Shannon thought obscene. Sometimes she investigated; Mr. Foster *did* work at the library–as one of the strolling commissionaires who rousted sleeping drunks out of the comfortable chairs in the magazine section. A month or two later: "Say hello to Gary. He bought me a new couch."

"On occasion she goes around with younger men," Shannon says. "I mean *way* younger men." And this, for Shannon, is the worst. Her mother-in-law showed her the thong she'd bought for thirty-year-old Michael's benefit: red, transparent, barely there. Eleanor owned sexier underwear than *she* did; there was not a word in the entire flotilla of possibilities to sufficiently articulate how this revelation– plus Eleanor's imparting of sexual particulars–made Shannon feel.

Monica's son tears through the kitchen. "Jory, put the brakes on! There's people living downstairs." Poor Jory, Shannon thinks. Not even a yard to race around in now. She looks at the Oreos. Her kids used to peel half the chocolate away and lick off the creamy filling; she often remembers things like this.

"Wasn't Eleanor living with that Terry what's-his-name for a while?"

Shannon nods. "She's shacked up in a trailer court with Bob, in a bachelor suite with Earl, and yes, above the laundromat with Terry." Eleanor was especially keen on Terry, Shannon recalls. In his younger days, he rode his 1957 Panhead Chopper–"that's a Harley, Shannon"–all the way down to Tijuana, Mexico. "You've had quite the exciting life, haven't ya, Hon?" Eleanor'd said, her hand in the back pocket of his jeans. "Yes, you'd better believe it, Shan." Oh, Shannon could believe it. What she *couldn't* believe was that Eleanor'd stayed with Terry after he'd twisted her finger so violently he'd broken it. She "Couldn't live without him... *even if.*"

Eleanor also occasionally resided in Shannon and Andy's basement. Every night she'd fall asleep with a sitcom cranked up so loud the canned laughter floated through two floors, and Shannon'd have to elbow Andy to wake up, trot downstairs and shut the blessed thing off. *She* wasn't dealing with it.

Everything rankled, from the clack of heels on the hardwood to the way Eleanor'd wash just a few items of laundry at a time, even after Tegan harangued her about the fragile environment.

"What does Andy think about all this? I mean, it can't be easy. Jesus. My mother chews with her mouth open and I'm all over her," Monica says.

"He's always looked after his mom. St. Andy. He'd put two fifties in her hand when we didn't have enough money to buy the kids' winter coats. He lends her the car. He's ever around, available, and–this is the kicker–veritably shit upon for all his good deeds. No gratitude, whatsoever, but you should see how she regularly foams at the mouth over her dear little Cam. She even lies about his employment so the government can't garnishee his cheques for child support."

"That's dirty pool."

"And I'm pretty sure that every time Andy gives her money, at least half feeds Cam's debts and addictions."

Monica turns a video game on for Jory and the boy settles before it, tasers blasting. "What about the sister... what's her name?"

"Charlotte. Apparently they had the kind of mother-daughter blow-out where things are said that can never be taken back or forgotten. But Cam–who's broken into his mother's suite and stole her TV... totalled her car off... sucker punched her... walked out on his kid and regularly disappears from everyone's life for months– *that* son's the golden child."

Monica pours the third round of coffee. "Jesus. That must drive you."

"Friend," Shannon says, raising her mug and pausing, "it sends me into technicolour fits."

5.

They've been ninety minutes on the highway; the sunlight, curving roads and unfamiliar mountains are making her light-headed. "My blood sugar's dropping. Can we stop for a snack?" I sound like one of the kids, she thinks. The kids when they were little.

Andy adjusts the sun-visor. "Honey, we're almost there."

"But I'm so tired."

"*You're* tired! All you have to do is sit there–"

"And navigate, and check every few minutes that you're not falling asleep."

"So sleep. We've only got about half an hour left."

She would love a quick snooze but she'd feel guilty, and they might end up driving off a cliff. Plus, she really wants to see everything: who knows if they'll be out this way again.

Soon they're in Chase, and slightly mixed up. "I've heard of this town," she says. Andy drives west down the main drag. Buildings need paint, shops are boarded up. "It possesses the ambience of a resort town at the end of a long season, when all the merchants and regular folks have had enough already and just want to get on with their own quiet lives."

"Yet here it is, July Long… just the beginning. Frankly, I expected more from this place, too. How the hell does one get out?"

They drive to a tourist information centre. Andy wouldn't dream of asking a passerby for directions–something she routinely shouts out her window to do–but he has no aversion to tourist information centres. Plus, she knows, he appreciates the travel paraphernalia: tour books and free maps, with coupons for local businesses printed around the edges. Shannon either pitches it all as soon as he's not looking or starts fires with it.

An elderly employee reorients Andy and Shannon uses the washroom. It is exceptionally clean; this slightly elevates her opinion of Chase.

They swing the Volvo back up the hill out of town, and find a sign missed twice earlier that leads them across a bridge. The road winds through a chain of resort communities, and Shuswap Lake flashes between spruce trees and cottages with two-car garages. "Look at the diamonds on the water," she says, dreamily.

Several speedboats are marooned in paved driveways.

Andy asks: "Can you imagine?"

"Hardly." But she *can* imagine. She possesses a weakness for imagining. She sometimes suspects that the design of her life went askew, as though she missed a critical intersection somewhere along the way. The blueprints went up with the wind. One wrong move, and *now* look. Oh, but she's being ungenerous. It's not that bad. They got the kids safely through their teens. They still have good times together, and regular sex. She thinks of Monica. Actually, it's not bad at all. "This is taking longer than I thought. Is it three yet?"

"No, quarter to. We're right on schedule," Andy says, and Shannon's spirit lightens.

Perhaps it's the long weekend atmosphere, the iridescent water, spruces that climb the steep ledge on their left: a block of green she feels is the very epitome of the colour. "I've got *déjà vu,*" she says.

"Yeah?"

"This reminds me of Scotland." She'd made the trip after completing her third year of a Fine Arts degree, an education she never returned to but she harbours zero resentment over leaving. Work mattered more for a long time, and then there was Andy, and soon after, the children. One doesn't require a degree to paint, she maintains. And weren't there enough struggling artists in the world, already a glut of talent? She makes a fine town administrator. Plus, she likely attained what was most important from her education: her college offered a modest travel grant for Honours students who, in a proposal of no more than five hundred words, expressed interest in visiting important galleries abroad. "Have I ever told you about that?"

"Twenty or thirty times, but tell me again," Andy says. "What's once more?"

"We went to England first, then Scotland."

"You and... Florence, right?"

"Yes. She was a fellow art history student. Younger, and didn't seem to like me much, but she had an aunt with a vacant apartment in Edinburgh, and Flo's parents would only let her to go if she had a travelling companion."

"A much more mature and responsible companion. Like you."

"Her dad was the Anglican minister... she didn't get a lot of breaks. The plan was to fly to London, see the galleries, then leapfrog up to Edinburgh. In London, we stayed a few nights in a hotel near Victoria Station." The hotel smelled rank, she remembered, and Y-shaped cracks in the windows were highlighted with masking tape. Trash accumulated between one grey building and the next.

"We fed pigeons in Trafalgar Square. Of course we toured The National Gallery–that's why we were there, after all. And we walked for miles. In South Kensington we passed a residence with a plaque that announced *Benny Hill Lived Here*. They were everywhere, those blue plaques. *Vivien Leigh Lived Here. John Constable Lived Here*–"

"Apparently one does not need a tour guide in London."

"–Fleet Street.... Hyde Park.... Piccadilly Circus. It was all incredible to me."

Andy says what he always says at this point in the story: "I've never had a desire to go."

"Really? Huh. It seems that most of my childhood memories are somehow related to England–the nursery rhymes, the songs from *Mary Poppins*–" She begins singing: "Feed the birds, tuppence a bag–"

"I get the picture, Dear."

"Did you know that Humpty Dumpty was a large cannon used during the English Civil War in the Siege of Colchester? Funny I should remember that now. I learned that at the Tower of London tour."

"We're getting up there," Andy says. "Soon all we'll have left are longterm memories."

"Nice thought. Hey, better slow down."

They cruise past ice cream stands advertising triple-scoops at double-scoop rates, and grocery stores with filled parking lots.

There are signs for white water rafting, canoe rentals. Wet suits and water skis are displayed outside a cedar-sided beach hut. Both she and Andy are alert now, the multifarious commercial diversions providing instant rehabilitation. Andy slows to let a consortium of teenaged girls in Popsicle-coloured bikini tops and short-shorts cross the street to their boyfriends, who wait in Ford F-150s. They pass a sign for a provincial park with a public beach, and Shannon gathers her long hair in her hand. "I'm melting, Ands."

"I'd turn the air up, but my contacts… you know how it dries them out."

She opens her window. The air smells like cotton candy and shorelines.

Andy whistles. "Check out that mini golf." In the centre of the terraced course, a whale-sized pirate ship is on its side. "We'll have to come back here. Jackson would love it."

"He's probably already been."

"Yeah. Maybe."

Again that jab beneath her ribs. How *could* Cam? She remembers the summers between seven and nine, when Tegan and Brock flung open the screen door every morning and literally catapulted into the season. She wouldn't see them for hours. They grew up building forts and playing kick-the-can, climbing trees and getting bucked off horses and bikes. Entire days spent barefoot. They were all so happy then. "Cam doesn't know what he's missing." Andy, she's certain, will understand exactly what she means.

In a few minutes he straightens and says, "Hey, that must be it. There, on the left. Those trailers behind the trees. She said to look for a Boler." They drive toward the area where Jackson's other family–his *real* family, Shannon thinks–has set up. Beside the Boler, three shirtless young men in lawn chairs are assembling a pyramid of beer cans.

A black-haired kid in too-big shoes and shorts that reach well below his knees bolts toward the car. Jackson. He's hanging on her door before Andy's even stopped. He's so big, Shannon thinks. The boy torpedoes into her, squeezing and clinging. Whooping. "I missed you so much!" This is new, and most unexpected.

Don't cry, Shannon commands herself.

Andy swings around the end of the car. "Hey, Bud, do I get a hug, too?"

The boy gives her one more squeeze, then opens his suntanned arms to Uncle Andy. "I really love you guys, do you know that? I really missed you."

The shirtless drinkers and a few older children eyeball the spectacle. Shannon feels exposed.

6.

There'd been a lover in Europe. He'd followed them through the labyrinth of rooms at the National Gallery of Scotland. Green knit sweater, with unravelling sleeves. Was that the draw? He had thin lips, and wore thick, crooked glasses; he wasn't what anyone might consider conventionally attractive, Shannon guessed. She found herself alone with him in the Degas room. The artist had always been a favourite, but not for the works her mother admired– *L'Absinthe,* his ballerinas, and women in their bath. Shannon preferred the horse race paintings. Luminescent blues and greens, the angle of the brushstrokes, the elegant horses and dispassionate jockeys. She could imagine the weather, the collective torpor as all waited for the gun to start the race. She swung herself onto the viewing bench in the middle of the anteroom. The boy stood in front, his slim back effectively blocking her view.

7.

One of the shirtless men is an uncle, previously met. Winnipeg, just after Jackson's birth. The uncle would have been a boy then. Fifteen or sixteen. Now, she notes, he's all grown up, with a shaved head, a beer gut, a cinnamon-coloured goatee in a two inch braid. Jackson scrabbles across the grass and gives this uncle a belly punch, then skates in his clumsy shoes back to Andy.

The potential for avuncular friction worries her. Who does Jackson love more, and will he show it? Uncle Steve cracks another beer and shares something with his buddies. Bleats of laughter result. The guy on his right spits beer across his knees and says "Goddamn."

If it's going to be three against one, they'd better head back to Chase right now. Or maybe to Revelstoke, she thinks. Safety in distance.

"So," Andy says, with Jackson squirming on his knee, though the boy is clearly too big for this, and sweat beads above Andy's lip like water blisters. "What should we do?"

Steve casts a corrosive eye. Well, Shannon can understand. Andy's brother caused nothing but misery for Steve's sister. The MacKenzies as a collective, then, are an infection.

A man with a yellow-checked handkerchief sitting on top of his head adds another can to the pyramid and the thing crashes. It sounds amazingly like a car accident, Shannon thinks. The way they sometimes conclude in a snap.

"Ha ha!" Jackson singsongs.

The third man jolts out of his chair as if cattle prodded, and starts crushing the cans with his boot heel in a macabre jig. The three of them could be meth addicts, Shannon supposes. Or neo-Nazis.

And she'd promised Jackson they'd stay three nights.

8.

Winnipeg, north end. A game of Michigan Rummy's begun in Cam and Kerry's apartment, and the new baby is fussing. Steve, Kerry's teen-aged brother, is there, and Eleanor.

"You're good parents," Cam is saying. "Your kids have turned out just great. I tell everyone what excellent parents you are. I want you to be Jackson's godparents."

Shannon notes the ascendance in adjectives. She accepts that Cam had the charlatan's way with words–in another time and place, he'd have sold a lot of liniment–still, she's hungry for compliments, and laps these ones up.

"Geez, thanks," Andy says, "that's an honour."

"Yes, thanks," Shannon says, and the baby offers his cacophonic best. "Wow."

An hour passes, and the baby does not settle. He lets out a wail that makes her jump.

"What the hell does he want now?" Cam fires at Kerry, who's been walking between kitchen and living room as if on a track, the baby hugged close to her chest. "Christ, you just fed him. Even *I'm* not that greedy." He smirks, and Andy laughs a little with his brother in a friendly show of fraternity: here they are, both of them fathers now.

Cam slides a cigarette from his mother's pack. Eleanor strikes a flame, then lights one for herself. The baby releases a piercing scream. Cam pounds the table. "Jesus Christ. Sounds like a coyote caught in a trap."

"Want me to take him?" Shannon offers, and stands. "I don't have to play. You can take my place–"

"Sit." Cam tugs her arm, then solicitously pats the back of her head. Like one would a puppy, Shannon thinks. "No one's quitting."

He peels the cigarette off his lip and calls over his shoulder: "Kerry, put him to bed. He's getting spoiled."

"He's only a few weeks old," Andy says, flatly. "Baby's cry."

"Not my kid. I'm not raising no spoiled brat."

Eleanor's at the fridge, pouring another round. "Cam's right. Sometimes you've just got to put them in their crib and let them cry it out. They learn soon enough."

Shannon checks Kerry's reaction. Her skin's the palest of flesh-tones after the trauma of a three day labour and awkward birth, her green eyes larger than ever.

"I.... I think he's just got a little colic. I'll try the gripe water again." The young mother opens the fridge; Cam strikes a leg out and shuts the door with his foot before she's able to reach the remedy.

"Put him to bed." His tone suggests: *Or else*. Shannon knows about the jaws he's cracked, the offset noses he's responsible for. The cops got involved when he took a baseball bat to another man's knees. She nudges Andy beneath the table.

Kerry leaves for the nursery with the trilling baby but quickly returns, and leans against the counter. Cam slaps his thigh and she obediently slumps onto it. She appears for all the world like she might scream herself, Shannon thinks. She seems to be having trouble keeping her eyes open. Every few minutes, Cam bounces her like a child.

"You look exhausted," Andy says. "Why don't you get some sleep? We'll keep it down out here."

Kerry doesn't meet their eyes. "I'm dead, but it's okay." Bounce, bounce.

Behind the door, Jackson continues crying. It feels to Shannon like an interminably long stretch, then he hiccups, as if trying to catch his breath before the next performance. And no one budges.

The game gets rolling again. Andy wins the King and Ace of Diamonds pot, a big one. He waterfalls the cup of pennies into his Corelle bowl of winnings. Cam keeps making unfunny jokes about Indians, and Eleanor encourages him with constant fawning and goosy laughter. The boy, Steve, says he's going to watch TV.

The baby's screeching now, and Shannon thinks he really *does* sound like an injured animal. A cat, maybe. Or a foal. When Cam rises to *siphon the python,* she whispers to Andy: "Do something." He looks at her, as if to ask *What?*

Eleanor's shuffling the deck. A few cards drop to the floor, and her long nails thwack the table's chrome edge as she bends for them. "Damn it! I tore one."

Kerry jumps. "I better check–" and Eleanor thrusts a wiry arm out to stop her.

"Leave him be. His dad said."

"Mom," Andy says.

And Cam returns. "My turn to win the big one." Kerry's repositioned on his knee, and the bouncing continues, and the drinking, and the cries behind the door come again and again, like punches. Each time Kerry rises, Cam pins her down.

When the night ends and they can talk in private in the Fort Garry Hotel, she batters Andy: "Goddamn it, why didn't you *do* something? Don't you see what's going on over there? Don't you *feel* it? Jesus. That bouncing on his knee. And your mother! Don't you feel *anything*? Somebody's going to get hurt."

9.
It is decided that the four of them–"Auntie and Uncle from Saskatchewan," Jackson and Kerry–will go for a drive to Frog Lake. "It's my favourite place," the boy informs them, "I caught five frogs there last year!"

"Four frogs and a toad," Kerry corrects. "That big one was a toad."

"Is it far?" Andy asks. "I don't mind driving, but I'll need to top up the gas."

"It's up the mountain, not far," she says, good-naturedly. "There's a gas station on the way."

Shannon hardly knows the boy's mother, yet she feels an affinity. Perhaps it's her calmness. She'd not freaked out when she'd called to tell them, the first time, that Cam had tried to hit her while she was holding the baby, and, a year later, that he'd disappeared with their rent money, a garbage bag of clothes, and a six pack of Bud. All this before Jackson was even out of diapers. Shannon likes this girl with the no-nonsense ponytail and Nike Air running shoes. A small blue heart is tattooed above her ankle bone, like an iota of hope. Shannon'd had to look twice; at first glance she thought it was a fly.

"Frog Lake! Frog Lake! Frog Lake!" Andy buckles Jackson into the passenger seat. So much making up to do, Shannon thinks. She slides into the back beside Kerry. Stones spit from their tires as they leave the camp, and the beer drinkers crane. Shannon tries not to notice.

"Oops…. didn't mean to do that," Andy says. "This car has more power than I thought."

"Race and rally! Race and rally!" Jackson rocks in his seat.

Kerry just laughs.

10.

His name was Finlay, and he drove her up to Loch Ness, where she'd braved her shins to the frigid water. In the Highlands they hiked an hour up Ben Nevis before her raging headache had them turning around. Then it was off to St. Andrew's, where his brother was studying.

She brought him home, to Canada. It was the kind of thing women in fiction did, she thought. And why not?

11.

A one-lane gravel path curls its way around the mountain. She has no idea how high they've climbed; a tangle of spruce and deciduous trees close them in, eliminating visibility. "Take it easy, Ands." She prays they do not meet another vehicle. "I'm not very good in a back seat, I'm afraid," she says to Kerry. "I'm sorry about the dust, but I have to open this window."

"Same here. I get car sick real easy. No worries." Kerry finds the button that controls her window, too.

Jackson's turned the music up so they can't hear the front seat discussion. Shannon closes her eyes. She hopes she's not going to be expected to initiate all the conversation this weekend, as she usually does. She wants nothing to be required of her. Already she's had to do too much internal cheerleading in preparation for spending this weekend with a seven-year-old, whom, she expects, is fairly starved for attention. Eleanor will call Jackson on his birthday—*Grandma loves you!*—and she's sent a card along, but she could come visit the boy once in a while, couldn't she? Help share the load? Shannon checks herself. Not the *joy*, but the *load*.

They greet a black half-ton. Andy comes to a full stop, then pulls over as far as he can without propelling them into the spear-like treetops. Jackson cries: "We're gonna go over!"

"No we're not," Kerry says. "Uncle has to concentrate on the road and you're making it hard for him."

Oh, bless her. Jackson's mother, after all she's been through, is all right. Nice. Would Jackson would take advantage of this? She wondered if his father, even in absentia, would manifest in the boy in dark and worrisome ways.

12.

Her mother approved of Finlay. "His hair's like Bob Dylan's during his 'Blonde on Blonde' years," she whispered. But for all her mom's pampering and her own zeal in revealing the small fascinations of Weyburn, Saskatchewan–including the notorious former mental hospital, now crawling with ghosts, and once a premiere destination for lobotomies, electric shock, and LSD experiments–within two weeks, Finlay turned homesick.

She drove him to the Regina airport, sat on his knee in the departure gate and hugged him hard, then drove home, thinking, *Well,* that *was something.*

In the decades to come, she would wonder how he looked with age. Did he get Lasik eye surgery? Have a family? Was he happy? She seriously doubted he was the missed turn in her life, if in fact there was such a thing. What she felt was an almost maternal fondness for her brief lover. And like all men she has known, she used him as a measure: *he* would not have *abandoned his own son,* or raised a hand against the woman who loved him best.

13.

"Here we are!" Andy parks in the shade.

"It seems small," Kerry is saying, "but it actually goes back around those trees there."

It does seem small, Shannon thinks, and more slough than lake. She approaches the shore; the water is the colour of root beer. A concrete pad gently slopes into the lake, meaning boat launch. Fishing. Meaning *something to do with Jackson.* Maybe they can rent rods and tackle at one of the shops they passed, spend a good part of these next three days casting off the dock. It wouldn't matter if they caught anything.

Andy and Jackson walk to the end of the rough dock, which undulates beneath their feet like a suspension bridge. The sun is bright and hotter now, Shannon notes, as if being on the mountain–closer to that burning star–has increased its intensity.

"There's a big log over there," Kerry says, walking toward it, "if you want to sit down."

Shannon follows. They sit in the sand and rest their backs against the rough bark. Shannon holds her hand up to make a visor. Andy has a branch and is poking at something in the murky water. Jackson's looking carefully over the edge. Can he swim? Has he ever had a lesson? So much she does not know about this child, this godson of hers. He is, she thinks, a cautious boy, and she hopes to hell it will serve him well in the high-wire years to come.

"I've gone back to school," Kerry says. "After I get my GED I'm going to register for the Early Childhood Education Program at Thompson Rivers University."

"That's awesome, Kerry," Shannon says. "Good for you."

A dragonfly lights between them. Its face, Shannon thinks, is like an old Chinese scholar. It helicopters off again. "Would you work part-time while taking classes?"

"I'd have to."

Shannon does not detect malice, but there seems to be some inference in these words. Something financial, and concerning them. Fuck. Ender and Charlotte could write a cheque and make a real difference here, she thinks. Forego the heated ceramic tiles–Italian imports, no less–and change the direction of their nephew's life. He is, after all, Charlotte's blood, too. But no, it's all on them. The boy's somehow become Andy's responsibility.

She looks at the child. He's hopping. Alternate knees rising in a pantomime of some ancestral dance. She thinks of hot coals. Why did people need to prove themselves in such bizarre ways?

The water beneath the dock makes a squelching sound; small waves ripple the lake's brown skin and quickly dissipate. Last night Andy played Monopoly for hours with the boy. Tomorrow there will be mini golf, and although it's expensive—and something they'd never have spent money on with their own kids—white water rafting is promised. He is so good with him, she thinks. But what choice does he have? Cam will never be in this child's life again. When asked, apparently Jackson says *I don't have a dad.*

There is shouting now, a commotion on the dock. They've found something in Frog Lake. Kerry is up and running toward her yelping son. Shannon stands but does not race after her. The dock leans into the water, then rights itself. A boat on high seas.

Jackson calls to her: "Look, Auntie! I'm holding it! I'm holding the snake!"

A garter is looped across the branch. Jackson shrills again, but keeps the snake at a distance. Well behind him, at the end of the perilous dock, Andy is on his knees, hands masking his face. A godson. Not a *real* son, but close enough. She looks at her husband's heaving shoulders as he weeps. Oh. This is better than a five frog day, and no one has even brought a camera.

THE LAY OF THE LAND

"I told you to pack light." Jack faces his resolute daughter, who has grown longer since the last visit, you notice, and imagine pull taffy, the girl's adolescent limbs becoming loose and flamingo gangly, much like her father's, an image that parallels–and is no doubt blandly informed by–the metaphorical tugging in opposite directions by her estranged parents, the pair now so many years apart they are as much separated by ideology and lifestyle as geography or time. But girls are bigger in general now, you think. And at least physically more mature. Twelve-year-olds like Karina flaunt breasts and know better than you what to do with a wand of mascara and palettes of eye shadow; they could easily pass for seventeen. There are many ways in which they trump you.

There has been a plan, and it is this: to meet his ex and daughters at a gas station on the outskirts of some town you've never heard of, approximately equidistant between the two independent cities the one-time husband and wife now reside in–and *you* reside in–the initial, shared city of a million evidently too small for all to continue to inhabit. Marie Louise was twenty minutes late and you are absolutely fine with that. You stand with your back against the hot car, smoking–you are not quite ready to kick this particular habit–and storing up the quiet before the saucy and perpetually bickering ten and twelve-year-olds join you, and you collectively ensue–a new little knot of family–down the highway and across two provinces toward Manitoba, your family's cottage, where the sour-smelling mattresses and mouse-tunnelled walls won't know what kind of storm has hit them.

"*That*," Jack motions toward his eldest daughter's luggage—a suitcase the size and weight of a pirate's treasure chest—"is the antithesis of light."

The girls stand awkwardly between the poles of father and mother while you pay acute attention to a yellow dragonfly, mangled, but still flicking a diaphanous wing in the car's grill. Smoke pours from your mouth. Is it perverse to enjoy these moments as the proverbial fifth wheel while the "real" family discusses the ever-changing logistics of the girls' week-long visit? New meds, new concerns, new rules. The Decourseys have been in divorce limbo for six years; a settlement regarding US rental property the pair jointly own is stymied in an expensive legal gridlock. Vacation rental condos in Vegas and Arizona, destinations you have zero desire to visit. All that business is rallied about in quasi-libellous e-mails Mr. and Mrs. shoot back and forth like flaming arrows, but they sport a talent for vanquishing their antagonism in the company of their girls. Bloody admirable, you think. It just disappears. There should be medals. Folks used to say that for the measure of a man, one need only regard how he treated his mother. You know a better gauge: assess how he treats his ex.

"You'll just have to sit with it across your laps," Jack is saying now, calmly, this man you are connected to, or is it *with*? You guess this is the tone he adopted during the single year he taught school—in Ottawa, before he learned what devils junior high boys of a privileged class can be, and abruptly abandoned any fantasies he'd harboured about being one of those fabled, Hollywood box office-type teachers who make a life-changing difference for their charges and have streets or public buildings named after them.

The girls scuttle into the car, limb over limb. There are complaints. And sisterly slaps. They must each suffer a layer of canned goods at their feet, and you can see that Haley is trying to adjust a fishing rod so it won't poke her eye out. She is the one you could learn to like. When she phones for her father she says hello first. The other one bleats: *Is my dad there?* He is unsuccessfully wedging the suitcase in. You grind the cigarette beneath your sandal, a little belly dance move you do with your right hip. Now he is adopting a different strategy. Watching this makes you think of that plastic geometric toy one gives toddlers to aid motor skill coordination: fit the circle, square, rectangle, star, moon or triangle into the corresponding shape. Ah, what a smart boy!

"Jack, they can't–" An errant breeze has caught the single wisp of blonde hair that's strayed from the wife's black hair band and lifts it, a kite string. An elegant woman, even in cut-off shorts and a wrinkled linen blouse, someone you expect will become exquisite with age, contract an aggressive form of cancer, deal with it valiantly and *sans* complaint, and be immortalized. Sainted. Though you will definitely outlive her, you will never live up to her. "You have four hours of driving ahead of you," she says.

"Actually, five," he corrects, manoeuvring the ungainly suitcase that contains god knows what. A pony? A pipe organ? "It's a lesson. The girls need to take me seriously. There are consequences–"

The wife is looking at you now. She has voluptuous hair, like Ukrainian bread, but you see that she's misbuttoned the bottom of her blouse, so you can like her. What's she thinking, and what does she think in general about you, the new woman in Jack's life? You've appeared as suddenly as an apparition or a meteorite, and moved your unspectacular and predominantly black wardrobe into the closet husband and wife once shared, your Prius into her side of the double garage, your car's motor directly over the spot where *her* car's motor left an amoeba-shaped oil stain on the slab. Are you vapour to this woman, or granite? You've crossed paths only a half dozen times, never in one another's company for more than fifteen minutes, conversation always self-consciously light and perhaps overly polite–like a tea party–but currently you glean that this older woman, this first wife, feels something like pity toward you. *You have to deal with him now,* her eyes seem to say, and my god they're blue as birds. *You poor, naïve, childless thing.*

How much has he told her, or anyone? You don't care who knows or exactly how far they twist the story away from the truth: you met in a pizza restaurant, Tony's, one of the city's most authentic, if only because the micro-hipped, froth-haired waiters treat customers with undisguised contempt when the patrons–quite innocently–request pineapples or other non-Italian-esque toppings, and within ten minutes–the time allotted for exchanges in the speed dating club you resorted to after a crippling year alone; you dared not attempt pedestrian bridge crossings–you and Jack decided to spend the rest of your days together. You linked chains. You selected the best of your individual furnishings. You walked through his door, and stayed.

Karina is wailing: "I can't feel my legs!" At least she's not whining "Dad" at the moment. You want to stamp and snort and behave like a prodded bull each time she manipulates the simple word into three separate syllables and two distinct octaves: up, down, up. *Da... a... duh.* You do not express the agony this causes you. There is a repertory, a silo of behaviours that you are silently swallowing. If you were the parent, you would have nipped this girl's tone in the bud.

He closes the car door. The daughters are now sufficiently pinned beneath the stupefying suitcase, and they are mostly hidden. No longer clearly seen, but still audaciously heard. You spy only the crown of Haley's alopecia-plagued head; Karina is obliterated, and suffers only hay fever. If you didn't know you'd be hearing about this second-seat injustice for the next several hours, perhaps you could find the situation semi-comical. If *you* had children, they wouldn't need to be told twice. Momma says pack light? The little dolls would arrive with a solitary bag each, light as a lap dog.

"Call me when you get there," Marie Louise is saying. You've heard this particular tremolo before. An ancient high school home economics teacher. You scored F+ for a blackened soufflé. *You burned it, you eat it.* The mother waves at her daughters who cannot wave back.

Jack opens the door for you and you scoot into the leather seat, sliding it as far forward as possible because it's the least, the very least, you can do. "I'll send a text," he says to his former bride.

"Call." Marie Louise looks deflated against the backdrop of gas pumps and the misty expanse of crop dust and a pinkish grey sky. You wonder if she'll cry. It will only be a week; Christ, she should be celebrating.

Jack turns the key in the ignition and the air conditioning blasts, instantly nailing your contact lenses to your eyeballs, which were irritated even before the cool assault. He tilts his head out the window. "I said I'll text."

This will not, you decide, be a good time to tell him there is no cell service at the cottage.

§

You think in terms of weight and solidity when you consider Jack's life and experience. He procures a slightly rigid disposition and is someone you may not have liked when he was a younger man. Too conservative. Too *safe*. Stalwart, like a ship with sails prim and erect. He believes too much in modelling, a word he uses at least weekly, the way other people become attached to *ascertain*, or phrases, like *Not to be competitive, but*.... You know it has been two decades since he's led a class, but he never tires of including a lesson each time he speaks to the girls, regardless of the diatribe's irrelevance. "See how I pass on a curve," he says, as the landscape morphs from occasional brush and farmland to occasional farmland and great vistas of forest. You scan the hunter green fringe for bear, moose, coyotes. You always expect them but rarely perceive them. Maybe once, maybe one time, near Banff, you saw a grizzly lumber out of the trees and turn his big dumb head in slow-motion toward the highway. For some things, once is enough to keep you believing.

"Girls, quit kicking my seat." It is not both girls, it is one girl. Karina. Haley is kicking *your* seat, but that goes into the silo to keep the other misdemeanours company. The clouds are rolling around like bowling balls across the panoramic sky. This is how you feel. Cumulous-ine. The opposite of solid. You are not railroad tracks. You are not a hockey arena. You sit on the sky's open palm while the wind purses his lips. You let him blow you around.

Will you arrive? Alberta becomes Saskatchewan and the roads get worse. Sometimes there is no one to inform you which side of the construction you're to attempt. The highway is thick sandy mush, with a ridge in the middle that could take out a lesser car. "Which side?" Jack asks, but his words don't reach the man in the grader, they don't get beyond the windshield flecked in fly guts. Jack throws his hands up, and just picks a side. It is the wrong side. The grader comes straight for you, and Jack can't help himself, even with the girls in the back, those impressionable pierced ears, he says, "Fuck! You fucker!" and gives the driver the finger, and you put your hand on his arm like you know what might calm him, and he steers the car precariously over the ridge and it is like going over a body, the way it bumps, the scrape of it, and you think about that word, his word, modelling, and add another opportunity to the silo.

There are bathroom breaks, and juice boxes with periscopic straws, and soggy ham sandwiches, and Haley's gelatinous slice squirms free of its bread and splats onto the roadside grit, and Jack says something about the two second rule but doesn't make her eat it, and you're glad. "It looks like processed skin," you say, "like something made in a lab, for burn victims." You pick it up and press the clean side over your forearm. Haley and Karina gawk at each other and then look at their father. You think they are thinking: *Dad, she's totally weird. Weird* has never been popular. You remember.

Each stop necessitates new engineering with the space-hogging luggage, and then, like a beacon, a new provincial border sign, and more fields, and aspen woods with strobed sunlight that makes you first dizzy then nauseous; and geese, two dead deer being desiccated by raggedy crows, and one flattened porcupine with its mouth open as if singing the "Hallelujah" chorus–"No, we can't stop to take a picture," Jack tells the girls, "and turn down your music, you'll blow your drums." This makes them screech and laugh, and when they laugh they inadvertently kick your seat and you say maybe it's time to pull over for a pee break, but really, what it's time for is a fast-smoked and profoundly-inhaled cigarette, and some furious but covert ground-pawing.

The daughters' music gives you that bull feeling. Not that you can clearly hear it, but what is emanating from iPod earbuds sounds like mosquitoes, like a dream of mosquitoes enveloping your body after you've broken a leg because you've fallen in the swampy forest where you've been forced by the rightwing government to plant conifers and sleep in army tents with all the other leftwing, neo-hippies in the world.

So maybe you sleep a little or a lot, because when you open your eyes again the queasy feeling in your throat is gone and you are on the lake road, the last road, the final echelon before freedom. "Is this the right way?" Jack asks, because he hasn't been here before.

He is new to Manitoba and to women who smoke and sleep with men on a second date, and–let's be honest here–sometimes a first.

"It's the right road," you assure him, "just keep following it and where it dips and there's a place where you can turn left or right, go left. We're the fifth cabin in, an A-frame, well, you've seen the pictures."

"Thank you," he says, and you know he's not talking about the directions.

§

You have brought so many different men here now–six, or is it eight?–over three decades, you no longer remember who possesses which particular knowledge about the place and its environs. The lay of the land. You have to be careful about this. You have to be Nancy Drew. Something's happening to your memory. It's gone south and turned kaleidoscopic, particularly when you travel and the air takes on that smell that's a combination of laundry soap and hibiscus, or the ocean spring's yellow-white blossoms look pinch-me familiar, or a tower-glazed urban-scape in one city transports you to other cities on the map you've been to, exactly the same, except on different continents. Pender Island is alternately northern Georgia and northern Italy. Victoria impersonates parts of Scotland. Venezuela insinuates Montreal. You wonder if this is normal or if it's unique to you and then you remember that nothing is unique–your own thoughts are often reflected in the books you read, and it seems impossible that those literary strangers have been inside your head, your thoughts, your ever-thinning skin, and it is simultaneously delightful and spooky, like seeing horses copulate.

§

"It's a bit of a work-in-progress," you say, as Jack kills the engine and you open doors and stretch and twist to get the kinks out and the blood flowing, and Jack pulls the imprisoning but edifying suitcase off the girls, who begin their own calisthenics. You fear the week will be a trial and try to sweep that thought away like crumbs beneath a carpet when you haven't time for an adequate house cleaning. Company's coming. Company's arrived.

"I thought it's been in your family for years," he says, releasing the trunk. Things spill out onto pine-needles.

"Yes," you say, "it has been." You are ten steps away from your favourite room in the world: the large screened porch that culls most of the afternoon sun. No one in your family dares add or subtract to it, except imperceptibly. At one end, a stuffed burgundy velvet couch perhaps no one has ever sat on is plunked beneath a window like an abandoned car. Above this hangs a rope upon which towels and wet bathing suits drip dry. There's an assortment of hats–free for the wearing–hung on common nails. A sweat-stained navy blue visor. An orange ball cap advertising a minor boy's football team. Your mother's old, collapsing sun hats. A cowboy hat. Even a toque. Beside the sofa there's an ancient wooden cabinet that comes up to your waist. "What's in here?" Haley's asking. "Any good stuff?" The perennial tubes of tennis balls, a lantern, a can of Muskol. Look up and there's the requisite candelabraic deer antlers. Where did they come from? There's the table that's round without a leaf, and four chairs that do not match, a combination of painted wood and aluminum and fabric. The table is covered, usually, in a vinyl cloth, and you see the current one bears a design of Italian postcards and the word *Olives* written in script across the green background. There are fishing rods and spools of line, and those fish hooks you call "spoons" that the jackfish go for at the west end of the lake, in the cattails. Sand pails, a mattress that may or may not hold air. "This pail is for baling water from the canoe, or putting out campfires," you tell the girls, who you think are not listening or don't care, then Haley says: "There's a canoe?"

There are tennis racquets, horseshoes, lawn darts, and a broom, and games of Scrabble and Monopoly.

"Can we play?" Haley asks, and her father says maybe later. You breathe, and tip your head back. Above you the cotton candy of pink insulation is stuffed between the gaps in the bare board ceiling. "Yuck," Karina says, "dead flies." Yes, there they are, impressive amounts of dead flies, *musca domestica,* stuck like pieces of gum into the corners of the windows that wrap three sides of the verandah. A heavy pair of bronze beavers rest on the window ledge: not specific enough to be considered artful, too short to be practical as bookends, and no one weights papers out here.

"If these beavers had eyes they'd see the traffic–human, dog, and deer–that parades past the cabin. It's fun to watch," you tell the girls, who most certainly are not listening now. "Campers and other cottages owners," you tell Jack, "en route to the mini golf or the main beach." Where you grew up.

"There's a mini golf?" Karina says.

Soon there's a mélange of shoes on the porch floor–the girls' flip-flops and sneakers, Jack's ugly leather sandals, and your own summer footwear: one pair of black flip-flops, one pair of white, and a pair of sneakers in case you're hiking and have forgotten the bear bells and are tied of yelling "Hey, bear!" as you round every corner, and then there's a black bear–scrawny, hungry-looking, probably territorial–and you have to book it out of there.

"I call top bunk!" Karina yells, and you say that's fair, she's oldest, and you have a premonition that she tosses in sleep and splats to the floor, tender child, breaking her collarbone, and Marie Louise is just an angel about the whole thing.

"There's loads of fun stuff to do both indoors and out, so we're covered no matter what the weather delivers," you say, and you wonder at your diction, at who you're becoming, but Jack likes this you, he gives this you a little tap on the bottom as you're unpacking the Libby's beans and mayonnaise, and he squeezes your boob in the hall.

"Can we go to the beach?" Haley asks. She is already in her bikini, red and white stripes–maybe she had it on beneath her clothes–and you recall the adolescent elation of arriving here; and the heart-freezing, head-blasting joy of plowing directly into the lake and diving under, then out, like a porpoise, a style so different from the inch-by-inch tiptoeing into the water you do now, and only when the sun's positively searing. All your bikinis are past tense and you never had one that was red and white, like the flag, as if deliberately selected to demonstrate patriotism on this Canada Day weekend.

Karina wheeled her suitcase into the heart of the living room then stole into the bathroom. "Why is she taking so long" Jack asks, but you guess it has something to do with the tampon-sized object she was clutching as she brushed past, a white string dangling from her fist. A mouse tail. If you had a daughter, she would tell you when she's menstruating. And the first time you would have made a ceremony. Each of you holding the end of a length of gold or pale blue satin ribbon, treading lightly and barefoot across an empire of lawn, then waltzing into a field of daisies as if there were music. Birds would invent songs.

"We must check the mousetraps," you say, and Jack asks where they are. You feel he should know this, and then remember: this is his first time, he's a virgin, you are virgins here, as a couple, together, and everything must be explained, and you would like to lie down already, you would like a good, old-fashioned afternoon nap in the double bed where you parents sleep, and your brother and his wife. If you had children, you would let them tuck in with you. You would wait out thunderstorms and calm them after they watched the horror movies lined up on the shelf in VHS tape; you watch them still, every year, "Carrie" and the rest, and jump at the same gory parts. "There's one behind the couch in the porch, one behind the fridge, another behind the stove. I don't think there's anything in the bedrooms. Maybe check?"

He is a good partner. The trapline comes up empty, but you know that if there were any mice he would deal with the infrastructure of small bones and bloodied fur, he would do it in a flash, before you could even be tempted to look.

§

"Da-a-*duh*... some kids on the beach told us we missed the sandcastle competition!" Karina speaks with her mouth full of corn from cobs roasted over the rock-ringed campfire. She turns and drills you with her eyes: "Why didn't you tell us?" Even with the niblet-jammed mouth she is loud, louder than any girl, anywhere, in the entire history of girls. Or so you think. You hear her all the time, everywhere. She pounds. Her feet hit the ground like wood blocks. She makes the sound of a complete summer camp.

The accusation is fired at you, bull's-eye, and this is the first time you've taken a direct missile, which must mean you are accepted now, or it could mean you've just risen to the stature of target.

"Don't talk with your mouth full," Jack says, but he is a happy dad; he has taught the girls how to build a campfire, teepee-style. He didn't notice that it was you who gathered all the kindling.

"I'm sorry," you say, "but Jack, didn't I tell you to check the announcement board to see what was going on this weekend?" Sure you did. You know you did. At least twice.

"What board," he says, "where?"

Sound the trumpets. It is squarely your fault that the girls were robbed of participation in the sandcastle competition and potentially lost the once-in-a-lifetime opportunity to make new best friends forever, and win prizes for their ingenious turrets and popsicle stick work, their palatial pebble-stone designs. You gave the announcement board instruction as a given, as if he knew where to find it in the park, by the change rooms, near the beach. Silly you. Of course he wouldn't know where it was, and now the girls are angry and he is perturbed, and what is there left to do except spend money on ice cream cones and, once again, the Dutch-themed miniature golf?

But at night everyone sleeps, even you, the career insomniac. And you love where you are, even with the children playing inane music and slapping each other's thighs with sandy towels that you know will result in your having to vacuum the carpet on hands and knees, nozzle directly digging at the ground-in grains. Still. You have moments when you feel your blood slow, your shoulders settle to where they belong. Loons have something to do with it. And the lit-from-within coals. The mummifying hammock, strung in the shade behind the cottage. Jack snaps lawn chairs at the squirrels when they come too close, and you think it's crazy how you've met this man, still hardly know him, yet he correctly intuits all these facts about you. Squirrels are terrifying. And the porch is a balm.

Karina meets a boy who was born in Germany and wears something like braces on his teeth. "But they're clear-coloured. He has them for two more years. He's a ginger," she says, "and the hottest guy ever. Dad, can I get braces?" She begins planning her wedding and listing which of her friends will be invited, and which ones she hates this week and thus will not be inviting. You have never planned a wedding, not even when you were twelve.

Haley brings you wild daisies nodding on flimsy stalks, and you trim them, and stick them in an empty soup can on the table in the porch. *"Voilà,"* you say, and then she says *"voilà,"* too. *"Pirouette... Alouette... tête-à-tête,"* you say, and she parrots. You tell her that her hair is growing back, and you like the way it looks now, like a golden sheen over her skull. Like something special. If you had a daughter.... You reach for her, pull her close on the cottage's front step. You stroke the child's head. "It's like a peach," you say, "it's wonderful. Maybe you'll start a new trend. I bet all the girls in your grade will want a style like this."

She looks up at you. You see her. You met her father in a pizza parlour. The lights were low, and there was a murmur of nervous hilarity. Underdressed or overdressed: no one got it right. Everyone was drinking draft beer. Two men used their ten minutes up trying too hard to make you laugh. One had a moustache so unruly you imagined a caricaturist portraying him as a muskrat. The best looking one asked if you swallowed or spit. And one had two daughters, "They can be a challenge at times." He confessed that he wasn't handy, and was almost divorced. He could cook, but did not garden. "You look like someone who plays violin," he said, and it did not sound like a line. No one had ever said that to you before. You told him you knew the major chords on guitar. "Other languages?" he asked, and you said you were the kind who never forgot the French bored into you at school. He claimed to be "Still learning English."

He'd been an athlete, and now he was not. The stupidest thing he'd ever done was challenge a co-worker to run over his foot with a forklift. "Hence the limp," he said. His name tag read *Jack,* and you thought it a solid name, a name for grandfathers and presidents. Jack. Yes. This one was just exactly right.

WE DON'T SAY *NEGRO* ANYMORE

Our second eldest daughter loved to play dress-up and did so–in my housecoats and gauzy scarves, my suede stilettos and white go-go boots–with an almost breathless zeal from the time she was three. An imaginative child, as second children often are, April amused herself for hours before the full-length mirror, the entire contents of my dresser puddled around her ankles or flung across the bed's headboard as if left by hasty lovers. Sometimes she made a party of it, inviting playmates to sift through my underwear drawer and yank clothes off closet hangers.

I'm certain that my wardrobe–mostly shirtwaist dresses, polyester sweaters that attracted static cling, brassieres engineered to separate and lift, and the odd black slip which doubled as a negligee–was no more tantalizing than any other mother's, but April found adventure in it. Even at sixteen, when she was partial to slamming doors and javelining sharp objects at her teasing siblings–she stuck Bonnie, the eldest, with a dart–I'd find her on the phone in my room, the tails of my blue satin blouse twisted in a knot below her ribs.

It was the sixties. I expected this child to assume a career in fashion design, or maybe–because it was clear in the regal way she carried herself and shook her bangs over one hazel eye that she would be the beautiful one–she'd become a model. She's twenty-nine now, and lives happily in baggy overalls and shapeless T-shirts with her husband and fraternal twin daughters in Prince Albert, Saskatchewan. She and Cal are teachers of chemistry (him) and typing (her). Or, *computer applications,* rather. *We're not in the '60s anymore, Mother!*

My husband and I share the ability to mortify each of our five children simply by opening our mouths. Jeff, middle of the pack and the only one to roll the family car, claims I say *warsh* instead of *wash*. I swear that Tam, Jeff's co-conspirator and closest sibling both in age and sentiment, traps me into saying it. *See!* she squeals to her new boyfriend, who seems somewhat leery of us (and we of him, taken so soon after Tam's divorce), *I told you!* What was once funny to all of them is now a bone of contention. *Don't worry, Mom. We'll get you trained some day.*

I've been publicly reprimanded by Bonnie for saying *stewardess*. Garrett, our youngest, threw a seventeen-year-old tantrum over *crippled*. We've endured monologues fit for the stage on the wrongful use of superlatives, and *mailman* drives them mad.

Cliff and I are of an age now where the most fun we've had in a long time was the day we went for an impromptu drive in the country and came home with an antique dresser wedged into the trunk of the car. Of course we paid too much for it and didn't realize how cloudy the mirror really was until we'd squeezed it through the doorway of what was once Bonnie and April's room. We'd been intoxicated with the beauty of swaths drying in autumn fields, with a sky so brilliant it burned our eyes; with our good fortune at having stopped at that doomed highway town for a fill-up, whereupon we spotted the Antique Auction sign pinned on the wall above the motor oil display.

We're of an age now where we say things like *whereupon* and *we're of an age,* but only when the children are beyond earshot. Neither of us knows how phrases like this crept into our vocabularies, but I am quite certain of the period, not so long ago, when my interests and concerns–who cared if I'd gone up a few sizes since we married, or company was coming and I hadn't scrubbed the bathroom down–became decidedly middle-aged.

My interests have changed in other ways, too. I've developed a taste for the finer things: kid leather gloves instead of the cheap vinyl I've always worn; a bottle of good merlot with dinner. I love the symphony and live theatre, and Cliff's learned that he does, too. For much of my adult life I scrimped and saved and put everything into the one big pot that was always for the children: swimming lessons and hockey tournaments, jazz dance and ballet shoes, the electric guitar when Jeff took an interest, April's parade of stray dogs requiring veterinary attention, contact lenses for Bonnie and Tam, money just so *they* could have money, because I didn't want them to be the only kids who couldn't chip in for pizza or keep up with the ever-changing blue jeans as they metamorphosed from wide leg to boot cut to skin tight and flare, back to wide leg again.

I'm also of an age where I can almost completely exhale, knowing my children are finding their way in the world, with or without partners, with or without addictions (Tam does drink a little more than she should; Jeff's never been able to settle for any one woman for longer than six consecutive months), and that they are generally personable adults with unique interests (Bonnie's learning German, April raises Siberian huskies) and abilities. Garrett, our late-breaking news–he arrived eight years after Tam–is the only one still at home and resents ever being born.

Cliff is so close to retirement it's never far from our minds, and we speak about the fun things we'll do–he's always wanted a kayak, I'd like to learn Bridge–as if they might occur next week, not two years from now. I paint prairie landscapes that occasionally find themselves on the walls of banks and dentists' offices (my work has that kind of appeal), and therefore will never retire.

My own mother, *seventy-six years young!* as she says in the way that only those who've aged well can get away with, is also an artist of some repute. Her gallery show, *Nudes in Various States of Repose: The Senior Body Beautiful,* was the subject of a documentary for a national television network and a few months of celebrity ensued.

She is currently at work and, I hope, getting some rest, too, at Lake Chapala, Mexico. While she's away, I'm her chief plant waterer and light turner-oner. I retrieve mail and set it in neat piles on the round oak table in her dining room. Her cat, a scrappy old gal with one ear, is boarding with a neighbour more compassionate than me.

Today I don't feel like working and avoid passing the back stairs that lead to my studio. My own house seems too large for my thoughts, which are as windswept and grey as any November can be. This might become one of those afternoons when I find myself wiping tears off my face without knowing, really, why they're there. I never expected to become the kind of woman who would mourn all the noise and craziness that once filled her house, peace-seeker–if not *maker*–that I've always been among husband and five children, trying to find a little space in the centre of it all with just enough room for my paints and the angles of my own body, but that's it, exactly, today.

I need to get out. I leave a note for Garrett and then, worrying that he'll miss it, press *memo* on our telephone answering machine and read the same words into it. Later my grim son with the bleached blond hair will confront me: *Why'd you leave the same message twice? No... don't tell me.* He'll press his fingertips to his temples, like a mindreader. *I know. You've got no confidence in me.*

I blame myself for all that ails Garrett. We thought we'd stop at four, and almost the very moment Tam was out of diapers and into daycare, I began to enjoy a string of good fortune: my first one woman show, a generous arts grant (it bought boards, drywall and paint for the addition which became my studio, braces for Bonnie, and another year of daycare services), and several lucrative commissions fell quickly into place. I had an overwhelming sense of *this is as good as it gets,* and I was right. I rode that wave for five years, producing the work I would continue to sell for the next ten. I was thirty-five, riding high on the fumes of success, and newly pregnant with a child I couldn't be sure was Cliff's. My energy for midnight feedings and rocking babies to sleep had all been spent on Tam, the colicky one, whom a two-year-old Jeff almost managed to smother with a pillow. It was supposed to be *my* time now.

I consulted no one before I made the appointment with a gynecologist whom I knew–perhaps women instinctively know these things–could set me free. But I couldn't go through with it, and later that year, when Cliff held Garrett's cheek next to his own–just to *breathe* beside him, I knew I'd done the right thing. The doubt, though, the days spent vacillating on a park bench, have come to haunt me: Garrett, never believing he's good enough, never believing enough in himself to join a team or even to ask a girl to dance.

§

In my mother's house I liberally douse plants which defy the laws of nature. A slim and unsightly four foot cactus I bought for her sixty-fifth birthday, when it was the size of a thumb, is not even rooted. It rests on top of its mix of sand and soil, happy and healthy as it leans against its friend, the fig tree. I kneel on the carpet, scratch all the dried and fallen leaves into a pile and make three trips to the kitchen garbage can with my palms full. Mom is an impossible gardener, but her various house plants invariably thrive on her brand of neglect.

In her kitchen I automatically open the fridge and dump out half a litre of bad milk. Then I start in on the bits of atrophied cheese and wieners, a bag of saggy carrots and oranges with the texture of petrified wood. What goes around; my girls do the same thing in my fridge. Bonnie says, *Hey, look, everyone! This salad dressing predates computers. Yuck,* April says, dumping a bottle even though it's only one month past the Best Before date, then continues, incredulously: *Thousand Islands. Don't you know there's a whole new world of exciting salad dressings to explore? Come on, guys, live a little.*

After Mom's fridge I move on to her cupboards; I'm really procrastinating today. In this kitchen every drawer is a junk drawer. In one I find a zipper, a half pack of Tums, sixteen pennies, and a six cent stamp in a nest of cotton pulled from the tops of her estragon pill bottles–she doesn't take anything else. In the lazy-Susan: a crystal vase, a fly swatter, a lone red sock, and a flashlight share space with twelve cans of Campbell's soup.

I wander through all her rooms, turn the television on, then off, I've never been able to stand TV. Besides, it was hardly necessary, with my own family providing all the drama, intrigue and laughter–thank God for the laughter–I ever desired. It's a wonder there weren't more disasters, like on television. More blood and broken bones and surgeries. I am grateful for that. I wrote a minimal amount of notes to teachers: *April won't be in school for a few days. She has chicken pox. Garrett will be late for Biology; he's having two teeth filled.* I do wonder though, if television hasn't subconsciously influenced my kids' career choices. Bonnie, who loved shows set in news rooms, is a newspaper reporter in Kamloops. She's always the one with a camera around her neck, casually arranging us for photos at family gatherings–*Garrett, come on, smile*–or yelling *Freeze!* when we're not expecting it. I dropped Cliff's birthday cake once, a three-tiered masterpiece with caramel pudding between the layers, when she jumped out from behind a door and a flash exploded in my face. Jeff, who was always wild about speed and adventure, fights fires in Calgary. Tam, who coveted her position as the baby for eight years, and was, admittedly, spoiled more than the others, was slow to decide upon the path her life would take, married impetuously, and is finding life much more difficult than it should be for a twenty-five-year-old with higher than average intelligence and a killer wit. "It's one thing to have a good sense of humour," Cliff had told her, when she was sixteen and we'd had a call from the vice-principal, who explained that Tam had *shredded* an English teacher in front of the entire class, "but you must use it wisely. Not everyone appreciates your sarcasm, Missy." Cliff made her write an apology and marched her over to the teacher's house. It was a dark day she's never really forgiven him for, and although he's tried to make it up to her in a hundred ways, Tam's always the last to arrive for Christmas and Easter and, guaranteed, she's the first to leave.

In Mom's bedroom almost everything is white: comforter, curtains, candles. Even the furniture is that pale wood that's become so popular, but to me just looks like it needs a good coat of stain. It's a strange thing, I think, all this white in the room of a woman, an artist, who lives and breathes colour. She says the room clears her thoughts; it's meditative. I open her closet and find the blast of colour inside a relief, like the sound of another human voice after you've spent a few days alone.

She's fortunate that she's tall, stands straight–she harped at me about posture all through my own adolescence–and has good enough legs to wear short skirts, though she favours long, waistless dresses these days. I drag the back of my hand along the clothes, some as familiar as my own teeth, others new or simply never worn. I pull out a rayon dress with a scooped neck, three cloth-covered buttons on the bodice and a skirt that falls to mid-calf. Predominantly puddle brown, the fabric is brightened with teal porpoises leaping across it in pairs. I slip out of my blouse and unbelt my slacks. (*Slacks* sends the kids into hysterics.) The dress feels cool against my arms and back. I finger comb my grey-blonde hair up and away from my eyes, remove my glasses, find some dangly earrings in Mom's jewelry box. There's a tube of lipstick with no lid in the dresser drawer where she keeps such things. I wipe off crumbs of indiscriminate nature and slide it across my lips.

I wiggle out of that dress and slide my arms through one patterned with fist-sized pink and purple peonies. I lift the skirt and sit properly on the edge of the bed, crossing one leg demurely, like an actress (actor, *Mom, nobody says* actress *anymore!*) in a turn-of-the-century English drama. In the far right of the closet I find a red plaid poncho–seventy percent mohair; thirty percent wool–that I recognize from three decades ago. I'm surprised by a metallic blouse with silver threads that shimmer in the light–far too audacious for a woman *seventy-six years young!* even if she *is* an artist, and is given a certain amount of leeway. I slip the blouse over my shoulders, but it's misshapen from hanging for too many years on a metal hanger that did not fit its shoulders squarely and it humps in the back, making me think of Tam's slight–*Honey, no one would even know*–scoliosis. There are a few purple and green track suits (my mother was not immune to the 1970s Participaction craze), several white blouses with delicately embroidered yokes, beige and taupe dress slacks with elasticized waistbands and a rack of scarves.

I'm drawn to one that's hand-painted in the colours of the prism. ROY G BIV. Once upon a time–I don't dare count the years–a science teacher told us to remember the colours in the prism that way, as if it's a name. It's one of the few things from high school that's stuck with me. I twist the scarf around my neck, then pull it up under the back of my head to catch my hair. I try it again wrapped like a bandanna over my flat crown *(Isn't that an oxymoron, Mom?)*, then flip it off and try it in various angles around my body, as one might see such a scarf wrapped around a slim woman on a beach.

The clock in the hall gongs four times, hours that have passed as smoothly as silk between my fingers. Now I get it: all the hours, weeks, years April traipsed through my own closets and found treasures. What a simple thing, becoming a girl again.

Driving home, I remember a deadline for a commission I've not yet begun, and the realization of how little time I have left brings a blunt pain, like a hammer blow, hard and fast, in the chest. I'm feeling less and less passion for my work, and it terrifies me. I know it's not uncommon for anyone who makes their living in the arts to suffer periods of self-doubt, but my interludes are lasting longer than they used to, and they visit more often. You become known for a little while for something you have little control over, because when it's working best you're just the woman with a brush at an easel and the work takes on its own life, and you slowly begin to believe you are who the art magazines and newspaper reviewers say you are–*an artist of some regard*–and then you're stuck. Somebody quotes you in your optimistic, early years saying, "I'm going to paint for the rest of my life." How can you ever stop?

I sometimes wonder what the world might have held if I'd have explored more. Did the children resent my one track life? Did I do them serious psychological damage because of the times I went away for a week or two to paint, to be alone, to sit beside a lake or a tree and wait for inspiration to ride up like a knight?

Where my family's concerned, if I had to do it all over again, I would, though that's not to say there weren't times, *many* times, when I desired only to be a million miles from any of them–their laundry and kitchen messes, their rants, neuroses and needs. It was worth the blow ups and long silences, the days I had so little energy I could scarcely roll out of my own bed, the desperate nights spent running back and forth to the window, hoping, praying, that my teenaged children would come back to me whole and undamaged from bush parties, back seats, and fragmented love. I admire their differences, respect the choices they make, acknowledge their faults

(Bonnie can be ostentatious, Jeff's too loose with money), and try to be their friend. This is most necessary where Garrett's concerned, the child who recoils from embraces and wilts from words of praise, and has no idea I love him best of all. I graciously accept that their father and I are often the brunts of their jokes and the source of their fury: we don't say *negro* anymore.

I am also of an age where the warm weight of Cliff's leg thrown casually over my own in the moments we allow ourselves before we rise means more than a dozen nights of lovemaking. For years it was as if we deprived ourselves of even that basic human need: not sex, but the simple reassurance of skin against skin. I'd felt, until these last few years, that *partners* fit us better than *lovers* ever did. We were in this together, heads bent over heating and automotive repair bills wondering *How will we ever?* Deliberating behind the bathroom or bedroom door over how to deal with Tam when she got caught shoplifting, or what to do when a dog sniffed out dope in Garrett's locker. (*Not* dope, drugs. Pot. *Call a spade a spade.*) We got through it that way, brushing shoulders in halls and doorways as our words slid past each other. Brief meetings. All those years in the same house and so little time together.

§

"If you knew you were terminal and had, say, eighteen months to live, what would you want to do?" I ask Cliff, reading in bed beside me. We tucked in early this evening, each engrossed in our books. The red satin bathrobe he began wearing a few years ago–the kids call him Hefner, and get a kick out of it–hangs from a newel post.

It's rained off and on. This is spring: a breeze gently lifting the sheers.

"I don't know. Travel, I suppose." He rubs the left side of his face, smoothing out laugh-lines. "Maybe get one of those around-the-world tickets where you pick the countries and they map it all out for you."

"That's nice. I remember a game I played as a child with my grandfather's electric globe. I'd spin it, close my eyes and stop it with one finger. Whichever country my finger landed on was the place I'd one day live." I pause, remembering how those hours chimed with all my possibilities, though the topography felt like scars. "I don't know what happened to that ancient globe, but it would no doubt be obsolete now anyway, with all the countries that have merged, or changed names, or perhaps just vanished altogether, like Atlantis."

"And here you are," Cliff says, "just blocks from where you played that childhood game, after all."

And here I am. And it's my husband of so many years beside me, not Garrett's father–a much younger, fellow painter–who once took my foot in his hand and drew a single red heart in the arch.

"Listen," I say, and Cliff turns to me, our pillows bunched together. I don't have to say anything more.

APPLES BY AN OPEN WINDOW

"So I saw this new patient a few weeks ago. Very young." Simon pincers the roach and hoots. High-hands it across the pillow to me. Exhaling, his mouth forms a slightly squashed O, as if he's been chopped in the spleen or is lip-synching to some soulful Anita Baker number: "Ooo-ooh, ooo-ooo-ooh. You're the best thing yet... to ever come... in... to... my li-iife."

"Real fuck-up?" I draw the smoke in, hold it for five Mississippis.

"They're all 'fuck-ups,' Sweetie. I'm in the business of fuck-ups. The stock portfolio, time share in Florida... all *merci beaucoup* to the–"

"Fuck-ups." I exhale a cloud, sniff the air. "Ever notice how pot smells like roast turkey?"

Simon raises an eyebrow.

"It's true," I continue. "Getting high's reminiscent of Christmas dinner."

You know that doctor-patient confidentiality thing oft-cited on TV dramas? Those docs who wouldn't betray a confidence if their *own* life depended upon it? Bullocks. I've been dating the doctor for two years, living with him for one, and I could spill the case histories of twenty of his most remarkable patients. Mostly he counsels a whack of menopausal women with low-grade depression and weight gain. There are your run-of-the-mill agoraphobics, bi-polars, the post-traumatic stress disorderees and obsessive-compulsives, but he also counsels certifiable nutcases, like Jerome, the paraphiliac who can only reach orgasm if his partner whispers sweet nothings in a cartoon voice. She must really dig him to go along with it. See, that's what I don't get–not that these looney-tunes exist, but that they actually find partners, mate, help their offspring do math homework at the kitchen table.

"So this new case... the boy is fifteen, and bright. An over-achiever, in fact. His mother found him hanging in his closet, naked and turning blue. He had two fingers stuck between the rope and his neck"–Simon demonstrates–"which was the only thing that gave her hope. Of course he didn't really want to die, she reasoned, and I'm inclined to agree... there was a *Hustler* on the floor beneath him, the centerfold thoroughly rippled from who knows how many previous episodes of autoerotic asphyxiation."

"His mother said 'thoroughly rippled?'"

"*I* said that. She *implied*. Please, let me finish."

Simon hates to be interrupted once he starts riffing. In fact, these professional purges are not for my benefit at all; this is how he sorts things out. His *modus operandus,* if you will.

I manage a final toke and squish the remains into the ashtray balanced on my breastbone. "Proceed."

"He's tall for his age, a good-looking boy."

I set the ashtray on the side table before it spills across skin and sheets.

"Define 'good-looking.' I need a visual."

Simon grunts. "If I must. Let's see... thick, brunette, side-parted hair swept across blue eyes, barely-there freckles across a nicely-proportioned nose."

"Like one of those Kennedy-types they use in American Eagle ads? Striped polo shirt, vaguely resembles Prince Harry?"

Simon smiles. "Yes, I suppose. Even has the cool name to go with it: Luke. Anyway, his self-inflicted ring-around-the-collar was faded, but still apparent."

"Mmm." The radio clicks on. A twelve-year-old Hutterite girl has gone missing near Riding Mountain, Manitoba. *At approximately six p.m. Thursday, RCMP received a call that Sarah Hofer of the Parkview Hutterite Colony disappeared, and rescuers fear she may have become lost in Manitoba's dense Riding Mountain National Park. RCMP and fire department officials, along with hundreds of volunteers, have begun searching.*

Simon slaps the snooze button. "Do you mind?"

"I didn't want to sleep in." I tap my wrist. "It's June, remember? The wedding month? I'm swamped."

Simon plonks a heavy leg across my knees and continues. "The boy stands there skulking, hands jammed in his pockets. He's not going to open up until he's ready–"

"A hard *nut* to crack?"

He pinches my arm.

"Ouch! Sorry, but in your profession, opportunities abound."

The doctor resumes. "His eyes sweep the room and he pauses at the leather settee. 'Guatemalan?' he asks. I'm thinking, Jesus, this kid's good. I fib, say it's Peruvian. 'No kidding,' Luke says, 'because the iconography definitely looks Mayan. The figures participating in a Mayan ball game... also, these glyphs here.' He points to some scribbles. 'Definitely Mayan-like.'"

"An eye for art," I say. "'Interesting. Have a seat.' He chooses the sling chair, sinks in it, and gives me a canny look, ostensibly because I'm sitting higher than him and he's acknowledging the power imbalance–"

"But I bet he was impressed that you're not some ostentatious dick behind an oak desk, and you're dressed like Joe Regular in chinos–"

"And an un-ironed shirt," Simon deadpans. Winks.

"Is that a passive-aggressive slam?"

He traps my hand like a scuttling crab and holds it next to his heart. The story continues. "'Your kid do those?' the boy asks, about the wall art. Again I lie. 'No, I don't have children.'"

Simon has a ten-year-old with a slight hearing impairment he may still grow out of. Nathan lives with Simon's ex-wife and her slightly pigeon-toed lover in a house insulated with bales. Their goal's to be off-the-grid within five years. We have the boy Wednesdays and most Sundays. When we were first getting acquainted, Simon shared that he'd never wanted kids; in university the sudden death of his cat, Morley–a grey, raccoon-sized Persian who never left the house–devastated him. Simon came home from class and found Morley paws up beside her cat dish; rigor mortis had begun its amusing trick. "So why'd you lie?"

"No idea, really. Just came out that way."

I snuggle in close. "My goodness, doctor… you're *not* perfect?"

"Apparently not, but don't tell my delusional girlfriend."

"Ha ha." I peek at the time. "Then what?"

"'So tell me about yourself, Luke,' I began, and he says, 'How about I talk about my mother.' 'I'm more interested in you,' I say, because the pretension's getting old already, 'and regardless of what you may have seen on TV or in the movies–' then the kid cuts me off, says: 'I don't watch TV or waste time on cinematic escapism.'"

I raise my eyebrows. "Wow, so young to be eschewing pop culture, your Luke. Bet that makes him really popular in his, what, *tenth* grade class?"

"Twelfth, actually." Simon carries on in the same rhythmic tone. "'Then you're an usual creature, a rare breed, you are. We'll get to what you *do* like to do in a bit. I was about to say that the stereotypical 'lie on the couch and talk about your mother' style-of-therapy is not what I do here. We're not going to beat around the bush–'"

"Pardon the pun," I say, and cackle. Simon's on a roll now. He wouldn't skip a beat if I left the bed, slipped out for a paper, whipped up a cappuccino then accidentally charley-horsed him when I crawled back in. At least he's entertaining, not like my sister's husband who tortures guests with slides of all the golf courses he's played.

"'Now why don't you tell me why you're here,'" I said. "'Oh, I'm pretty sure you can figure that out,' the kid says, and he makes the universal distress signal for choking. He says 'I was halfway across the River Styx and thoroughly enjoying the journey when my mother crashed my party, cut me down with hedge clippers and called 911.'"

"'That's good, now we're getting somewhere, though I'm concerned with what I'm hearing. Perhaps it wasn't the sexual gratification you were after in that closet, perhaps you were flirting with death–'"

"'Flirting? Ah, no sir, we were all out dating. We'd been going steady for months.'"

The radio again. "Sweetheart," I say, lifting my head off Simon's chest. I can see up his nostrils; they're two completely different shapes, one like a kidney bean, the other nearly round. "This is scintillating and all, but I've got to be at a wedding in…" I lean across him to check the time again, "an hour and a half. The abridged version, *por favor?*"

He scowls. At forty-six he's had enough disappointments to master the brow-bunching. "Okay. So I learn that Luke is like this savant who's already taking college classes, but he exists in an anti-social bubble. No friends, none of the usual adolescent hobbies. Add the abnormal sexual proclivities *and* possible suicidal tendencies… he's suffering from Disorganized Episodic Aggression."

"So lots of kids are loners," I say, standing now. At the mirror I pick at a nugget of sleep in my left eye. "Why was he trying to kill himself while jacking off? Why not enjoy the real thing, get a prostitute or something? I mean, hey, it sounds like he just needed a good–"

"That's what I don't quite understand." Simon pauses. "He doesn't fit the profile. Suicidal patients report having felt humiliated by important others prior to attempting–apparently nothing like that going on here. Many report having felt emotionally abused, treated like an object, devaluated as a human being. Again, I'm not getting that from Luke. As far as the autoerotic asphyxiation's concerned–"

"Yes?" I turn to so he can zip my dress, a blue and purple floral on a white background. Blossoms big as splayed hands. Rayon fabric: long and loose so I can move freely, but smart enough for formal events. Simon sits and zips me up. He's a tall drink of water, whereas I'm a half-pint. My high school nickname was *Peanut*.

"Well, the truth is, it seems to be some sort of trend. I'm talking to more and more men who actually prefer the company of their own hand."

"You're kidding. Have you seen my keys?"

"I'm serious, and no. These men say they can't even reach orgasm with women anymore. Furthermore, they say it's just too much of a bother to try. Check the dresser."

"Lazy bastards." I paw through the laundered clothes on the dresser. Keys! I also snag my wallet and wedge it into my camera bag. My tripod, lights, props and other accessories stay in the van. "Give us a kiss, Love. I'll be home in about four hours. Dinner in or out?"

Simon's hand on my neck is a brief but welcome heat, like when you're on the beach and it's overcast but the sun breaks away for a few heartbeats before another cloud slides across it like a lens.

"Out. I feel like Indian."

"I feel like Canadian," I say, monosyllabically.

§

Another week pans by and I'm up to my eyeballs. Not much to say about my work. I am a wedding photographer who hates weddings. I mean I really, really can't abide them, especially the brides. Forget radiant. When I look at these gals, I see old-fashioned Barbie dolls—before pliable limbs and waists that twist. *Muy* Stepford. The whole thing screams artificial. The weepy mothers, the best men who drink far too much and make inarticulate toasts that people will laugh at anyway. And all that symbolic white. Fuck, I hate the white. It can be a bugger to get the contrast right on a bright day. And the whole virginal symbolism thing is such a mockery, as if each of these guys has not been "entering parliament" from the get-go. And the women'd be damn stupid not to let them. I mean, what if there's no fire? What if the intended's hung like a breakfast sausage and she needs a salami to feel anything at all? But this is what I do. I stand the brides and their attendants beneath rose-twined arbours and beside wagon wheels, lift arms, adjust hair, position legs. It's mechanics, really. The kiss. The twirl. The bouquet. The still-life with rings and pearls. The half-starved bride facing a stone wall, her head turned just so in profile, skin barely covering the jutting, boomerang-like blades of her back. Why doesn't anyone ask why the bride's facing a wall? I pine for that day. I shoot close-ups of the groom's hand over hers (unless he possesses small or offensively hairy hands, warts or amputations) and arrange the light to accentuate her diamond, which he probably couldn't afford and will eventually begrudge purchasing. He could have pimped his ride, Man, or paid cash for a big-screen TV. He could have bought a little trailer and lived on a few sunny acres with a soft-hearted German shepherd who'd be happier than hell with the minimums: a scratch beneath his collar, a corner of the couch. With each click of the camera's shutter—digital, I'm no purist—I'm contributing to one of the longest-standing lies in the world.

June is a surreal blur for wedding photographers, and the weather smacks you full in the face. May's just a bunch of false starts: a few consecutive days of high UV indexes followed by frost warnings, then the calendar flips and you're in the middle of the freaking savannah, thick with flies and bees so proficient at disturbing the peace you'd think they were equipped with twin outboards. Either that or you're trying to shoot in the rain, or before a funnel cloud touches down: gotta love the Prairies.

I am perturbed today. Bohdanko Kosokovich, father of one of the Barbies, has demanded a discount. This after I stood in the holy heat of the Ukrainian Orthodox Church for the two-hour-plus ceremony. Jesus. Even the saints were sweating (old joke, not mine, though I regularly take credit for it).

"You purposely shot pictures of our guests looking their worst," Kosokovich accused.

"How could I? I don't know them. I don't know their worst." I'd caught grandpa scratching his balls.

"My wife... that one of my wife."

"Which one?"

"You know which one."

Near the end of the night, about the time the DJ started playing lid-droppers like "You've Lost That Loving Feeling" to clear the crowd, the mother-of-the-bride was resting her bosom shelf on the head table. This nudged her boobs up beneath her ample chin, and with her head plopped forward—and the low-cut neckline providing a perfect frame—it looked as if she were feasting on her own unflattering flesh. "Listen, if you dislike any photos in particular, you don't order them. Simple."

"I want a refund. Thirty percent."

Hmm. Must have had a bad crop last year. "With all due respect, that's ridiculous."

"Fifteen, then. Or I Facebook my friends about this. Tell them you're a rip off."

Oh, Christmas. The Facebook threat. Not the first. So I won't get anymore marathon Ukrainian Orthodox weddings. "I'm hanging up now. If your daughter would like to discuss these or any other photos, she has my number. No discounts. I shoot what I see."

"And that sacrilege in the church, the priest–"

I hang up, pour a bourbon, retreat to the deck. Simon sidles into the shade beside me and makes a sound like he's pitching an anchor off a sinking boat. "Wow," I say. "And I thought *I* had a bad day."

"It's that kid, Luke."

"Still uppermost on your mind, eh?" I stroke his arm. "How many times have you seen him now?"

"Maybe ten. You know, he seems perfectly normal, has the whole world with handles on it. He comes in and, well, to tell you the truth, we have these dynamite conversations."

"Darling, he's fifteen."

Simon stretches his long legs. "I know, I could be his great uncle–"

"Or his grandpa, if we were in Utah."

"True, but he knows way too much for his age, about everything from Sidney Bechet–"

"Sidney who?"

"Bechet... the legendary New Orleans jazz artist who put the soprano sax on the map." There's a whiff of exasperation in the air. "Where was I?"

"He knows about everything from Bechet to...."

"To xeriscaping. He says he can *get by* in four languages, and–"

"Whoa back. He knows about xeriscaping? He's a baby. How is that possible?" I consider the struggling yard. The neighbours' weimaranar, Oscar, keeps jumping the fence. Oscar apparently doesn't drink enough water and thus his 100% Proof urine has effectively obliterated the sod we laid last year. The *Farmer's Almanac* calls for drought: I overhead this at the Ukrainian wedding.

"He confided that the first time he tried AEA it was like experiencing nirvana. Way, *way* better than drugs. He was soon addicted. Sure, it sometimes goes wrong–"

"Michael Hutchense, INXS." Rock and roll is the only *Jeopardy* category I can cream Simon in.

"So they say, and numerous others we never hear about. Did you know the practice even has a literary historicity?"

Literary Historicity? Well aren't *we* getting la-di-da. This is no longer Simon talking; this must be that pedantic lad Luke.

"In fact, Luke was first introduced to asphyxophilia when he read Beckett's *Waiting For Godot*... that scene where Estragon suggests to Vladimir, 'What about hanging ourselves?' and Vladimir responds, 'Hmmm. It'd give us an erection.' Some discussion follows, then Estragon says, 'Let's hang ourselves immediately!' Well, being a bright light, Luke immediately gleaned the reference, tried it at home, found nirvana, and–"

"Very educational, I'm sure, but more to the point, was Luke really trying to kill himself, or just have a *crème-de-la-crème* jizz?"

Simon spins to face me. "You know, you really can be crude sometimes. Honestly, what comes across those lips." His face is reddening, and this is only our first drink.

"Careful, or there'll be soon be considerably *less* coming across these lips." I give him an I-don't-really-mean-it squeeze.

§

They say you can't judge anyone until you've walked a mile in his or her kicks. Example: you think it'd be exciting to be a cop, then you learn they spend most of their time writing reports. You hear writers don't get to spend months alone writing in garrets after all. I didn't want to photograph weddings, I stumbled into it by default. The snaps taken at my own wedding, oh so long ago, were abysmal. Out of focus, grainy, too many shots of the bridal party sitting semi-circular on the church lawn with legs tucked beneath the bonny bells of skirts, too many of me floating down the aisle on my papa's arm; not enough of the guests, the accidents, the small tragedies happening in the bathrooms and the back seats out in the parking lot. What was missing was the whole picture. Sure you need a few close-ups, but I would have appreciated a smattering of long shots as well–wide angle views of the hall, decorated in little cauliflowers of tissue paper that spelled out our names, as if those flowers alone staked some kind of a claim on happiness; the dance hall series, including the expressions on my waltzing parents' faces, now that their oldest–whom they worried was promiscuous because I changed boyfriends every three years–had finally fixed a knot. That kind of thing.

So was the bride happy? That day, sure. Positively aglow. Ten years later, I kept asking myself what the hell was wrong. I wasn't *un*happy. Friends said Wilson and I seemed the very poster of marital bliss, with our evening walks and handholding, our decorous dinner parties, but what, exactly, *was* bliss? I kept trying to find some emotional yardstick to measure it against. There was nothing wrong with Wilson. There was nothing wrong with anything. And that, it seemed, proved to be the key. I needed something to *not* work. I could handle imperfection, it was this running-along-as-efficiently-as-a-Swiss-clock business that quite literally threw me into a tailspin.

One February day I was driving out of town to shoot a winter wedding. White on white. The worst. In the city the snow was like a fine dusting of flour across a cake pan: hardly there. I got on the highway and the story changed. High winds had slicked up the surface, and beneath the blowing snow and a median of slush: black ice.

What do I remember? Tires locking. Lifting my hands off the steering wheel but letting them hover just above it. Crazed spinning, the ice accelerating my speed. Then the sideways slam into the ditch, snow obscuring everything. For a moment I thought "Gee, at least there's no damage to my car yet," and in the next, "Gee, I wonder if I'm going to roll." Then the slow-motion amusement park ride of a four door sedan leaving earth's gravitational pull and rolling, rolling, rolling.

It was the most peaceful thing.

I woke in the hospital, certain I was dead. And it would have been okay, you know, if I had been. Really. It would have been absolutely fine.

§

"I've invited Luke to dinner." Simon is straightening magazines on the shelf below the coffee table. Thursday evening is clean-up-the-house night.

"What?" I'm sweeping dead leaves from beneath the palm tree, and drop the broom. "Christ, Simon. Isn't that unprofessional? He's your patient! Should he even know where you *live*?" I realize I'm sounding slightly Machiavellian.

Simon stiffens, as if each vertebrae is instantly fusing. And again: that flushing. A new thing. "The invitation's been made, Louise." I hear the full stop at the end of the sentence: a declaration. His house; his rules. "Not this Saturday but next, at seven. If you're uncomfortable with it, you could–"

I could find my own place. Be alone. "No, I'm okay," I say, thankful for the multitude of brown and withered palm fronds that have earned my rapt attention.

§

Two weeks. In two weeks Simon and Luke have had another ten sessions together. Guess his folks have a good medical plan. Or maybe Simon's pulling a *pro bono*. Christ, he almost doesn't give his own kid this much attention, though he does spoil the sweet, frail boy, and is especially keen on giving him gifts that require electricity. These little things; he thinks no one notices? Show me a human being that really does walk through this world with a heart and core of pure kindness, and I've got some stills from a few, um, *interesting* weddings to sell you, and no, they're not blurry, that's intentional. That's *art*.

I don't dwell on the dinner date until the day arrives, and Simon asks me to remove my Nora Roberts novels from the bookshelf, and clear the fridge of magnets pasting down dollar off coupons for WeightWatchers soup, and Bizarro cartoons clipped from the paper: a Zen monk reading a birthday card inscribed "Not thinking of you" and the one about the cyber suitor at the door meeting his date for the first time, flowers in hand: she says, "You look different in your online profile," and he says, "I was impressing you with my Photoshop skills." This is funny shit! Guess our Luke doesn't have a sense of humour.

At the intended hour and minute, the doorbell chimes. Simon seems a tad uncomfortable at the greeting: he's either intentionally blocking me or legitimately doesn't know where to stand. He'd already started into the drinks, and I see he's spilled a little on his beige cashmere sweater. It'll soak in soon. "Luke, my partner, Louise."

I step in front of Simon and Luke grasps my hand, grips tightly and for three seconds too long. Pins and needles when I get my hand back. I had a boyfriend who judged people by their handshakes. He'd have thought Luke potentially violent. "Pleased to meet you," I mouth, though I'm sure my countenance reveals I'm anything but copasetic with this whole deal.

From the neck up, the boy genius is, as I'd imagined, one of those Kennedy-types, but he's dressed like an unsuccessful door-to-door Jewish salesmen circa 1955 Montreal. Mismatched navy suit jacket and dress pants with a grey vest beneath, slip-on black leather shoes with a weave over the toe. His pants are two inches too short. *This* is the great savant?

Simon steers us into the dining room, to the table, set with our–well, *his*–best plates: creamy white, to showcase the soon-to-be-served food. He sits then jumps up for more wine. I rearrange my napkin, and ask Luke how he thinks he'll find college next year, at such a young age. He looks down his faultless nose at me and answers, "Well, I'll leave my house, walk to the end of the block and catch the no. 15 to the main station, then I'll transfer to the no. 6 and ride it for about ten minutes. It stops in front of the campus library, and I'll disembark. I'll go through the door and down the escalator, across the food court, and up a few steps. Then I'll walk down a long hall and pass many students who may or may not give me a second thought, and then, presto–the doorway into my first class."

Little shit. I could slap him.

Simon returns. He touches books and knick-knacks as he circumnavigates the room before settling again, like one of his OCD or ADHD patients.

"I'll bring in dinner," I say. "You two can talk shop." I can't help myself.

I take a little longer than necessary arranging the food on a serving trolley, and wheel it in like I'm providing room service. Luke tucks his napkin into his collar rather than unfolding it and placing it in his lap, and Simon, on cue, does the same: two bibbed, blue-eyed, oversized babies. First is a cold cucumber soup served in flattened bowls. I'm particularly proud of this, but no one comments. The gastronomic carnival continues with roast beef and a potato/carrot/onion medley, stewed in the beef juice, Waldorf salad, and sweet buns from the IGA bakery. Nothing fancy. I rarely have time for fancy.

"So how do you define yourself, Louise?" Luke asks.

I almost choke on a walnut. "I'm sorry?" *Say what?*

Luke dangles his water-filled wine glass between thumb and middle finger. "I mean, what do you do for a living?"

Jesus. "I'm a photographer."

"Are you represented by a gallery?"

I shoot a glance at Simon.

"She's not that kind of a photographer," he answers for me.

"I'm a wedding photographer," I say, all on my own accord. This kid makes me feel like I'm in the principal's office, about to be blasted for pulling boys into the girls' washroom. "You know, rings and bridesmaids and *By the power vested in me.*"

"Ah, not art then," Luke says, swirling his ice water.

Oh, to have innate wit–like Jann Arden or Ellen; I can't think of a damn thing to adequately retort with. "No, nothing like art."

I'm galaxies away while my dinner partners discuss Liszt and the paintings of Jasper Johns. I fade in and out, remove plates, march in the apple crumble, drink. My night adds up like that John Lee Hooker song. Three generous glasses of wine, then: one bourbon, one scotch, and one beer. Time contracts until I hear Simon's: "You're sure we can't give you a lift home?"

I cock an ear, puppy-like. Mother of God, it's almost over.

"No, no, I like to walk," Luke's saying. Simon's helping him into his coat, one of those large black cape-draping things popular with Goths and Dracula.

"If you're sure, then. Oh, I was going to lend you that Stan Getz CD. Just a sec–" and Simon's off again.

I'm standing there, drunk but not sideways, when Luke leans into me and whispers what I think is this: "You're just like me."

Spinning. I've left the ground and am not feeling a thing.

§

Nathan visits for a full weekend and I give father and son miles of room. Simon's a pretty terrific dad—perhaps that's one of the positive offshoots of divorce: sometimes the pendulum swings in favour of the kid. Love in the smallest things: how he dabs Nathan's chin when the boy dribbles ice cream. Watching juvenile programs that rely heavily on scatalogical humour. The way he speaks extra clearly and always faces his son, making certain Nathan catches every word. He patiently repeats himself if necessary.

It's tucking-in time. I don't usually interlope, but I hear them discussing the news story about the little Hutterite girl—still sporadically in the news, though it's been six weeks now—and I park outside the door, brace against the wall for this strange bedtime topic.

"Do you think they'll ever find her, Dad? There's bears out there. And wolves. They keep looking and looking but they can't find her. I bet she's sleeping in some soft deep grass beneath a big tree. That's what I'd do. Or I'd build a fort."

"Me, too. I bet she's found a nice soft place to sleep. When put to the test, people often demonstrate amazing survival skills."

"But it would be cold, wouldn't it?"

"It would be cool, but it's July. It's not too-too bad. There's dogs, and planes and even people on horseback looking for her. They're not giving up."

I peek, see Simon snug the blankets up beneath Nathan's chin, and kiss his forehead. When the boy was a fussy baby, Simon says he'd rock him for hours and sing John Lennon's "Beautiful Boy." How could I not love this man?

I've been following the missing girl story, too. The searchers have already gone over the area countless times. The prospect of her being found alive has grown exponentially slimmer. There *are* bears, and thunderstorms, and bad people. The child has mostly likely been snatched. For some reason, the fact that she's Hutterite makes an abduction seem all the more obscene.

"Dad, that girl is only two years older than me. How come so many bad things happen?"

At this point I creep away: I don't want to know how Simon will handle this one. Really, what does one say? Because life's a game of Russian Roulette? You wait a few moments longer at a stop sign and avoid the head-on collision. You step five feet to the left and get struck by lightning. A question like Nathan's could stump Aristotle. Thank god the boy hasn't put this question to me, a woman of mediocre intelligence who is *not that kind of photographer.*

§

I thought we had a pretty decent rhythm in the bedroom, but things have begun to change. Simon is inexplicably taking a long time to come these days, and when he does, he holds his breath so long during orgasm it's almost scaring me. I've asked: "Is this some kind of Tantric sex thing you learned about in yoga class?" He keeps his eyes closed, continues methodically breathing in through his mouth, out through his nose, but something's not clicking: he's barely hard enough to manage the job.

Tonight, after a session that's gone on so long I've already had two perfectly adequate orgasms and am beginning to chafe, he says: "Put your hands around my neck."

"Beg your pardon?" I'm on top. The curtains are parted so we can see the shapes of each other, but no details. There's a bottle of ylang-ylang oil on the bedside table. And a black vibrator–the sales clerk at the sex shop volunteered that she really enjoys this model–just in case. I stop grinding.

"Choke me, Louise. Not hard, just push your thumbs down with medium pressure."

I buck off him. I'm all for fun and games, but not this. "Too weird, Simon. What's up with you lately?"

He throws his forearm over his eyes. Apparently ponying up about this new kink is difficult for him, and it should be. He waits a few moments, screwing up his nerve, I expect. "You know, it's not so strange. Anthropologists report asphyxial practices in various cultures. Asians, for example, often strangle to heighten sexual pleasure. The Yahgans in South America do it, and the Celts."

"Then you can bloody well fuck the Celts!"

He's not ready to let it go. "Okay, I'll do it on my own. I'll secure a towel around my neck first, and you can be right here, in case anything happens."

"Yeah, I'll be right here *this* time. What happens when you get the urge to do it again, and I'm working, or visiting my sister in Illinois, or picking up the dry cleaning? Simon, you're a therapist. What's happening to you?" I will not make it any easier.

"Just one time, with you here. I promise."

"No."

"Please."

"No."

"It could be–"

"Listen," I say, grabbing his head and forcing him to confront me. We're almost nose to nose. "Let me make it perfectly clear for you. Absolutely no fucking way."

He gets up and pounds into the ensuite. Slams the door. I hear the shower spray. So, it's come to this, then. I am not enough anymore.

§

There's a wedding I can actually tolerate. Second time round for both, so hallelujah–none of that kitschy white-gown-and-veil business. They've gone the JP-in-the-hotel-room route; no flower girl, no penguin-suited ushers at the door. It's unreservedly sane and refreshing.

I bring up the photos on my screen and decide there's something unique about this particular set of shots, about these people. He's fifty, give or take, grey on top, white at the temples. She might have been pretty for a few days when she was sixteen; a tall, long-haired gal who bends slightly forward at the hips when she walks. She strikes me as the kind of woman who always waves her gratitude *and* mouths *thank you* when walking and a driver stops to let her cross at uncontrolled intersections. I examine the candid shots, see a sort of contented resignation around the eyes of both partners, a look that seems to say *I'm glad I found you, let's enjoy the ride as long as we can and have the wisdom to know and admit when it's over.* That's maturity. It's two adults–not Barbie and Ken–recognizing love everlasting for the fairytale it surely is.

The bride has a droop to the right side of her mouth. It would be so easy to perform digital surgery, but she's better this way, I think. It's our oddities that make us remarkable. The scars that tell the stories of our lives, the pronounced veins, fractured bones and ligaments that stitch themselves together against innumerable odds. And what you can't see. The idiosyncrasies, the proclivities. The closets.

Tonight I also have to print an album of 4 × 6s: a bridal shower I shot Wednesday night. I download the prints, open Photoshop and a clip-file compiled of hundreds of random physical attributes and deformities. The bride-to-be–a skinny blonde knock-out with dental veneers–gets a furry set of muttonchops. Her best friend and maid-of-honour develops hydrocephalus. When I stop laughing, something else creeps in: the possibility that I am well and truly fucking sick.

§

Simon beats me home.

I slip off my shoes at the front entrance, sense an unfamiliar heaviness in the air. It's like walking into my favourite Thai restaurant and smelling Greek ribs or pizza: something is off. I find him on the couch, head in his hands in a caricature of hopelessness. I sit in the studded leather club chair across from him. He looks up, and his lips move but nothing comes out.

"You look like you're going to ask me something," I say.

"He–"

"He?"

"He did it again."

"Who did what?" Like I don't know who and can't imagine what. "You don't mean... Luke? Oh, Simon, I'm so sorry." If this were recorded and played back, I know I would sound utterly genuine.

He nods, and a choked cry escapes him.

"Is he–?"

"No, his father found him this time, but perhaps not soon enough... there might be brain damage. We won't know for maybe a week. God, what a waste. That brilliant, brilliant boy. I failed him. I... I've been–"

I reach over and tuck his head beneath my chin. Stroke his thinning hair. "It's not your fault. You are not responsible for him... you're not responsible for any of them." I move around to kneel before him, my hands on his knees to let him know I'm serious. I'm the real deal. "You can't stop a person who's hell-bent on ending his life. For whatever reason, Luke doesn't want the things most people want."

Simon squeezes the inner corners of his eyes between thumb and forefinger. "He's fifteen, for Christ's sake."

"Yes, but years ahead of himself." I crawl back up, sling my arm around Simon's back. Offer my shoulder this time. There, there.

"I thought I had him, you know? I deceived myself into believing we were making progress."

Making progress. When I first sat in the sling chair, it seemed nothing was beyond fixing as long as this kind, earnest, slightly stocky man in rumpled chinos was willing to help me sort out the knots in my life. I close my eyes, remembering my initial appointment, see as if for the first time Nathan's crude still-life of apples by an open window; the Guatemalan settee; the library of Zen meditation books, spine by spine, on the self-help shelf. Simon taught me how to breathe: hand on your diaphragm, inhale slowly and deeply, hold it, then exhale completely, hold it, and repeat until the universe starts to feel right. Post-traumatic anxiety: the accident had made me fearful. That's what I said. But I knew the highways would be treacherous. I was driving too fast, and when I crossed the slushy median I simultaneously slammed the brake and yanked the wheel. But that's all behind me now. "Baby," I say.

The patio doors are ajar, the day growing late. I'm compelled to throw open all the windows, too. Air this melancholy out like smoke, but I don't move. A few houses away, someone starts a lawnmower. We need to mellow out. I know there's a little weed in the house. I'm about to suggest we roll it, but then Simon gets up and mixes drinks.

I turn the TV news on, the volume just high enough to be audible. Top story: the little Hutterite girl has been found safe and relatively unscathed after all these weeks of wandering alone in the Manitoba wilds. A modern day miracle. "Simon, you've got to see this." I increase the volume; there's an onsite interview. The dark forest is a menacing backdrop against the cardinal red serge of the RCMP officer who led the search efforts. "It's good news," he is saying, an unruly moustache hiding his upper lip. "It's a nice ending to the story."

The camera pans back to the female reporter, her curls sprayed in place like a bride's. "At 8:45 p.m., two women from Dauphin were hiking in the park and they located Sarah just outside the search area. The girl was weak and dehydrated, but otherwise appeared to have suffered no major ill-effects. She apparently collected rain water and ate roots and berries to survive, and she'd constructed a shelter with leaves and branches. The shelter saved her from the elements, but made it difficult for rescuers to locate her in the dense area."

Jump-cut back to the officer, with the reporter's hand and microphone in the shot. "A lot of times these kids haven't made it when we find them," the sergeant says, "but this is excellent, an excellent ending to this story."

"Wow." Simon hands me a glass, chiming with ice. "Nathan's going to be so relieved."

I glance out the patio doors: dusk's creeping upon us. "Her parents... *they're* going to be so relieved." We listen to the other news items. Woodland caribou need the government to protect forests from industry. The death toll tops ten thousand in the latest Indonesian earthquake, and terrorists are lurking in our quiet Canadian cities.

"Sometimes the world is a spinning ball of shit," Simon says.

"Hmm... no argument here."

It's become one of those early summer evenings where the light is the colour of a fading bruise; briefly perfect for shooting photos. I reach for the remote, mute the TV. The lawnmower, further away now, sounds exactly like every lawnmower I've ever heard. It could be my own father out there, religiously mowing our square of lawn every few days whether it needed it or not. Life seemed more ordered then. I reel back the years, think about my childhood. Myself at fifteen. Those backlit summers before I became restless, and reckless, and my life spun off the rails. I never imagined an existence like the one I've fluked into. Flawless, no, but the scale tips mostly the right way.

"Imagine," Simon says, "a lone child surviving for weeks in the Canadian wilderness."

"Yes," I say, "some stories have rare and excellent endings." I am going to cling to that.

Shelley A. Leedahl calls three provinces home. She's Saskatchewan born and has lived in Saskatoon and numerous small communities (including Meadow Lake and Middle Lake); in Edmonton, Calgary and Medicine Hat; and she currently lives in Sechelt on BC's Sunshine Coast.

Her critically well-received titles include *Wretched Beast*, *The House of the Easily Amused*, *Orchestra of the Lost Steps,* and *Talking Down the Northern Lights*. She is the author of the multi-award-winning children's book *The Bone Talker* (illustrator Bill Slavin) and the popular juvenile novel *Riding Planet Earth*.

Leedahl frequently presents her work and leads writing workshops across the country. She also freelances, edits, and works as an advertising copywriter for two Edmonton radio stations. She has received international retreat Fellowships for Hawthornden Castle (Scotland), The Hambidge Centre for Creative Arts and Sciences (Georgia, US), and Fundación Valparaíso, (Spain). Her poetry, essays and short stories are often anthologized, most recently in *Slice Me Some Truth: An Anthology of Canadian Creative Nonfiction*.

See www.writersunion.ca for more information.